MASTERMIND

a novel by

KAT FROST

Printed in the United States of America
First Printing, 2017

ISBN (Trade Paperback): 978-0-9982941-0-0
ISBN (E-book): 978-0-9982941-1-7

Back cover photo credit: Ariana Johnson Photography

Phoenix Press
morethanivebeen.wordpress.com

To the Phoenix;

The King Who guides me,
The Spirit Who drives me,
The Heart Who holds me,
The Shepherd Who enfolds me,
The Captain Who leads me,
My Savior Who frees me!

Sometimes you reach what's real just by making believe

...

Each happy ending's a brand new beginning

- "Ever Ever After" by Carrie Underwood

SKIP THIS

HAHAHA! You rebel! You couldn't help yourself, could you? Ever heard the expression "curiosity killed the cat"? Well, as it turns out, these words are poisonously enchanted, so that by the time you've finished reading this, you will be seized by the poison's power and die. Sorry, tried to warn you.

Now, to those of you who kept reading anyway, that above part was a lie. It's the trap to scare away all but the die hards (heh heh), because I want only the stout of heart to read on and discover my treasure map.

That's right, you heard me. There's a treasure map in here, but you see, it's in code. Here we go:

When I was little, I was annoyed by what I decided was an unacceptable lack of good written material on the market for kids my age. So I determined that when I grew up, I would change that. I would put something out there that other kids like me would want to read.

(Shh, I know what you're thinking: "Where's the treasure map, punk?!" Hang in there.)

When I got older, I was possessed by the question of what to share. What story could I possibly tell that has never been told before? What can I write that will touch people in profound ways, speak to them with what they need to hear most?

I journeyed to the heights of writerdom ("I've got some crazy talent!") to the very lowest ("I can NEVER do this! That's it. I'm quitting and becoming a seamstress!"). And in the end, I realized the epiphany that everyone eventually makes: What I was searching for was inside me the whole time. What I needed to do was write from my heart. And if I did that, then *someone* would hear it. Someone who needed it would get my message in a bottle. Sharing my own struggles and battles, my own thoughts and feelings, is the only way to make that incredible writer/character/reader connection. So I began to write, really write, from the heart.

(Seriously, cool it, peeps. Treasure map is on the way. Estimated time of delivery: the next paragraph)

This book is the culmination of a dream. A dream I've had for more than half my life. A dream I believe in. But it doesn't have to stop here. I will keep going, and I ask you to join me. What are your dreams? Go out and live them. Realize that making your dreams a reality starts with you. Commit to them, pursue them, make them come true. Dreams are powerful and beautiful. And they start with you.

I told you I'd give you a treasure map. And now I am. This book is my map. And the treasure is you.

Sic parvis magna.

~ Kat

CHAPTER 1

I expected pain. That's what you'd usually expect after being thrown headlong off a horse into a tree without a helmet. The problem: I didn't feel any pain at all.

I figured I was dead, and I decided that was outrageously unfair. Who gets killed by a tree? Sure, the one time I forgot to wear a helmet I get conked by a conifer. So what? The most I should have is a concussion. Maybe a broken bone or two.

I peeled my eyes open and propped myself up on my elbow. Sunlight greeted me, strong and tingling, mitigated by a cool breeze smelling of dreams. Bigger problem: I had no idea where I was. Oh, I knew where I was supposed to be: I lived in Texas. But this was not Texas. *Texas is big and empty and flat. Texas is kinda barren; the sky is big from horizon to horizon. Nothing blocks the sight of the place where the sky meets the earth. I am battered and bruised and wish I could be dead, lying on the ground by some old tree, waiting for someone to come find me. I'll take the pain, just please, please, don't let this be real.*

So wishing it away didn't really work. Vainly, I tried not to panic. Where was I? What was I doing here? This place was so alive, so green! Vivid, growing green that shouted of life in the grass stretching all around me, in the waving leaves of the deciduous trees on every side, in the delicate flowers more brightly colored than any I had ever seen before. They seemed to sing, lifting their nodding blooms joyously to the golden sun, which was larger and brighter here than I'd seen anywhere. I had no words to describe the color of the sky, for it was a deeper blue than a Texas sky could be. Was this Heaven? I had never seen anything like this place ever in my life, but for all its beauty, I was terrified.

1

Scrambling to my feet, I made a hasty evaluation of myself. "Okay, okay, Alex. Stay calm and think!" I was freaking out, and my bad pep talking wasn't helping. I appeared to be in normal, scrawny condition: my whitewashed skin wasn't scraped or cut at all. I patted my face and hair, inspecting every inch of myself as best I could. My scraggly brown hair was surprisingly un-messed-up and un-dirt-filled, my features felt unbroken and my gray eyes hadn't had their gradient bars dragged to black, at least if the lack of aching and swelling told the truth. Check. I was in perfect health. Actually, in better condition than I tended to be, considering I was a twelve-year-old girl and lived on a ranch. So what had happened?

I closed my eyes, remembering the accident. *A secluded trail. Flying out of the saddle, screaming. Impact. And then…* Nothing. The next thing was opening my eyes in this place. I backed up and tried again. *Riding my favorite horse, Starr. Mom telling me to be back from the trails by five. Elliot, my brother…*

At that thought, I wanted to cry. I had spent so much time annoyed by him, trying to get away from him, ignoring him, and now I was dead. I would never see him again or be able to tell him I was sorry. I'd even go back to the day that he had executed one of my Barbies as Marie Antoinette, when I had wished I'd never had a brother.

He begged me to let him ride with me. And I refused. For the hundredth time. Now I'll never get the chance. Alex, you're a jerk!

I tried frantically to remember anything that might help when waking up and not knowing where I was. It was like Worst-Case Scenario Survival come to life. I could hear no sounds of life, not so much as the buzzing of insects. Of course, I'd heard that lots of predatory creatures like tigers stalked with absolute silence and you didn't know they were there until they were on top of you.

I hugged my arms, trying to look everywhere at once for any sign of danger. I knew I should find water and shelter and all that, but part of me didn't want to leave where I was. Who knew what might be out there? Maybe I was in the safest place right here, and leaving it I'd walk into a pack of mountain lions… or something worse. Oncoming panic painted the world in stark detail, every tree hiding a menace, every shadow cloaking a hungry predator. My throat began to close. I bolted.

If I stayed on the move, nothing could catch me, I told myself, believing I was reasoning and not in full-blown-panic mode. I'm not altogether sure what one is expected to do in situations like this. Sit calmly and wait for everything to work itself out? Pinch themselves black-and-blue trying to wake up (tried that and failed)? Look for help in a seemingly life-barren place?

The sound of water pierced my fog. I was terribly thirsty. I slowed, letting the sweat prickle against my skin in the breeze, and soon found myself on the bank of a perfectly clear river romping over a bed of stones. I knelt beside it, scooping up the water and drinking in agonizingly small doses. It was so cold it hurt my stomach, but good. I hoped I wouldn't die of typhoid.

The breeze stopped. A warmth enveloped me, along with a wild, rich smell, spicy and fragrant and utterly unlike any other smell I'd smelled before. It made the blood pound in my ears and my heart race with a new fear, and excitement like I hadn't felt in a very long time.

Slowly, terrified but unable to not, I turned. A ball of fire, bright as the sun and burning in a million colors, more than I knew existed, was falling from the sky. My body felt numb and slow as I tried to cry out and leap back. My feet splashed in the water, shoes and all, and a squeak escaped my lips. The orb struck the ground, whooshing that same warm scented air over me, more powerful and intoxicating than before. The earth didn't flinch when the fire touched down. The ball spun faster and faster, changing shape, and in only a few seconds, a Phoenix spread its wings and called to the sky.

There was no question about what it was. Its cry kicked my heart into my mouth, as if I didn't already sense that I was in the presence of a mighty eternal being, full of strength and kindness, power and love. I collapsed vaguely to my knees, my legs simply unable to hold me up.

The Phoenix cocked a golden eye down at me, folding its fiery wings behind its red-gold back. A beautiful terror coursed through me, a sweet pain so sharp and overwhelming it pierced my heart like a dagger. I caught my breath, my head light and my lungs not filling or releasing. The pain was terrible, but somehow, I didn't want it to stop. I wanted to stay in that forever. But it passed. I was still filled with that beautiful terror, and it was mixed with a love and longing that felt distantly familiar, as if in another lifetime I'd sensed the shadow of this feeling. Now, I was at the feet of the real thing. Then, the Phoenix spoke.

"Child," he said, and his voice thrilled through me, vibrating my soul like a plucked string, musical and mighty like the voice of the earth itself, only bigger. More. Like hearing the voice of the one who made the earth. "You've made bad decisions; in this your judgment of your past is correct. Such is the nature of fallen man. But you are repenting them, and that is good. It is the only way for healing and change. You must learn from the past and shape a better future with your present."

I tried to speak, but my voice was gone. Then I tried again. "Please, Lord Phoenix, sir, who... who are you?"

"You know me already." The Phoenix fixed me in his eye again. "You will know me better still in future."

Something about his eyes made me trust him. Well, it wasn't that I thought he was a safe cuddly pet to be around, but I stunned myself to realize that, afraid though I was, it didn't matter to me whether he intended to eat me or not. I felt drawn to him, like right here, at his feet, was where I truly belonged, was at home and at peace. It simply didn't matter to me.

I swallowed. "Where am I? Am I dead? Can I go home?"

"You are not dead, child. I have simply called you. I am he who creates and who heals, who ends and avenges. A time for change and for reckoning is at hand, and you are my messenger."

"Texas?" I managed. "Home?" I was having trouble making sense, but the Phoenix seemed to understand.

"In time, perhaps you shall return. But my child, there are worse things than to lose what you had."

A crushing sadness descended on me as I thought about not being dead and yet unable to return. The more I thought about it, the more I wanted to go back, if just for a little, at least to make things right and say goodbye. The Phoenix stooped his head to me, and this time in the smell I caught something that tingled a sadness down my spine. A sadness bigger, deeper, more ancient than my own, but tinged with a bright spark of hope. His sadness. The sun overhead dimmed and then brightened, as if sensing my feelings and reacting in sympathy.

"There is always hope, child. Even in the darkest night, there is always hope for a sunrise. Come! There is work to do, worlds that need your help. Change must be made."

"What do you mean?" I realized he had said "worlds." Goosebumps erupted up my arms, and a little of the old fear, a not-pleasant-fear, poked at my heart again.

"Three worlds await, hovering on the brink of darkness, or for some, already plunged into its depths. Change must be made. And it must begin with you." The word *you* swirled around me in a warm tingle. "You must go to the worlds and set change in motion, put the worlds on the path of healing, or an end. Only then will your task be complete."

"Why me?" My fear was shouting in my ears to yell at the guy that I couldn't do it, that I wasn't the hero type, that I would die within two minutes. "How can I..." I trailed off, gesturing vaguely. I didn't even have words to articulate my feelings.

Again, the Phoenix knew my meaning without words. "You shall have help, child. As long as there is a single person whose heart does not serve the darkness, I shall send someone to aid you. You will find help in even the most unexpected places if you look for it. And I shall guide you and show you what must be done. As for why you..." He shook his golden head, sending a shiver down his neck feathers, scattering light like jewels over the grass. "That you must realize for yourself. You are in need of change and healing as much as these worlds. You must find it for yourself."

Great. I didn't know what to think or feel. Currently, it was just scared, and very, very small. Water sloshed around my legs, but I barely noticed. The Phoenix tucked his feathers with his beak, and drew out a gem that flashed and sparkled, catching the light and flinging it back with all the colors of the rainbow. It was small enough that I could have clenched it in my fist and it would be invisible, and it was strung on a fine chain made of something like silver. He dropped it around my neck, and a feeling of peace washed over me from him.

"Take this diamond from the ancient forges beneath Mount Sinai. Be careful who you tell about it, and avoid revealing it as much as possible. When you clutch it tight, it will show you all you need to know to accomplish your mission. It is how I will guide you, my child. But be warned: your mind will not like the invasion of the diamond's message, and will revolt. Your mind may become muddled and in pain for a time; no great thing comes without cost. So be careful, and be wise."

I gulped and nodded, slipping the diamond behind my shirt. I tried to feel strong, to feel a thrill of excitement over the coming adventure, to feel confident and fearless. I still felt like a beetle. I tried to find my feet, but my legs still felt like Jell-O and objected at the idea of standing up, filing a complaint like "*but he's just too much! We can't handle it, not yet. Give us a few... something... until he's gone.*"

"Excuse me, but just one last thing: I'm not a hero by a long shot."

5

I swallowed. Just thinking about some of the things I might have to face was making me sick to my stomach. "I'm afraid. Like, *really* afraid. Fear thinks it's besties with me, actually. It's like my Achilles heel." I was babbling now. "I can't do this if I have to deal with it like always being there, never giving me a break. I mean, I won't stand a chance as it is, and I know I can't always be without fear, but could you just like take it away for while I'm doing this mission thing?"

"My child, fear is not a curse to anyone unless they let it rule them. You must learn to master your fear. You must create the change yourself. Fearlessness is no virtue; courage in the face of fear is. You must choose: will you serve fear or let it serve you?"

"I'll...I'll do my best," I said, biting my lip. I had a feeling this was going to get very ugly and wasn't going to end well.

"Farewell, my little Mastermind. You have strength you do not understand." The Phoenix bent his head and fixed his golden eyes on mine. All the world melted away. "You shall not walk alone, child. This burden you will not have to bear alone, not the whole way. She will be with you, even when others are not."

I wanted to look and see who he meant, but I couldn't take my eyes from his. I wanted to open my mouth and ask him, but I couldn't speak.

"And though you may not see me, I am always with you. Farewell." He erupted into a geyser of flames, collapsing down into the ground. Me, all the colors, the entire world along with my *self*, folded in and were sucked after him.

CHAPTER II

I'm not sure if I lost consciousness; certainly for a while I felt as though I had left my body far, far behind. Gradually I became aware of light. Not as bright as it was in that last green and living place, but sparkly in its radiance. Was I falling, or was I flying? Colors blurred, light grew intense about me, swirling in a myriad of rainbows. I was kneeling on grass, breathing hard, my head spinning, but I had not felt the impact of landing. I tried to sort my thoughts out, but they were in a hopeless muddle. A Phoenix had spoken to me... I remembered how I had felt in his presence, but it felt very distant and far off, like a dream. Somewhere in the back of my mind, fear hollered: *Hell-o, lady! I'm right here! Are you going to listen to me or what? We're in a hopeless mess and we're going to die! Do you even* care?

Shut up, I thought. *Give me a sec.* The voice had said something about my fear... What exactly had it been?

"Will you serve fear or let it serve you?"

I straightened. Had I actually heard a voice speaking, or was it only in my head? I narrowed my eyes and scanned the field around me, my pupils still adjusting to the light. Grass, studded with sweet-smelling blossoms, more waving grass, more flowers, and a patch of black and white fur lying on the ground directly behind me. A dog, a border collie actually. She thumped her tail.

"Uh... was that *you*?" Surely it couldn't be!

"'Course, silly." The dog cocked her head and wagged. *"I'm the one the Phoenix sent to be with you through thick and thin to the bitter end and all that. How do you expect that to work if we can't talk? Isn't this exciting?"*

Um, I thought back, *it's weird right now, and scary. I don't think it's*

7

exciting at all. What I tried to not let her know I was thinking was that I didn't think anything dangerous with a dog on top of it could be anywhere near my ability to cope with. I didn't know much about dogs and had always been kind of afraid of them and their wicked-looking teeth.

"Hey, it can't be that bad. We're going to get along fine, just you wait. What's your name, anyway?"

Alex, I thought fiercely. Far too many people called me by my full name, Alexandria, and this dog was not going to join the club. She already could read my thoughts, including the ones I tried to keep from her. *What's yours?*

"I – I don't think I have one." She dropped her head and, padding up to me, butted it gently against my chest, looking up into my eyes, her wide brown liquid ones pleading. *"Would you please give me one? Please? I've always wanted a name!"*

I thought for a minute, my mind straying to Texas and my home (no, Texas was not *at all* a good name for her). I thought of dogs in books. And then I smiled, tentatively scratching her silky ears. *How do you like… Dixie, girl?*

She raced off into the swaying grass, play-bowed to a shadow, leapt in the air and barked with joy. *"Dixie!"*

I sat back and crossed my legs, watching Dixie frolic in the sunlight. Then my fear finally had its audience. I realized I was in another strange world. A completely unknown world. Instinctively, I curled my knees to my chest, hugging them close as I scanned for threats and tried not to freak out.

"Stop freaking out," Dixie called casually to me. *"I'll let you know if trouble's coming."*

The inspiring view of grass and flowers and more grass at least offered little hiding for dangers. And it did nothing to conceal the castle ahead and to the right of where I sat. I'd missed it before, but now that I saw it, I couldn't stop seeing it. I imagined guards marching around in it, goose-stepping and barking orders. I could see prisoners in my mind's eye, languishing in cells for no other crime than being magically zapped into the castle's territory without a passport. I squinted, trying to make out the distant gate, waiting for it to open and troops to pour out, coming to take one small, frightened, vulnerable girl and an airheaded dog prisoner.

Dixie sniffed indignantly. *"I don't agree with your evaluation of me. But if you're so worried, let's get out of here before they spot us! We'll find cover and go from there. Maybe figure out what we need to do here for starters."*

I stood, trying to stay low against the horizon, suddenly aware for the first time that my hair, instead of falling to my shoulder blades as it had on Earth, dangled to my knees in two braids, each as thick as one of my normal ones. Blinking in surprise at them, I saw they were golden as firelight, and my skin too was a dark brown more befitting a Mexican than a plain American like me. I was also outrageously tall, towering over Dixie and the ground at a height that would have easily dwarfed my six-foot-two dad. And on top of all that, I was wearing a ridiculous sky blue silk dress that hung to my ankles and had ruffly sleeves that tickled. Okay, seriously, what kind of adventure gear was this? I could only hope that my magical luck improved in the other worlds, and I got something more practical.

"This way!" Dixie barked, bounding off to the left of the westering sun, nose to the ground. *"I can smell trees and a forest of wonderful things growing!"*

I stalked off after her, feeling in body like some goddess crudely painted in primary colors, and inside like an egg being used as a ping pong ball by doubt and fear.

Dixie was right. Ahead, the shadowy eaves of a forest loomed, getting closer with each step, colors difficult to distinguish in the gathering twilight. The smells coming from it definitely were a strange mix, and not all the sorts of smells one usually smells when approaching a wood. Food.

Entering under its eves, I looked around, greeted by dangling loaves of cinnamon toast, a blossoming donut tree, cactus-like plants with granola clusters pinned on each spine. Rice crispies hung from branches, candies of every kind studded the underbrush like sticky gems, and the centerpiece of this junk food Eden was an Easy Cheese tree. Cheese-Its bunched and dangled where leaves should have been, and where the branches had broken off or the trunk was punctured, old dried Easy Cheese plugged the hole.

A torrent of memories assaulted me as I stood there. *Chariot rides, a white stallion, lots of dragons over and over again, princesses in towers...* The place reminded me of something I'd once invented. From the time I was a very little girl, I had imaginary adventures in worlds I invented, saving the day over and over again (a thing I knew was really only possible in my imagination). I'd invented three worlds over the course

9

of my adventuring, each one getting more complex and harder to "survive" and save as I got older, each becoming darker and darker as I upped the ante on myself. At the guppy level, the world with training wheels (named Bliss – I'd created it when I was six and abandoned it two years later), I'd put in something I called a fwood or food wood. It was so that adventurers like me could have easy food on the road. It also put a lot of people like farmers out of a job, but I hadn't thought of that at six. Now, I was just grateful that my fwood idea hadn't been an original thought, and that in this world they had something like it. The food looked a little gross, but it was something. At least we wouldn't have to be afraid of starving to death. One way of dying crossed off the possibilities list, seven hundred more to go.

I sat and rested for a while, trying to trust myself to Dixie and quell the fear in my stomach. Of course, my fear thought it would be smart to point out that getting eaten by wild animals or captured by hostile soldiers was the least of our worries, and that we still had no idea what we were doing here or why we were here. I had to agree with that last part.

I pressed my forehead against my knees, struggling not to cry as I thought of my family, wondering whether they thought I was dead, hovering anxiously around my unconscious body in a hospital room maybe. Or maybe I looked dead to them. Maybe they'd bury me in a coffin somewhere, and they'd have a funeral… I wanted to think about them, but it hurt so much. And the Phoenix had sent me here for a reason. Me. Why? I had to figure that out for myself.

I ate a little, but it wasn't very appetizing and I soon gave up. Walking back to the edge of the trees, I peered out, back to where the fiery light of early sunset bathed the castle in stark outlines. I could just see it from here. I stared, harder and harder. It looked familiar. I wasn't sure why. I searched my memory for famous castles, coming up blank. I finally decided I was too tired.

"You sleep, Alex." Dixie's voice was gentle as her wet nose snuffled at my ankle. *"I'll keep watch, just in case."*

I nodded wearily, too exhausted and drained from all the emotions ravaging me to consider protesting. Curling up in the shade of a donut tree, I arranged my awkward dress more comfortably, and almost immediately fell asleep.

The Rallies. I know them well. Being homeschooled, we go to monthly

Rallies to learn things from other homeschooling parents who enjoy teaching a particular subject. I hate them, not least because of Mr. Filips. He teaches what he fondly calls "Storybuilding," and does it with vigor. Class participation is mandatory, and everyone always has to bring a ten-page story to read in front of the entire class. He makes the Rallies a nightmare for me.

I'm in his class now, of course. You never get to dream about your favorite teachers, like Mr. Mackintosh. I'm standing nervously, trying to control my panic. I've written ten pages, but it's not very interesting, all about me squashing all my enemies very heroically in my imaginary world. I wasn't clear though whether it was placed in Bliss or in Secret, my second world.

"Alex!" Mr. Filips bellows. He bellows everything as if we're all hard of hearing. My heart stops beating as I move forward, the sea of faces surges, trying to drown me, and I think I'm going to die right here. Tentatively, I begin to read.

"Give it more soul, sweetheart!" he bellows. "Tell your story like you mean it! And you took what I said about making stakes high and the future looking dark way too far. I'm not sure which side I'm supposed to be rooting for in this story!"

I feel very small. In fact, I've shrunk to be no taller than his knee. "But I need to make it dark so that I can be really heroic," I protest. "If the world isn't overrun by evil, then what do they need me for? They can take care of it themselves. This is the only way that I can feel strong and brave and... needed."

I'd never say that. Oh, gosh, please tell me I never actually said that. It's the truth, but something I've never fully articulated it, not even to myself.

Mr. Filips shakes his bald head. "Girl, that story is depressing. Stories are meant to make you feel victorious, to remind us of hope in the real world. That feels like the freaking *end* of the world. There's no light to counter the darkness, no hope to counter the despair. Show me some hope, sweetheart, and not just the hope being you riding in on a golden chariot and saving the day."

I look down at the pages clutched in my hands, feeling more hopeless myself than I've ever felt before. And crushed. When I try to keep reading, my tears blur the words. I stammer, frantically trying to blink them away as Mr. Filips shifts impatiently. The words won't sharpen, even when I clear the tears. They get blurrier and blurrier and then they aren't there. I stop helplessly,

"That's enough for this week, Alex. Bring us a better story next week."

I slink back to my seat, wishing I could die of shame. I wad up the papers, wanting to throw them at Mr. Filips, and shrink down into my chair. Mr. Filips takes out his pencil, breaking it in half. Easy Cheese squirts out, and he hoses it over a pile of Cheese-Its. I stare as he starts to munch, and he throws the other half of his pencil at me.

"Come up with something tastier!" he bellows, his mouth full of pulped fake cheese products.

"I – I'm sorry," I stammer. "I didn't think – I didn't realize – I didn't know. I should've known better. I'm sorry." I'm not sure what I'm talking about, because I don't mean the Easy Cheese. I don't have time to sort my thoughts.

Mr. Filips straightens and barks. Then he yells: "We look in the diamond or we go to the castle!"

I awoke with a start.

CHAPTER III

Dixie sat above me, staring solemnly down into my face. *"Seriously, Alex, I've been thinking this over."*

I sat up, rubbing the sleep from my eyes. As much as I hated my dream, and revisiting Mr. Filips and the Rallies, I hated coming back to reality more. Stuck in a strange world with unknown dangers and not a clue yet what I had to do or why I was here. And I had to help this world and several others before I could go home. Currently, that was all I really cared about, and there was no "skip this step" option on helping the worlds.

Early morning sunlight slipped through the foody leaves and branches and fell around me. I sprang to my feet, charged suddenly with fear as I remembered the castle. Had anyone sallied out to capture us? I raced to the gap in the trees and scanned the field of grass between us and the castle. It was perfectly empty. I breathed a sigh of relief.

Again I eyed the castle, trying to shake the feeling of eerie familiarity. Disney-esque, I decided. That was why. It just looked like all the Disney castles in the fairytale movies. I briefly wondered if the moviemakers had visited this world themselves and used that castle as a prototype. I turned to Dixie.

Okay, so what are you talking about?

"We don't have a clue about anything. We know literally zero about this world. So you look in that diamond and at least get us something to start with, or we go spy on that castle, maybe knock on the gate, find stuff out. We don't have much choice. We can't take forever on these missions, and don't you want to get home?"

Of course! I retorted angrily, eyes stinging. I viciously plucked a handful of granola clusters from a cactus and chewed them ferociously.

"We've got to start somewhere. We need to get someone on the inside, someone who knows a lot about this world and everything, and get help from them. Why not start with the castle? There has to be a reason we were dumped so close to it."

I considered that. It seemed likely. The Phoenix didn't seem like the sort that would do anything by accident. He had promised to guide me. What had I been expecting, a trail of golden light or the occasional flash of fiery wings? No, he used more subtlety than that, I was pretty sure. He was leaving a lot of it to me to figure out and handle on my own, which I supposed made sense. Otherwise I was just a kind of slave, even with a kindly master. But still, I couldn't help wishing for a little more handholding.

Experimentally, I broke off part of the stem of the cactus, holding it carefully with the spines. I was rewarded by discovering the inside was filled with milk, and I quickly quenched my raging thirst. "I'm not so sure that's the best idea. I mean, yes, I agree about starting somewhere and needing someone knowledgeable, but just walking up to the castle seems like a crazy risk."

"Then we look in the diamond."

"But…" I remembered about what the Phoenix had warned me, that it could drain me and cause me mental and maybe physical pain. I didn't like the idea of doing that out here in the middle of a strange place with no real place to hide and being left helpless. Then again, Dixie was right. It was that or go up to the castle. I pounded my forehead. Why? I wondered. Why did the choices have to be so bad?

"I'll look," I said at last.

I sat down and made myself as comfortable as I could, folding my legs up under me. Then I gestured for Dixie to curl up next to me, and she rested her head in my lap. My heart was beating double time, and my hands shook as I pulled at the silver chain. The diamond fell out, flashing and sparkling just like it had when I first got it. I took a deep breath, then another.

"For heaven's sake, just get it over with, Alex!" Dixie said, her voice drenched in nervousness, but not half as strong as my own. She wasn't the one who would get an incapacitating headache at the end.

There was nothing for it. Putting it off was only making it worse, now that I had decided to do it. I bent over it, gripping it tight, and as I held it, the light that reflected from it spun and morphed from random colors into distinct pictures. The jumble of light danced and rearranged itself, filling my vision as it became images and meanings I

14

could understand. I felt dizzy, lost. I was aware of nothing, not Dixie, not my body, only the diamond and the things it showed. I saw a barren rock mountain so small it didn't dream that snow could crown it. An instant later I felt I was swooping over a forest that glinted with gossamers, like, *way* bigger than any others until it whirled out of sight, replaced by a woman, tall and fair. Her hands were clasped together, and I had the impression that she was saying something, but in the swirl of overpowering images I couldn't catch any words. Yet somehow, I knew my mission here had something to do with her. The flow of images grew faster and faster, whizzing by in a blur before I could decipher them. I felt sick and weak. My head was a pounding roar, and I thought my brain was about to explode. *Let go!* I screamed at myself. I felt my clutching fingers again, and slowly, doing everything I could to block out the diamond and its message, I forced my fingers away. The diamond fell from them.

The pictures were gone. I drifted in darkness, away from the pain, away from memory and awareness. The darkness was better. With a sigh, I embraced it.

* * *

"Never mind the code!" an animated voice said. "Technically she didn't ask for solace or refuge, so we aren't bound by it."

"That's the letter of the law," an impatient female voice responded. "The spirit is to extend hospitality and help those in need. That's what Queen Rowenna was after when she first instituted the code. We should honor that."

"Yeah, well, in times like these, we have to look after our own, not go taking in a bunch of strangers. We'll all die anyway. What's the point? We're all doomed to the dragon."

"Talking like that will only guarantee it," the girl's voice said tartly. "Go run off and take care of your own. *I'll* act like a true daughter of Bliss and look after her."

A door closed. Irate footsteps snapped back and forth across the room. Water poured. I swam up through my mind fog and opened my eyes.

The room wobbled in and out of focus. Blood drummed in my head and my chest felt crushed. I tried to piece together where I was and how I got here, but the last thing I remembered was looking in the diamond. A wet slobbery tongue swiped my hand, and I looked around to see a black and white Dixie blob curled beside me on the wide, cushioned bed. I sat up groggily. The blood roared louder and I momentarily lost my vision. I fell back on the cushions.

"So. You're awake." The girl's voice still had a tart edge, but she spoke gently enough. Then she appeared in my vision, holding a glass of water. She had long blonde braids like mine, and her frame was just as fragile, but the strength with which she easily lifted me to a sitting position showed that she was much, much stronger than she looked. She put the glass in my hand. "I'd like to know who you are. My name is Kya, and though I'm just a servant girl, I can probably help you with whatever you need. Just let me know. Unlike my grouchy companion, I believe we should help one another, including strangers like yourself. Now, who are you?"

"Alex," I slurred, gulping down the water. My head cleared a little, but I still sounded to myself like I was speaking underwater. "Twelve. Texas." Important information delivered.

I glanced down quickly, and saw the diamond was tucked safely under my dress and out of sight.

"You did it before you passed out. You don't remember? The servants came to pick food, and they found you blacked out. They brought you here, to the castle, and have been looking out for you."

How long? I asked.

"Only an hour or so, don't worry. And that girl's a good sort. She's been looking after you."

I remembered the conversation I'd overheard waking up, with the two arguing voices. Then a chill ran down my spine. I looked at Kya, at her big cobalt blue eyes, her ready-for-anything expression, and remembered what she had told the other person: *I'll be a true daughter of Bliss.*

It was impossible. But now that I realized it, I felt stupid. The big-eyed, string-bean-Hercules people, myself included, the familiar, Disneyish castle, the fwood… I was *in* Bliss. The world I'd imagined when I was six years old.

"Why are you staring at me like that?" Kya demanded.

"This world…" I stammered. "Is this… is it called Bliss?"

"Uh, *yes*. What hole did you spring from? No offense, I mean," she added quickly.

I glanced around at the stone walls, at the narrow window not much wider than my shoulders, letting in the bright sunlight. My world. I swung my feet over the edge and stood carefully, steadying myself against the cool stones.

"Queen Rowenna, the code; that's about giving shelter to non-criminal travelers who ask for it, right?" I was so rusty. I couldn't recall a scrap of geography.

"Yeah." Kya looked at me like I was crazy. "Seriously, don't you know all this stuff? Everyone does."

I blew out a long breath. In my imagined adventures, I'd made a point not to tell anyone that I made the world. I was just their goddess-like heroine who rode in and saved the day when things got bad. Because of how I'd designed it, that happened a lot. It made a need for me, and if I'd actually created the worlds in imagining them, I wondered how they had survived this long since I abandoned them. The evil things I usually crushed should have swept them away easily by now.

"Kya," I began, staring at the wall and not her, my eyes beginning to cooperate more. "I... I made this world. I come from another place. It's only been six years there, but a lot longer here if I understand right. My full name is actually Alexandria, the same adventurer who'd help you guys out in the old days." I winced. "I used to imagine I had adventures here, and turns out it was all real. I somehow made it happen by imagining it." I looked up at her face, trying to see how she was taking this. She was just staring blankly at me, her expression unreadable. "I'm sorry. I shouldn't have made so much evil for you guys to fight, even though I didn't know I was actually creating a world. It wasn't right. I hope it's not too late to change."

Kya's face softened. "You didn't know... and a whole world created, just like that?" She looked a little impressed. "This must be quite a shock for you."

I nodded and looked away. Overwhelming guilt poured over me. What had I done?

"I'm here to help create change and healing," I said at last, refocusing on the Phoenix and the job he'd given me. "Tell me what's the matter."

Kya puffed out her cheeks and almost laughed. "What isn't the matter? We thought we had evil dragons in the past, but now there's this one... Well, he's the only one of his kind, but he's worse than any ever before. He has magic like all the dragons did, but unlike them, he's smart enough to use it, really use it. Just for starters, he's created these huge spiders —" she indicated with her hands a size that would have put a fair-sized bean bag to shame "— and they do his bidding. He's also captured the Relic of Shakira and woven it into his power so that he has more magic than any other dragon dreamed of. And without the Relic, we have no magic to use against him, so we're helpless. He's building up for something, has been for years, and any day, the dam will break, and he'll sweep us away. We'll be subjugated to his rule, eaten for food or fed to his spiders, enslaved to his darkness, who knows?"

She sighed and threw back her shoulders determinedly. "Sorry, I just kind of whined all about our doom and gloom. Probably didn't make much sense to you."

"It made enough," I said, thinking hard. I was trying to remember what I could about Bliss, which unfortunately was precious little.

I knew it was a fairytale princess world with dragons and princesses in every story, and usually a gallant knight to ride to their rescue. I'd given the dragons magic and humans none, as that made things harder to beat the bad guys. Shakira, a sort of wizard, had been the only human ever to possess magic, and before she died, she took all her power and encased it in a magical orb the size of a soccer ball. It had belonged to the royal house of Bliss for eons, and they had used it to keep back the dragons. Perhaps that was the saving grace that had preserved the world after I stopped returning to ride in and save the day. But if the dragons had it now… well, no wonder the world was on the brink of being plunged into darkness.

"*So what do we do?*" Dixie asked in my head. "*We have a mountain, a forest, and a woman. How is that supposed to help us? Too bad you didn't watch the vision to its completion.*"

I was about to fly apart, Dixie! I thought back with some irritation. *Would you rather I died?*

"*'Course not, silly. I was just saying too bad. But if we want anything helpful, we may have to look again sometime. Just, you know, saying.*"

My shoulders slumped. The mountain… I had known it. Dragons. A mountain. "We start with Dragon Mountain," I said suddenly. Kya jumped.

"Start what?"

I gave her a long, contemplative look. Dixie had said we'd need someone on the inside, and my memory was nowhere near going to cut it.

"Kya, how do you feel about risking your life to save the world?"

She didn't hesitate. "In a heartbeat, especially if it saves my queen. I want her back, and a happier world with her. I'll do whatever I have to for that."

"Then I'll need a change of clothes, something I can rough around in, and supplies and a guide out of this castle." I paused, realizing what she had said. "Wait. What's the matter with the queen?"

Kya glanced at the door. "Later. I'll get what we need and we'll go at sunset. Try to sleep." Then she left the room.

CHAPTER IV

I was exhausted, now that I thought about it. Being unconscious seemed to have drained more than rested me. My emotions were in a turmoil and I still felt a little sick from the diamond. Flinging myself face down on the bed, I buried my head in the pillow and let it all come loose in hot tears. When my sobs subsided to the occasional sniffle, my mind turned to thoughts of my family. To my parents, who were always there for me to guide and protect me, and to my little brother Elliot, who shadowed me and taught me so much without either of us realizing it. Oh, why hadn't I been a better sister? Where were they? Were they worrying about whether I would live through the night? They would never guess that I was in a different world that I had made up and needed to help change. If only I could see them, tell them I was all right! Was that even true?

At some point, I fell away into a deep, dreamless sleep, and didn't wake up until I heard a low voice by my head.

"Wake up!"

I sat up with a jerk, heart pounding in my throat. "What? What is it?"

"Shh, keep it down, will you?" Kya hissed back. She was standing right beside my bed. "The castle people think you're a crazed wanderer and very dangerous. They won't do anything too drastic, on account of the code, but they intend to keep a close watch on you and basically keep you a prisoner until they figure out more about you."

"What?" I asked incredulously. Me, a guest under protection of the code, a prisoner in Castle Bliss itself? It was unheard of!

"It's true. That's what took me so long. I was trying to make the arrangements unnoticed. I think I succeeded."

"Arrangements for what?"

"Our escape?" She seemed baffled that I hadn't figured it out on my own. "Anyway, I didn't want any of them knowing that we're leaving tonight."

"You're sure you want to help me?" I asked, hoping desperately she would but not wanting to force her. I needed every ally I could get, and I was already starting to depend on her. "You'll probably get in trouble if you do."

Kya chuckled humorlessly. "Maybe, but if we don't do something, the world is basically going to end, and we'll probably all die, which means getting in trouble will be the least of my worries. And if somehow we manage to pull off some kind of miracle, then getting in trouble will be a small price to pay." She puffed a strand of hair out of her face. "And if I ever was unsure about helping you, I have no doubt now." She paused, looking at me out of the corner of her eye. I waited. "I had a... a vision," she said quietly. "A wonderful, fiery Phoenix spoke to me, telling me I was meant to help you. So I'm going to."

I smiled faintly. "The Phoenix. Yeah, I've seen him too."

She really smiled for the first time and straightened, holding out a bundle to me. She cleared her throat softly. "Here. I got you a change of clothes. I hope it doesn't offend your dignity or anything, but it was the best I could get."

"I'm sick of dignity. I want to be normal again. Just call me Alex, won't you?"

"Sure. Oh, and we're going out the window." She grinned, backed quietly to the door, and waved. "I'm getting us horses," she whispered, and disappeared.

I unpacked the bundle on the bed. Compared to my current clothes situation, what Kya brought me was a breath of fresh air, and it certainly could have been worse. A soldier surcoat, marked with the emblem of the royal house of Bliss (a swooping white-gray dove on green), a loose, pant-like garment that I thought was structured more like trash bags sewn together than anything that should be worn, and a pair of boots, a bit latent. My feet were already sore and blistered from the walking I had done in silky slippers. Thankfully, Kya had had the forethought to put thick knitted socks in the pile, so my blisters would at least have some cushioning. Quickly, and as quietly as I could, I changed my clothes and ate some of the food and water that had been left on a side table in the room.

Somewhat satisfied and with nothing else to do, I moved to the window to wait, trying not to pace. Kya had said we would leave by the window, but I doubted what method she could have devised to get both of us and Dixie out of the room. Dixie watched me through hooded eyes, sprawled luxuriously on the bed by herself. I gazed out and watched the sunset, the sun gone behind the horizon and only its memory streaking the sky in a myriad of hues.

When Kya did return, it was just as I suspected. "It'll be simple enough," she explained quietly. "I managed to slip out unobserved with two horses. I could be a thief." She flashed a grin. "They're waiting outside the outer wall right now. It doesn't really matter if they know how we left as long as we're gone by the time they discover it, so we can leave the rope knotted in here. I'll throw the other end over the outer wall and we can slide right down to the outside."

"Isn't it a little far from here to the outer wall?" I didn't relish the idea of sliding free over a great depth of space, picturing a sight almost like zip-lining across the Grand Canyon.

"No, it's only a foot or two. We'll be fine. You go first, and I'll follow."

I squinted out the window and saw that she was right. The outer wall did run close to the side of the castle here and there were no guards in sight... yet. Bravo, Alex. Well-designed castle.

"How do you plan to get Dixie down there?" I demanded, guessing the answer she was about to give.

Kya shrugged. "She'll have to stay behind. She wouldn't be able to keep up with the horses, anyway, not for long. They'll take great care of her, don't worry."

But I shook my head firmly. "No. Dixie comes, even if we have to waltz right down the stairs and out the main gate in front of every watching eye in the castle."

"And how do you plan to do that?" She crossed her arms.

"If you go down first and wait on the wall top, she can put me in a blanket sling and lower me down to you, and you can lower me to the ground. Then you can follow me and she can follow you. Also, with me as a counterweight, you won't have to worry so much about falling; my weight will keep the rope taut."

I stared at Dixie, marveling at her ingenuity. I turned to Kya and explained Dixie's idea, doing my best to act like I had thought of it

22

myself, as we had decided to keep our ability to communicate a secret if at all possible, just like the diamond. If the wrong sorts of people heard about it, they might find a way to use it against us.

"Are you sure it'll work?" Kya asked dubiously.

"Um…" I glanced swiftly at Dixie, immediately wished I hadn't and hoped Kya wouldn't put the two together, and repeated aloud what she thought at me. "If all goes as planned, scientifically and statistically speaking, we have every reason to believe that it should work as neatly as a –" I broke off before I said Dixie's simile aloud – *as neatly as a well-thrown ball.* "As the Pythagorean Theorem," I amended, reverting to mathematical expressions per one of my oldest habits.

Kya reluctantly agreed, apparently thinking this was at least a better idea than going down the stairs bold as brass. She tied one end of her rope to the bedpost, and leaning out the window, gave the other end an expert toss. It vanished over the outer wall.

"Off you go, Alex," she said, stepping back. I climbed onto the sill, feeling very sick and frightened and not at all as if I could do this.

CHAPTER U

Despite my fears, the climb was relatively easy, in no small part due to the incredible strength I had in this fragile body. In fact, if I had fallen even ten feet, I probably would have been badly injured and broken half my bones, but as long as I could use my record-breaking strength to *keep* myself from falling, I was in little danger. Dixie's plan did work, though I hadn't much doubted it. It seemed like forever before all three of us were standing together on good solid ground outside the walls beside two horses, saddled and packed for a trip.

"Here we go," I chuckled, still feeling queasy and shaken, but in my nervous state I was giggling like a teenager on her first day at a new school. I swung into the saddle, a motion that should have been familiar from all my ranch rides, but wasn't. I had way too much legs to put anywhere, and my torso seemed to tower from the saddle. Kya, beside me, was in a worse plight being older and taller, but she didn't seem to notice. Of course, for them this was normal. I pitied these people even more for the undeserved troubles my girlish fancies had flung on them.

Dixie, as I expected, kept pace with the horses easily, sometimes racing ahead and whisking around to wait for us to catch up, other times lingering over some intensely interesting smell only to put on a burst of speed to regain her lead, and all the while she maintained a constant stream of chatter. I was driven almost to distraction, but at least she didn't seem to mind whether her questions were answered or not and often moved on to another before I had time to think of the answer. I wondered if Kya guessed something was not completely normal in the relationship between Dixie and me. She kept sneaking glances at us when she thought I wouldn't see, and on these occasions I caught a glint of intense curiosity in her eyes, but she never asked any questions, which was good.

"So tell me what's up with the queen." I broke the silence at last, once the castle was long out of earshot and dwindling out of sight behind us.

"Oh." Kya's face darkened and she turned away from me, scanning the night shrouded landscape. "Yeah, well, the dragon kind of kidnapped her. All of them, actually. Queen Vida, her sister and her sister's sons, and all the great warriors and lords. All those who go after them to rescue them don't come back."

"Do they know where to look? I mean, are they all being held in his mountain cave or whatever? Can't you just overwhelm him with an army long enough to rescue them?" As soon as I said that, I felt stupid. *Of course* they would have thought of trying that. They would have thought of every possibility. Still, I'd said it, and I glanced at Kya to make sure I hadn't insulted her too much.

Her shoulders sagged. "You're forgetting the Cob Grove, Alex," she said softly.

"The, um... the what, exactly?" I asked, trying not to let the image from the diamond of a forest wound up with monstrous webs that no normal spider could have spun invade my memory.

"Those spiders I mentioned. They live in the Cob Grove... for now. They are the dragon's army. If they stood in force against us – which they would if we looked like we were so much as *dreaming* of attacking him – we wouldn't stand a chance. It'd be over before it started. Chances are, they stopped all those people who tried to find the queen and the lords." She blew out her breath and urged her horse on a little faster. I had to follow suit to keep up, and I only just caught what she murmured, half to herself. "And chances are, they'll try and stop *us* too."

My skin prickled up in goosebumps. *Told you so!* My fear shrieked in my ear. *You are so going to die. And did you listen to me? Nooooo. You didn't. Nitwit!*

"Shut up," I said aloud. "I have to do this. I owe it to Bliss for causing all this trouble to begin with, and the Phoenix sent me as his messenger. So just shut up already."

Kya stared at me. "Alex..." she began hesitantly. "Alex, are you... okay?"

I shook myself, remembering she was there. Dixie was laughing at me in my head. "Yeah, I'm fine, sorry. I was just talking to myself."

She was quiet for a minute. "I didn't know the Phoenix sent you," she said finally.

I grunted. "And I'm supposed to figure out why for myself. I mean, I have a guess that it's because I made this world, but I'd like to know for sure, you know what I mean?"

"Shh!" Kya hissed so suddenly I flinched.

"What?" I gulped around my hammering heart.

For answer, she pointed. Dragon Mountain was dead ahead of us, and in the dark, it had snuck far closer than we realized.

It was only fifteen miles from Castle Bliss to Dragon Mountain, as when I created it I wanted to put it at a convenient distance for the knights (unfortunately, that also made it convenient for the dragons). It was the dragons' lair through all the generations of diabolically evil magical dragons. It was also the mountain I'd seen in the diamond, so this was where we'd start.

I could see no firelight coming from the deeper-than-dark pock halfway up the mountainside that was, if I remembered right, the dragon's cave. Either he was asleep or away. I wasn't sure which I preferred.

We picketed the horses off to the side of the mountain, out of sight of the cave but it certainly didn't put it out of our minds. We'd have to wait until sunrise to investigate the cave, but it was only a few hours away. Neither of us much liked the idea of blundering around his cave in the dark, especially when we weren't certain where he was.

"There's food from the fwood in the saddlebags." Kya's voice was barely audible. We didn't dare speak aloud, for fear of drawing unwanted attention.

"Yeah, no thanks. I'm not hungry." I'd just eaten before leaving, and I didn't say what I was thinking: that after a few hours, when we poked around in the dragon's cave, I probably wouldn't need to eat again. Kya shrugged and settled down herself near the horses, and Dixie curled up near her. I lay down too, trying to mimic their easy breathing and instantaneous sleep, but I just couldn't. My mind kept returning to the unfinished diamond vision, and Dixie's words: *Too bad you didn't watch the vision to its completion.*

I rolled over and looked at the sleeping forms of my friends. No, I couldn't be that peaceful, not now, and I was beginning to think not ever. I found my feet and slipped around an outcropping of boulders as quietly as I could. I nestled down in a crook so I was almost completely hidden and drew out the diamond.

I wasn't really thinking about what I was going to do. At the moment, I was only vaguely scared of the awful crippling mental pain to come, and it didn't occur to me that this was probably the worst time I could do this. I was moving mechanically, drawn by the need to know, to decide. I was never meant to do these things! I worked best when I had someone else's clever thinking and decisions to rely on, and I stood on the outskirts watching. That was my job in life, to watch and dream and hide in my little turtle shell, only poking my head out if it was absolutely necessary. I peered into the diamond, waiting for the overpowering flow of images painted in light to flash in my vision and overwhelm me.

It came. Dragon Mountain, the very one I had my back against at this moment, slid into view just as it had before, but this time, there was a difference. This time, I heard words. A voice, actually. One I recognized. The Phoenix. I saw the forest again, the one I now knew was called Cob Grove.

"Cut off the body, the head will die. Free the lives locked in the Cob Grove's sinkhole. Set the torch to evil's roots, and set the magic in motion. So end Dragonkind and its evil and begin the change."

Good grief, what could all that possibly mean? But more was coming fast. I shot toward the mountain, no, *through* it. I saw the woman again, but now I could see she was surrounded by darkness, bound hand and foot, but still as regal as a queen. Her lips were moving faintly, but it wasn't her voice that spoke in my mind. "Vida knows the answer." Who knew what answer? What was the question? But the vision was ending. The images pulsed by faster and faster as my brain lost its grip on reality. The pictures became blurred and indistinct, and disappeared into darkness.

CHAPTER VI

"It's the queen!" I sat bolt upright. My head was drumming like it was hosting a band concert, and my vision was wavering again. I stumbled out from where I'd been sitting and pitched forward onto my hands and knees. Dawn grayed the eastern horizon as I got up and stumbled toward the others, hastily stuffing the diamond away.

Kya was on her feet, roused by my cry. "Shh, quiet, Alex! Not so loud. You'll wake the dragon!" she hissed desperately.

Dixie forced herself up, stretched, and shook her ears. "*What do you mean it's the queen? I don't see anyone.*"

"I mean the woman up there." I lowered my voice to an urgent half-whisper. "It's Queen Vida, and the dragon has her all trussed up in the back of his cave." The words spilled out of me in my groggy rush.

"What woman?" Kya asked. "You mean to tell me that you went exploring last night and didn't tell me or get my help? Well!" She looked something between aggrieved and awed.

"Oh no!" I actually flinched at the thought of doing such a thing. With any luck, I'd get this world all squared away and set to rights without seeing so much as a trail of smoke from the dragon. "I mean –"

"*You mean the woman in the diamond, I see, but shut up!*"

Dixie's last two words rang so loudly in my head I clicked my jaw shut instantly and bit my tongue. I stared at her as she slid in and out of focus, seeing her ears pricked and alert, eyes locked on me with an explanative look. I suddenly realized my near slip. I remembered what the Phoenix had said about avoiding revealing the diamond if at all possible.

"*Right. That was a close one, but I've got your back, Alex.*" She licked my face. "*Best be careful what you tell her.*" Her eyes slid to glance at Kya. "*She a good sort, I think, but she talks.*"

And you don't? I thought wryly. I sat down, more in possession of myself now, but concentrating hard to avoid another accident. That one had been too close.

Kya was watching me with a baffled impatience. "Well, what do you mean by 'the woman up there'? How can you know there's any woman up there, never mind her being the queen, if you didn't go poking around last night while I was asleep?"

"Kya," I said slowly, thinking out each word before I said it, "you told me you had a vision, right?"

She glanced away. Clearly the vision had affected her strongly, and she was still getting used to the idea. "Yeah. I did."

"Well…" I figured the diamond basically counted as a vision. "I had a vision, and saw a woman deep in the dragon's cave, all trussed up, who is Queen Vida herself."

"*Is that how you really know?*" Dixie asked, her head popping up from where it had been sniffing to look narrowly at me.

I'm surprised you haven't read my mind yet and found out, I thought, deliberately not looking at her this time.

"*It's tiring to go poking in someone else's mind, so I only do it if I need to. It's hard enough putting thoughts in.*"

I looked in the diamond again, and I got a little more, I told her.

"*What else did you get?*" Dixie asked eagerly, but our mental conversation was interrupted by Kya interjecting. Her voice was intense, but still low in volume.

"So did this vision of yours give us even a *clue* of what we're supposed to do? And does it have anything to do with your thing with you and Dixie?"

I stared at her, feigning complete incomprehension. I'm a horrible actress. "What about me and Dixie?"

"Don't give me that." She bestowed a particularly withering look on me. "You keep looking funny at each other. You were just staring at her for like, forever, ignoring me, doing nothing but gawk at your own dog. You've been vague and distracted ever since I met you, you laugh at bizarre moments, and you make the weirdest faces at the weirdest times, and you look at Dixie a lot when it happens. And anyone with half a nerve bundle for a brain could see that Dixie isn't any ordinary dog. So what's the big secret about you two? Is she someone enchanted or something?"

I looked at Dixie. *If we're not going to tell her, what can I say?*

"See, there you go again!" Kya pointed out, exasperated.

"Try deflecting back to the subject of the queen."

I lost no time taking Dixie's suggestion. "We were just talking about Dixie," I said innocently. "It's normal to look at something you're talking about. And speaking of which, suppose we go look and see if the queen is in that cave or not? It's about time we did something other than sit around in the shadow of a dangerous mountain and chat. Let's go."

"But you didn't answer my question!" Shoot. It wasn't going to work. "And what about the dragon?" Oh, nice. An out.

"He's not there," I said confidently, hoping I was right. "There's no smoke coming from the cave, so he must be out and about his dragonish business."

"How do you know?" Kya asked, sounding as nervous as I felt. I shrugged. The truth was, I didn't know. I was just guessing and hoping. "So we just walk up there and rescue the queen? Is that the plan?"

I shrugged again. "I guess. Supposedly she has the answer to something, but I'm not sure what."

Texas doesn't have mountains. Sometimes it likes to pretend it does, but I lived in real mountain country before I ever saw a grain of Texas soil. In the Northwest, we know what mountains are. Since I was only nine when we moved down to Texas, I hadn't done any mountain-climbing, but I had seen and heard some. Since it was in that last year there that I had begun to get bored with all things princess, I had actually taken some interest. I might be able to figure this thing out.

It was, as I might have guessed, not as easy as I thought. I kept losing track of where my arms or legs were. For some reason they seemed to have about as much to do with me as my clothes, and accidentally misplacing a limb while climbing resulted in a couple of close calls. Thanks to my goddess-like strength and the use of a rope, it was not as hard as it might have been to climb the four miles up a fairly smooth mountainside, though my strength didn't do much to reduce my fear. Kya, for her part, was doing excellently behind me, being an expert with using her own rope to her best advantage, but Dixie had informed me when I was ten feet off the ground that *"there is no way that I am doing that in any world under any sun. You go ahead and I'll keep watch and sniff."*

The first rays of sunlight had well breached the horizon when I staggered to my feet on the flat slope outside the dragon's cave. It was a broad, almost circular area, level for a mountainside, sinking back into darkness in a descent inwards. The place where I stood, and Kya too now, could hardly be more than a take-off point for the dragon, but there was not a sliver of doubt in my mind that he had been here, and not too long ago. Not only had this been the traditional home for dragonkind since I created this world, but I could smell his smoke, the reek he left fouling the pure mountain air, curse him. And into that cave we had to go. Somewhere down there was the queen, and she had the "answer" to something about my mission. I had to get to her or die in the attempt, and it would probably be the latter, I thought darkly. Shivering nervously, I glanced at Kya.

"Ready?" I asked. Her temper was a little hot apparently, and not improved by the climb.

"No, quite frankly, I'm not. I think this is a stupid reckless idea and we'll be killed when the dragon comes back and finds us in his den. But if my queen's in there, I'll do whatever I have to. This is a crazy idea." She paused for breath and looked at me. I waited, wondering what to say. If not for the fact that I had little choice, I would be as far away from this place here as I could get in this world. Personally, I wanted to wake up, find this a dream, and have the comfort of sheets to hide under and tremble in. I couldn't blame her if she wanted to back out now. "This is a crazy idea," Kya repeated, somewhat calmer, "but I'm not leaving you. I'm with you, Alex."

This girl was full of surprises. Abashed and confused, I gave a half shrug and turned quickly away to hide my blushing cheeks. I plunged into the utter darkness of the dragon's cave.

CHAPTER UII

I had neglected to account for my clichés. My foot hit something slippery, or more accurately a great heap of shifting things, and I skidded, slid, and rolled sideways down an ever-steepening bank of what I at last guessed to be coins. I crashed into a stash of spiky objects, tumbled over an embankment of very small, very sharp stones, and flopped in a battered heap at the bottom of the good old-fashioned dragon treasure hoard. There was no light. I tried to stand and call to Kya, but I was in too much of a bruised fog of pain.

Ever so slowly, my eyes began to perceive light. It was an eerie bluish light, radiating from patches on the walls on either hand. There was something totally unnatural about it, something whispering of lurking evil and sorcery. I shivered, and wished I was still blinded by darkness. In the patches of light that looked almost like imbedded crystal formations, I could see things. In one, a spearhead, in another, a grinning skull, a third showed an amulet. I wondered if these objects were actually imprisoned in the crystal, or if the strange light only showed things far off. It didn't matter. They radiated evil power.

Scrambling painfully to my feet, I was greeted by a shocking and disturbing discovery. I was starting to lose the sense and feel of my own limbs! I tripped over myself just trying to stand, and my ability to feel other parts of me with another appendage was marginal. I could as easily misplace an arm as anyone else would misplace car keys. I realized I had felt the beginnings of it while climbing the mountain, but now it was stronger, more extreme. Was I becoming less tangible somehow? Would I fade bit by bit until I was no more than a ghost? Was I already a ghost? I shoved the thoughts from my mind, trying desperately not to let my brain go there, too late.

"This is... this is evil!" Kya's voice sounded unnaturally loud beside me. I jumped at least a foot and clamped a hand on her mouth. She pushed my arm away but was quiet, and side by side, we crept farther in. I noticed that from each pulsing patch of light a slender thread ran out from the top, along the roof of the cave, and disappeared in the direction we were heading. Did that mean anything?

Here the hall-like cave was relatively clear for the most part, scattered only with the occasional jewel. We followed the sorcerous cord of light overhead deeper and deeper.

The light convened in another of the patches, but this one was different from all the others. The shapes in it spun and moved, sliding in and out of focus, getting bigger and seeming to emerge from the wall like a holograph, then shrinking and growing more distant. It didn't matter. I had seen it clear enough in the diamond to know exactly what it was: the Cob Grove. What did the pulsing light image mean? As overwhelmingly strong as the diamond's images were, it didn't feel evil, only too strong for my mind to hold. This was crawling evil, black sorcery, witchcraft if ever there was. What had I done, giving magic to those I created to be evil villains? I had handed the world over to their corrupt power lock stock and barrel, without so much as a second thought. Magic was a dangerous thing, not to be taken lightly. I stretched out a hand to the shifting vision of the Cob Grove, wanting to rip it out, destroy the dragon's power, to cripple their kind forever. Closer and closer my fingers got.

"Don't touch it!"

I jerked my hand back, startled by the unknown voice that spoke to my right. I half expected, in the split second that my brain registered that it was not Kya speaking, that it was the sibilant growl of the dragon, but an instant later processed the gentle sweetness of the voice. No, it was no dragon, though the speaker's tone was pierced with untold agony. Even before I turned, I knew who I would see. Sure enough, she was there, graceful and slender as a lily, hard as diamonds, regal as the queen she was.

"Oh, my queen!" Kya cried, throwing herself to her knees beside the queen. She was just as I had seen her in the diamond, bound, slumped against the wall seeming drained of strength, but her eyes were very much alive.

"Leave me!" she commanded. "Go, my friends, before the dragon returns and finds you here. You will not fare so well as I."

"But we have to free you!" Kya urged, and I saw tears in her eyes as she scrambled, searching for bindings to cut and a way to do it.

"No!" she said forcefully. "You must leave me here." She twisted, showing the back of her wrists, tied behind her. Out from the ropes that tied her spun a thread of the bluish light, sinking into the wall. "If you cut me loose, I will die. He is using my strength, my blood, to bind me and help control the magic of his precious talismans you see in the walls. I am one myself to him. His power holds me, and freeing me is not the way to break it. You must destroy his magic and then I will be free, not the other way around."

"But we don't know how to destroy his magic!" I interjected. Oh, if only this were a story I was writing! I could write the magic out of existence, write everything back to normal, write everyone home alive and well. I could unwrite all the things I had gotten wrong in the making. *Get out of the past, Alex! Focus! Lives depend on you now!* That didn't improve my ability to do things, knowing that lives depended on me. "Do you know how? Do I have to kill him?"

"If you destroy his magic, he will die. It will cut the ground from under him, and the last blood of the dragons will be no more than ash." She stopped, struggling for breath and strength to continue. *Cut off the body, the head will die,* I remembered. Was that what it meant? "You saw the grove," the queen went on, searching both of our faces with a pleading urgency. "In it are my family and the knights and lords of the royal order. They were snared by the spiders, trying to get the Relic of Shakira. The dragon keeps it in the heart of the grove, guarded by hundreds of his spiders. He wove the foundation of his power through it to gain more, and if it were destroyed, so would he be. At least, that was what we believed and hoped. But none of us succeeded. If those others still live, they are held prisoner there, in the center of the grove. Free them, please, and destroy the Relic."

"How do you know this?" I dropped to one knee beside Kya, leaning closer to hear the queen better.

She gave me a sad, wry smile. "I've been held here a long, long time."

"We'll rescue you first," Kya said firmly. "We'll set you free and then we'll destroy the dragon and his spiders, smash the Relic, whatever we have to do. But you're my queen, and I'm not leaving without you."

Vida smiled faintly. "Thank you. I know you mean well. But only by killing the dragon and his magic can I be freed. I will come to no more harm here than I have yet, but you must go. He may return any moment, and your lives he will not spare. You must go, find the sinkhole in the Cob Grove, rescue my kindred and destroy the Relic of Shakira. At the very least, you must go now! Go, go!"

Sinkhole in the Cob Grove! I was struck by the memory of the words I had heard while looking in the diamond, "Free the lives locked in the Cob Grove's sinkhole."

"How many are in the grove?" I asked quickly. I needed all the information I could get, and I wasn't sure what exactly the "answer" was that the queen supposedly had for me.

"My sister and her two little boys. As for the others, there might be a score or so of them." She closed her eyes and drew a shuddering breath.

"We will do everything we can to kill the dragon and save the others, Your Majesty. I hope we meet again." We needed to get out of here. Panic flooded my chest as I imagined the dragon getting closer and closer while we took too long.

Kya rounded on me, tears bubbling over and out of her eyes now. "How can you? We can't leave her, not alone, not like this! We have to do something! There has to be a way."

Hesitantly, I touched her arm. "I'm sorry, Kya, but she's right. The only way to free her is to kill the dragon. We have to go. But we'll come back, if we kill him, and rescue her."

She stood stiffly, as if her body were being pulled in opposite directions. Then, without a word, she turned and ran back toward the entrance. I wasted no time in following her.

Dixie's thought exploded in my brain. *"He's coming back! Get out, guys!"*

Loose the horses and go, Dixie! We're coming!

"The dragon's coming!" I panted frantically, catching up to Kya. "We have to get out of here!" We reached the entrance and were searching by hand for the rope Kya had left. She'd explained breathlessly how she had strung it down and used it to descend, leaving it for going back up. Finding it in the blind dark at last, I realized we were too late. The harsh rasp of leathery wings echoed around us, the light was blotted out, and Kya and I just managed to crowd together in the shelter of a pile of treasure before he slid down the heap of coins like a two-year-old at the park.

"Little human queen!" he bellowed, his voice making you want to clear your throat. "Your human stink profanes my cave! But not for long."

The queen said something I couldn't catch about idle threats.

"Ah, you think yourself clever, little human fool! No! When the sun next rises over your precious castle, I will begin the end! I will tear it down stone by stone. I will burn the woods and plains. The few I leave to survive will cower and serve me. But you shall not be one of them. Once your eyes have been tortured with these sights, you also shall find your end!"

Kya was quivering, either in anger or fear or both, I wasn't sure. I didn't know what to do. All rational thought had deserted me with the dragon's arrival. I huddled, hugging my own arms, unable to think about how to get out. The dragon was roaring with scornful laughter.

Kya pulled me to my feet, hustling me stealthily along. A rope was in my hands. She shoved me at the coin pile. Every nerve strained to snapping, I scrambled upward, freezing whenever silence perforated the cave, hurrying when the dragon laughed or bellowed.

Light. I was out. Slipping, stumbling, sobbing with relief, I somehow got off the mountain. I collapsed somewhere near our campsite, my mind a smudge of fear. I didn't remember about Kya or Dixie. I squeezed my eyes shut tight and forced the world away.

CHAPTER UIII

I opened my eyes to see Kya huddled beside me, close under the shadow of the mountain and out of the view of the cave. I rolled over and shut my eyes again. I was not ready to be awake.

"Are you all right?" Kya asked.

"No," I snapped. What did she think, that I had just been daisy-picking in the sunny fields?

"We only have until sunrise tomorrow to kill the dragon; did you hear that? Can you manage?"

I filled my lungs to bursting, savoring the breath. There was no use pushing away the world. It had come for me, ready or not. And Kya was right. We didn't have long, and I couldn't afford the luxury of hiding from the world.

"I think so. We need to make a plan." I sat up, and Dixie padded over, flopping down half in, half out of my lap.

"*We're going to be okay, you know that? I'm not sure how, but everything's going to work out in the end.*" I wished I could share her confidence.

"So we have until sunrise. It's what, sometime before noon?" I squinted up at the sky.

Kya shrugged and nodded. "Ish."

I considered the diamond's message. It seemed pretty simple: Step one, free the people in the Cob Grove. Step two, set it on fire. Step three, end dragonkind forever. Well, that really made things simple, I thought sarcastically.

"So we have that much time to get to the Cob Grove, rescue the prisoners, set it on fire, and kill the dragon…" I trailed off. Kya was staring at me, impressed.

"Where'd you get all that?"

"Same vision thing," I said vaguely. *Vida holds the answer… What was it?*

"So when we rescue everyone, we look for the Relic and destroy it, right? The queen said that should kill the dragon and free her."

It was my turn to stare at Kya. *That* was the answer Vida had had, it had to be! "Yeah," I said at last. "We do that."

"Oh, and I'm sorry I lost it about leaving the queen." Kya stared at the ground, twisting her finger around a strand of grass. "It's just that that was why I wanted to help you. I mean, mostly. I wanted the queen back, *and* a happier world. I didn't think I'd have to choose."

"I'm sorry," I said. I really was. I couldn't imagine being in her shoes. "Oh, and thanks for saving my life back there. I wouldn't have gotten out if it wasn't for you." I didn't mention that I felt terrible for being so lost in my own fear that I didn't even think to look and see if she got out alive.

Mostly to change the subject, I said, "So how far is it to the Cob Grove? Vida said the sinkhole was in the center, so I don't suppose it matters what angle we approach it from."

"About eight miles south, they say," Kya said, seeming grateful for the shift in topic. "Of course, no one likes to go closer than they can help to either here or the Cob Grove, but we know that what is now Cob Grove is what used to be Silverwood."

"Well then, what are we waiting for?" I sighed, pushing myself unsteadily to my feet. "Let's get to the Cob Grove." The idea of what we were about to do seemed almost worse than riding to Dragon Mountain had.

Did you save the horses? I asked Dixie, almost afraid to hope.

"*Well yeah, but they bolted, believe me. I got no idea where they are now, besides probably somewhere far, far away. Want me to track them and herd them back?*"

I glanced back up at the mountain nervously. *No. It would take longer than we can spare, and we really need to get out of here.*

"*You're going to walk?*" Even Dixie sounded impressed. Walking eight miles was a little intimidating.

We'll have to.

"*Yeah, and on the way you'd better think of something to tell that girl. She's catching on to our secret. Wanna just tell her?*" For some reason, Dixie never called Kya "Kya," but just "the girl" or "she." Come to think of it, so far as I could remember, I was the only person I had ever heard her call by name.

Are you sure? The question was for both parts of what she had said, but one glance at Kya's face answered.

"What are you doing?" she breathed, as if afraid to break an unseen spell.

"Can you keep a secret?" I asked abruptly.

She started to answer, stopped, and then cocked her head as if asking herself, "can I?," then took a second breath. "I think I could, if I had to."

I hoped this was true.

"Well," I said, trying to be as casual as possible, "you know Dixie and I came on a very special mission from another world..." Kya nodded. "You've been asking what my big secret is, though I think you have a guess."

"Uh-huh?" Her hands were clasped and her eyes sparked with anticipation as she leaned eagerly forward.

"So, it's like, Dixie and I have a sort of – understanding between us. She's a smart dog, smarter than me, and we can communicate in our minds. There's your big secret, but you can't tell anyone. We don't want it going to nasty ears."

Kya sank back, her eyes tick-tocking between Dixie and me. Then she drew a quick breath, shooting a glance up at the mountain. "I guess we'd better get going," she said. I couldn't agree more.

CHAPTER IX

Walking is boring. Particularly when you are constantly harangued by the fear that giant spiders will spring out of nowhere and attack you, or a dragon will come sailing out of the sky with your doom. And especially when you are walking eight miles with said fear, and know that you have exactly till sunrise the next day to save the world. And you are stuck walking. And walking. And walking.

I did not know until now that a person could feel as bone weary and in pain as I did and still somehow manage to go on, and I also was beginning to appreciate, quite ruefully, all the things I had put my imaginary characters through. I had never *walked* eight miles before, and my legs and feet made sure I knew that. All I wanted to do was crash on the ground.

When the Cob Grove had first come into distinct sight ahead, I had cheered up. We were almost there. I almost forgot the burning acid in my legs, the lead weights in my limbs, even the spikes driving into the bones of my feet with every step. But the Cob Grove stubbornly refused to get any closer, as if it delighted in tormenting us by being just close enough to be a terrifying threat, but far enough away that we couldn't do a thing about it, much less what we came for.

The sun was setting as we reached the fringe. I flopped onto the ground, my pulse throbbing through me, every inch of me screaming for relief. We had exactly one night to complete our three-step impossible feat.

I was certain by now that I was slowly but surely losing my tangibility, as you could call it. Was I dying in Texas? Would I be able to finish everything before I lost tangibility altogether?

Lost in these dark thoughts, I lay on the ground as dusk drew over us. Without particularly meaning to, I came to a decision and stood up painfully.

"Kya," I muttered, doing my best to pull myself into the heroic pose and tone of voice I imagined any gallant adventurer would put on, but I couldn't shake the feeling of utter stupidity I had about what I was going to do. Something niggled in me that this was not a good idea, and if I hadn't felt more certain that this was the right thing to do, smart or not, I would have given in.

"Kya," I said again, this time more authoritatively. She peeled her arm off her eyes and forced herself into a sitting position, looking almost as exhausted as I felt. "Stay here and get a fire going if you can, something substantial enough that we'll be able to torch the woods but small enough to not draw too much attention. Dixie will stay with you and guard you unless I need help, in which case she will come after me alone. If dawn is coming and I'm not back, torch the wood anyway." I drew a deep breath and exhaled slowly. I turned to the Cob Grove, only now realizing that Kya and I had not a weapon between us. Oh, well. It would be speed and stealth that would keep my skin in one piece, not actually battling spiders or dragons. That would be a decidedly losing battle.

"Wait! You can't go alone!" Kya was on her feet and leapt forward to stop me.

I turned to study her. Her face was drawn and pale beneath her brown skin. There was an almost desperate look in her eyes. "Why not?" I asked, surprised at the calmness in my own voice. This was not the me I knew.

"I don't care who goes in there, I don't think they should go alone. Anyway, you're not used to this world. Don't think I haven't seen the look in your eyes; you're in denial and you're not giving this everything you've got, I can tell. I mean, you're distracted and scattered, like what happened in the dragon's cave. I'm sorry, it's just the truth. So I don't think you should go in there – you'd be caught and trussed like the rest of them in no time. I'll go. Send Dixie with me if you want, but you stay and light the fire. Let me go instead."

In that moment, I came face-to-face with my dark side. In another time, another place, I would have thought that what Kya had just said would have left me crushed, shocked, and insulted. But I was only partly. And it wasn't because I accepted that she was right. No, it was because I saw a way out. Kya was so certain that what I thought was the right thing was wrong and resisted the idea of me going into the Cob Grove alone. It would be easy to give in, to let her deal with it, and I could stay snugly back here where it was safe and wait for the end of the story. I wouldn't have to worry, wouldn't have to face my own darkness, wouldn't have to get close to my fears. Cowardice. Yes, that was what I felt now. All my heroic pretenses, all my stories of my daring exploits, all my Alex-the-brave stuff, it was all because, deep inside, I had always known I was no hero. I was not brave. I was a failure, and I always would be. I had always hoped that if I pretended enough that I was brave I wouldn't have to be; that courage would come naturally to me or something. *Fearlessness is no virtue*, the Phoenix's words sounded as clearly as if I was hearing them again. *Courage in the face of fear is.* I froze then, understanding everything perfectly.

I knew what I had to do. I was right. I had to go. "No, no. That's why I have to go, don't you see? I have to do this or I'll die inside. I'll become a monster. Please," I urged, sweat breaking out on me as she tried to stop me again, "I can't explain. There's no time." Everything I'd have to say to get her to understand was too big. There was too much. We couldn't afford the time. "I have to go. It's a matter of who I am, saving my own character as much as the lives of those people. I know this is what I'm supposed to do, what I have to do. Please don't make it any harder." *You must choose: will you serve fear or let it serve you?* If I wanted to master my fear, if I wanted to *not* be a coward, I had to be courageous now, in the face of fear.

And if Kya didn't back me up, I knew I couldn't do it. I needed her support. I looked at Dixie, circling, sniffing the air and occasionally letting out a low growl. *Were you in my thoughts? Are you with me? Do you understand?*

"*Yeah, I was…*"

Then you know what a coward I am, I thought flatly. She was bound to find out sooner or later anyway, especially now that I myself was disenchanted from my own make-believe.

"*We all have to realize that we are cowards before we can be heroes*," Dixie replied cryptically. "*There's more in you than you believe, and I think you're right – you should go. But she is also right – you have to be careful. I'm not sure how ready you are for this, and oh, how to say it? It's like a hound going out on his first hunt. He can only be trained so much before he goes out on the real thing. But on that first hunt, it will be very easy for him to mess up. He has to be extra careful to remember his training and follow his instincts with discretion, because there's nothing more he can be taught to prepare him, but one slip and he blows the whole thing. After his first hunt, he will have some experience to work off of, but until then he's green and naïve. Anything might happen, and he can't risk blowing it. That's what it's like with you now. You're on your first hunt, and no more training will help you now. This is the real thing, so good luck, hunt hard, and come back!"*

I listened to Dixie's words of doggy wisdom, amazed that most people would take this beautiful creature for granted as just another herding dog. No one could know that a dog could have the kind of insight that Dixie had unless they had the gift we did, of being able to communicate.

I shot her a grateful look. *Thanks, Dixie. I'll remember. Where would I be without you?* I closed my eyes, tilting my head back, letting the cool evening breeze sweep across me. I wondered how much more of this kind of strain I could take; Dixie already had to bolster me up and urge me on. If things got too much tougher, I would become too heavy a burden for one dog to carry, however strong she might be.

"Kya?" I said at last, opening my eyes. Ever since I had made my last desperate plea she had stood stock still, staring at me, saying nothing. I needed to know if she was going to support me or not. I couldn't stand the suspense.

"You were conversing with Dixie," Kya answered. "I didn't want to interrupt."

"I'm not anymore." I tried not to look like I was holding my breath. "Do you understand now why I have to go?"

"No. I don't understand at all. But that doesn't matter. I don't need to understand. I trust that you know what you're doing, so even though I think this plan is more than harebrained, you know that and still intend to go on. Dixie agrees with you, I can see that much, so listen to her. I think this is above me. My fealty is to my queen, but I'm with you, as I said before. I still mean it. Tell me what you want me to do, and I will do it. I'll be with you to the end. That's all I have to say."

I try to never let anyone see me cry, but I didn't succeed this time. Kya's words brought tears to my eyes and no matter how I fought them they seemed intent on spilling down my cheeks. I turned quickly and brushed them away, hoping she hadn't noticed. Taking a deep breath, I regained control of myself.

"Light a fire like I said, that's all I ask," I told her, but I couldn't quite keep the knot out of my voice. I'm sure she heard it, but if she did, she didn't say anything.

CHAPTER X

Get yourself under control, Alex! I ordered myself. This is no time to melt down, there are lives at stake! That mantra was becoming ominously repetitive – I found myself saying it more and more. It wasn't exactly…reassuring.

I had ducked into the outer fringes of the trees and immediately encountered threads of spider webs. They were at least an inch in diameter, stretched carelessly from tree to tree, some high, some drooping low, at varying distances and for varying lengths. There was no particular rhyme or reason to the pattern; they were there to deter intruders, and catch any who might be foolish enough to pass. I was going to be one of those foolish ones; I could only hope the webs wouldn't catch me. And do my best to avoid them. It was grueling work, stepping gingerly over one here, slipping under another there, always afraid of bumping into one accidentally and getting stuck. So far, so good, but how far had I really come? A hundred feet? A mile? There was no way to know. I could only keep going as straight as I could and hope by nearly sheer luck to come upon a place the diamond and Queen Vida had called "the sinkhole in the grove." The strain from trying to be stealthy and dodge webs, on top of the tedious journey here in the first place, was making my limbs tremble. Sweat dripped into my eyes, and adrenaline raced in my veins – struggling valiantly to smudge away my fear in a single feeling of drive. It almost worked. But then, I hadn't yet seen a spider.

I'll never forget those hours, forcing my way through trees and dodging macabre webs. It was the stuff of nightmares, the kind where you wake up, all frightened and shaky, but only a vague ghost of dark memory remains of it, hovering on the edge of sleep. I only dimly remember the long trip inward, straining every nerve to keep a steady course, keep quiet, keep avoiding the webby snares, and keep a lookout for spiders.

I saw him – or it, or whatever – before it saw me, or I would be dead. Huge, black as night, monster: a spider of the Cob Grove. The thought occurred to me, even in that agonizingly terrifying moment as I crouched behind a needled pine, that if Shelob herself had descendants in the world, they could be no more horrible than these. It waddled on eight long furry legs not twenty feet away, undulating up and down as it shambled into the tree shade darkness ahead.

I fought down a whimper and tried rather unsuccessfully to steady my erratic breathing. When my trembling slackened, I reflected cynically that this was probably a very nasty "good" sign. I ought to be getting close to the middle of the grove by now, and this was the first spider I'd seen, so I guessed that I was on the right track. I wondered where all the other spiders were. Lying in wait in the sinkhole? Out on some deadly mission for the dragon? Or, as a chilling thought occurred to me, preparing for his apocalyptic attack at sunrise? How was I going to do this? There was no back-pocket resort, as there usually was in my stories, like giving your attacker a heart attack. I was not in control. I could only react to circumstances.

Okay, not much choice but go on. I can't do anything when I don't know how things are. But I had to dodge more spiders the farther I pushed forward. My mind struggled to block out their hideous appearance and focus on not being caught, either by a sharp-eyed spider or the webs, thicker here than before. By the time I came to the lip of the sinkhole, which I did uncounted hours after leaving Dixie and Kya, I was a complete emotional wreck. My nerves were at a fevered pitch, my whole body shook uncontrollably from the effort it had taken to get here, and I knew I was alarmingly close to letting out a very unheroic squeal if just one more spider startled me.

I vaguely remembered, peering down into the sinkhole at ruined stones that had been a foundation and tumbled sections of wall, that Silverwood had held at one point a prison for an enchanted princess and at another the stronghold of a great prince. It had been the same castle in two different times, I was pretty sure on that, and both of their fairytale stories felt worlds away in another age. Now, in the ruins of their home (and, it felt, all the happily-ever-afters *ever*) I could see a sight that made my stomach churn.

Lined up in rows like caterpillars in their cocoons were the unmistakable shapes of people, wrapped in layers and layers of the thick spider webs. Not one of them moved. Were they dead? But no, the diamond had called them "many lives." That meant they had to be alive, right?

But I had bigger problems at the moment. Hundreds of spiders squatted in a circle around the castle ruins several rows deep. It had to be all of them, there were so many. Or maybe that was just wishful thinking. They seemed to be waiting for something, and were content to sit and watch until a signal came to do something else. I closed my eyes and thought hard. I had to focus, had to get this right. I only had one shot. A plan was forming somewhere in the back of my mind. It was a little ridiculous, but sometimes ridiculous things actually worked. At least, they did in books. I desperately hoped this would work now. *Dixie*, I thought as hard as I could, as if my own effort could drive it into her brain, *I need a diversion. You'll have to be fast and you can't get tangled in the webs. I need you to draw like three-hundred spiders away from the sinkhole. Can you do that? For ten minutes…ish?*

"*On my way, Alex!*" Dixie had heard! She would be coming soon. I lay in the shadow of a tall tree, the moon stretching its shadow over me. I was in a race against time. Everything had to be timed just right, or the whole plan would collapse, not to mention that if we wasted too much time or if the plan didn't work, the world would basically end. If Dixie couldn't keep the spiders back for as long as it took me to free the people among the ruins and they began to return, me and some of the prisoners would be caught mid-escape. If Kya torched the wood too early before Dixie, me, and the rescued prisoners got out, we would burn to death with the spiders. And then of course there was the wild card of the dragon, but I couldn't plan for him.

I crossed my fingers as I waited, wishing I could turn invisible.

The shadows of the trees on my side of the sinkhole reached for the other side. They stretched and stretched, and as I lay, holding my breath, waiting for Dixie to draw the spiders off, they touched the roots of the farther trees. At that instant, as if it were a signal, the circle of motionless spiders moved. They did not crawl forward at all, moving only sideways, the first row rotating to the left, the second to the right, the third to the left, and so on. Their pace was steady, unwavering, and they moved as if it were a ghoulish dance or ritual they were performing. Slowly, the sound of a low guttural chant rose, throbbing in the night, sending shivers up my spine. Whatever they planned, it was not nice. I wondered if it was some sort of evil ritual to call up a blessing for the dragon's coup at sunrise.

One extraordinarily large spider seemed to be in command, occasionally emitting a rumbling grunt different from the chant, and all the spiders would change direction, sometimes speeding up at his command or slowing down. They were always in perfect time, never missing a step, never colliding with a fellow dancing spider. It was eerie, lying there alone in the darkness, watching the spiders dance.

It had gone on for some time, how long it was impossible to tell. I heard nothing over the chant, but the spiders did. Without warning, the movement stilled, every spider froze in place, bulbous bodies swaying gently. Then, at a roar from the lead spider, every single one of the hundreds split into three groups and rushed off into the trees. I had no idea how Dixie got them all to go, but at that moment, I didn't care. The time I had to work with was way too small for anything like comfort.

I darted out from my hiding place and moved among the web-swaddled figures. The first I looked at was child-sized, probably about five if my guess was anywhere close. I wondered if this was one of the queen's nephews, but if he was, he would be no good for what I hoped for. I hurried along past another small child-sized bundle and another I thought was a woman.

After what seemed like an eternity, though I think it was only a few seconds, I found a hulking figure of warrior proportions – a good bet. I quickly searched for a knot or fastening or any sort of place where the spiders' ropes ended. No, no, no! There had to be a way! I was losing precious seconds! I ripped frantically at the cords, sweating as the weight of passing time grew increasingly heavier. A single strand came loose, and as I worked it over the man's head, more followed. It was like unraveling a skein of yarn from the outside, very sticky, very tangly yarn. I pulled with all my strength at the cords, the man beneath the layers of web tumbling over and over like a slowly whirling top. More of him became visible. Mail, a helmet, a limp hand, a face. Then, to my relief, I found what I had needed – a dagger. I tore it from his belt and slashed at the webs. He rolled free, groaned, and lay still. Somehow, the magic must have sustained his life and little else. He was as limp as an overcooked noodle.

"Help me!" I said in an urgent undertone, but went to the next figure without wasting time on him. He would come around in his own time and mine was precious. I cut the woman free, discovering a face that looked a lot like Vida's, and the two child cocoons revealed two little boys. One by one, I cut warrior after warrior free. The first man whose dagger I had taken staggered to help me, using his sword carefully. They all were about as dexterous as drunks, wobbling around and trying to free one another with clumsy fingers.

I heard distant barking, and as I hauled the last warrior to his feet, Dixie bounded into sight, tongue lolling from her mouth, bits of webs stuck to her fur.

"Run! Go, go, go! They're all on my tail!"

Help me get them moving! They're going nowhere fast like this! I ran to the woman who I thought was the queen's sister and grabbed her shoulder. "We have to go. Order them to follow me if you value our lives!" She looked blearily at me, a boy on her hip and another held by the hand. She didn't seem to understand where she was or what I was saying. I might as well have been speaking Russian.

"Friends!" she shouted so suddenly I jumped and almost squeaked. She pointed at me. "Do whatever this girl says. Now!" The warriors oozed themselves into order, encouraged in no small part by Dixie's teeth.

"Draw your swords and let's cut our way out of here!" I yelled, pointing back the way I had come. *Keep them in line and heading in the right direction*, I thought at Dixie.

Of course, the shouting could not have passed unnoticed, especially by a few hundred spiders that were already hot and angry at Dixie. We were shuffling as swiftly as we could manage, which was painfully far from a run, and I was tailing at the back, helping Dixie make sure no one wandered off. I heard sounds behind me and looking over my shoulder, I saw the first of the enormous spiders thunder out from the trees on their long furry legs, glaring angrily at us. There was only a score or so of armed knights in no condition to fight, against hundreds of spiders, furious enough to kill.

CHAPTER XI

I wish I could say that in a burst of heroism I beat back the spiders unafraid and saved the day singlehandedly, or that I spoke fiery heartening words and rallied the people's spirits so that we outran the spiders. But it wouldn't be true. In fact, the time that followed is only a blur for me, spotted in places with moments in odd clarity. I remember stumbling after the group of prisoners I had just rescued – which in of itself didn't sound real, like it could be me – and glancing frequently over my shoulder at the always just-on-the-edge-of-sight spiders. The warriors ahead slashed at webs and branches alike, cutting down anything that stood in their way. We were exhausted, but we knew that stopping meant only death now. Once I looked back and saw the ugly black things just behind me, and another group circling from either side, racing grimly at us. I screamed in panic, the swordsmen turned, a black-and-white streak blazed in the night, and Dixie's thought burned in my head. I can't remember exactly what she said, but I knew what I had to do. I scooped one of the little boys up, Vida's sister carried the other, and together we fled, pushing through webs that tangled around us, clinging to my skin and giving me the urge to shudder if I'd had energy to spare for it.

We would have all been dead if not for Dixie. Once again, I don't know how she did it, but somehow she managed to help drive the spiders back whenever they tried to attack, herd the people on with all their speed out of the Cob Grove, and all the while maintaining a consistent course. I meanwhile knew my arms were going to fall off in approximately three point eight seconds from the weight of the boy in my arms and it was only a question of whether I could get out of the grove before they did. He couldn't have been more than five, while his brother must have been just over two years old. Still, as he banged along against my shoulder and my muscles burned from the strain, I wondered how a small person could be so heavy. Sweat dripped in my eyes, I stumbled but forced myself to go on, the fear of dying here and sacrificing this child's life, the fear of failing to do what I had been sent to do, charging me with energy I hadn't felt before, driving me on.

I ran forever. Then a voice, a flash of long blonde hair, and the weight gone from my arms. I was on the ground, utterly spent. Had the others gotten out? I hoped so. I couldn't move, couldn't do anything more. A strong wind dried the sweat to my skin and chilled my bones. Loud crashing and shouts behind me mingled with barks rippled dimly through my consciousness. *Ahem, X-cuze, me, lady, just thought I'd remind you... SPIDERS ARE COMING FOR YOU!* The voice of my fear in my head seemed to lack the strength it once had, and I ignored its warning. I had nothing more to give. If they got me they got me, and that would just be that. I no longer cared. I hadn't the strength to.

Whether I fell unconscious or fell asleep I'm not sure, but in the peacefulness of the dark that enfolded me, something prodded at the back of my mind.

Step one: rescue the people in the Cob Grove. Check. Step two: set it on fire... oh, great. Gotta do that. Step three: oh, no! I awoke with a jerk, and somehow managed to stand. The sounds of a fight were gone, replaced by harsh shrieks and yowls and the crackling of flames. My head was spinning, but I could see well enough to understand. Silverwood was burning! Kya had set fire to the ancient forest as I had told her to. Problem: I had forgotten to look for the Relic of Shakira. We would have to wait until the fire burned itself out before we could pick through the ashes to find it and destroy it somehow (I wasn't sure where to really begin when trying to destroy a magical Relic), and by then, it would be too late. The dragon had won.

The queen's sister and her sons lay sleeping near Kya's campfire, but no one else was in sight. *Dixie, where is everyone? What is happening? Are you okay?* I could only hope she answered. It was all I was good for until I'd pulled myself more together and figured out what to do. What could we do? I'd blown it.

"Hey Alex! The old cobsies are trying to get away from the fire. Apparently they don't like it too well. We're trying to keep them bottled up, but who knows where they might be getting out. Any ideas?"

51

I thought, fighting the throbbing in my skull. I supposed that we could at least do our best to cripple the dragon by making sure his spider army was destroyed, but if only there were more of us! *Split the group in two. Have them station themselves periodically around the perimeter to kill any spiders that try to escape, and close enough together to reinforce each other if the spiders rush them.* I'd read about that happening in books. I could never have dreamed I'd be using what I'd learned from them, not like this. *They can light fires at their stations to help keep back the spiders and encourage the forest fire. I'll head around to the far side to move it along there. It's the best we can do.*

Discouraged and feeling utterly defeated, I sighed. Silverwood wasn't huge, but it felt like a national forest as I walked around it, passing warrior after warrior as I did. After a while, I just guessed that I was on the other side, though I couldn't be sure. Borrowing a burning stick from a neighboring fire, I set to work.

I gathered some brush and sticks, building it against one of the cobwebbed trees. I wasn't too sure how to start a forest fire. It wasn't the sort of thing you watched on National Geographic: "Forest Fires: Starting Them in The Wild to Kill Giant Spiders." Still, I did what I could, dunked my smoldering branch into it, and backed away. It caught, burned, and began licking at the bark of the tree. A trailing strand of cobweb dribbled within reach. The flames touched it.

Instantly, as if it were paper soaked in oil, the fire shot along it, racing into the wood, leaving a trail of flaming carnage behind. I stared. Then, tentatively, I snatched a piece of burning wood back from my fire and, holding it out at arm's length, touched it to another web. The same burning destruction swept along it, and I knew our prospects had just improved.

I scrambled out of the grove, cupped my hands around my mouth, and yelled at the top of my lungs: "Light the webs!" My voice cracked as I screamed it, but I repeated it again anyway. I heard the cry taken up by stronger voices, saw trails of fire zipping through the trees, and backpedaled further. The fire was taking control of the wood.

Wind rippled around me, whipping through the trees first one way and then another. A storm was probably coming. *Please don't rain yet,* I pleaded silently. No rain came. The fire raged.

The east grew paler, but no shafts of sunlight fell on the plains. The wind had blown in thick clouds that blocked out the rising sun. It whipped my long braids in all directions, bowing trees, carrying to me the sounds of roaring fire, the sound of an unstoppable fire that is in complete control. It blew to me the sound of hoarse barking. Kya and Dixie came slowly into sight, heads down, exhausted but successful. They joined me, and we watched.

The heat was a force, beating us back far away from the wood. Fire eddied around the burning husks of trees. It was terrifyingly glorious. Thunder boomed, and I jumped, looking up to see the first fat drops of rain fall, and to see a huge angry scaled shape scar the glowering sky overhead. The dragon had come!

He circled the wood, and we stood, glued in place with fear. Beside me, Kya gasped faintly as she and Dixie realized what I already had. Step three had utterly failed. I hadn't found the Relic.

The dragon swooped over the forest fire a second time. "Who has done this? Who has dared to insult me like this?" he roared, his voice like an enormous rockslide. I trembled, trying to remember if I had made my dragons eat people and whether I had made them kill quickly or horribly. If I could tell anyone a last piece of advice right then before I died, it would be this: Be careful what you say, what you plan, and what you dream. You never know what might come of it, so don't do it carelessly. Love, Alex. I wanted to send a message to my family, to at least tell them goodbye and what happened to me.

"Who commanded this deed?" the dragon roared again, and I could see his hate-filled red eyes scanning the surrounding area.

My eyes fell to the fire, and the swirling colors, the power, the beautiful terror of it, reminded me of a far more real fire in a different place. It reminded me of the Phoenix, and I suddenly felt less afraid, or perhaps, a surge of courage pushing against my fear.

"The Phoenix commanded it!" I shouted, stepping forward. "He who creates and who heals, who ends and avenges. He sent me to make an end of your evil and to heal this world."

In one swift movement of his leathery wings, the dragon turned. I could feel those eyes on me, and the sheer hate in them seemed to pierce me, though I sensed most of it was aimed beyond me. To the one who sent me. He beat his wings, up and down, drawing closer all too quickly. I could feel Kya's nails digging into my arm, but I felt like I was floating. I was waiting for something, holding my breath as the seconds on my life ticked down to zero. I felt the heat of the fire on my face. I heard Dixie growl long and deep.

Then an explosion that made the earth tremble. A column of fire from somewhere near the center of the grove shot skyward, straight up like a geyser of flames, and it flickered and shone with all the colors of the rainbow, pearly and shimmering. In that moment, I knew what it was. I had no reason to, but I did. The Relic of Shakira, wherever it lay hidden in the grove, had been destroyed by the fire. The dragon gave an awful howl. The memory of the sound still haunts my nightmares. His wings hung loose, and he tumbled sideways in the sky, crashing into the inferno below.

The rain fell harder, hissing as it struck the fire. It became torrential, rain unlike any I had known when I created this world back in the Northwest of America. Within minutes the ground at my feet was a marsh, and I was sinking past my ankles. Lightning splintered the sky, thunder rumbled, and more rain fell, working valiantly to quench the fire. The wind slackened and died off, letting the rain fall almost straight. I sank to the soggy grass, too shaken to care if I got muddy and soaked. I wrapped my arms around Dixie's wet and tangled fur neck. She sat on the ground, solid as rock, her head drooping slightly, too worn out to position herself in one of her over-precise sits.

We did it, Dixie. We're alive and we did it.

"*Yeah, Alex. But are we done? Why are we still here?*"

I – I don't know. I'll check the diamond I guess. But not now. Not now. I'm so tired… Kneeling in the swishing muddy water, I clung to her, wishing I didn't ever have to let go. I closed my eyes, and somehow, slipped into sleep right there.

CHAPTER XII

How much can happen in a single day! I was learning this very quickly. After the dragon's death, Kya and a group of warriors had marched to his cave and found the queen freed from her magical bonds. They had brought her back in triumph and excitement, and Kya had fairly glowed when she saw me again. The party that had investigated the skeletal remains of Silverwood reported that only damp and drying ash covered the ground there now, and there was not a trace of spiders, dragon or Relic. Blackened stones were all that was left of the ruins that had been in the sinkhole of the grove that was now ash and burned husks.

It was now late afternoon of the day the dragon died, and I stood outside the walls of Castle Bliss. The sun shone as if in denial of the storm at dawn, the completely un-Bliss storm that had helped spread the fire before it put it out. That storm was the miracle that saved the surrounding lands from being burned. I had slept a little in the rain, but not much, and I was exhausted and hungry for real food. But I needed to know if my job was done here, and I couldn't stand the wait.

Kya came out from the castle and smiled when she saw me, walking quickly to join me. After my last stay in the castle, I had politely refused to return, despite the queen's urging.

"It won't ever happen again," I said when she got closer. "Dragonkind is gone forever, and with them their evil magic. You have your queen back, and happier world." I managed a smile, though I didn't like this. It meant we'd probably have to say goodbye soon. "That's what you wanted, isn't it?"

"Yeah, I guess. I mean, the queen's back and it's all great and I'm beyond glad and all that… it's just…"

"I think I know," I said wistfully.

"You have to go, don't you?" she asked quietly.

I nodded. "I think so. I know there's other worlds I have to help, and I've finished everything I was told to do here." I was a little surprised to realize I was sad to leave this world. I surveyed the beautiful land, the field studded with brilliant blossoms, the butterflies flitting through the air, carefree as ever, and the strong castle towering above me. Kya. I'd miss Kya a lot.

I whistled sharply, and a minute later Dixie bounded up, spunky as usual. I looked into Kya's eyes, trying to find words. I felt full of things I wanted to say, remembering all we had been through together, everything she was willing to sacrifice to help me, her grit that had pulled me through the hard times to victory. I would be dead if it weren't for her, but I had no words in me to say all the things I wanted to say. I swallowed, wishing I had my mom's tact and talent for moments like this.

"Well," I said finally, "I'll miss you, Kya."

"I'll miss you too, Alex." I was surprised to see tears in her eyes. I was even more surprised when she threw her arms around me and hugged me hard. "Good luck on your other missions."

I squeezed her just as hard, and when I let go, Kya dropped to her knees in front of Dixie, reaching out to scratch her ears. "I'll miss you too, girly-girl. You look after Alex, okay? She's going to need lots of looking after. You are a smart dog, Dix, and you'll need it all. I'll never forget you."

I stood still, watching the two of them, and felt Dixie feed a thought into my brain. "Kya?" I said. She glanced up at me, still stroking Dixie's fur. "Dixie said to tell you that she won't forget you either. She said you have a noble heart and a strong will, and as long as you remain true, nothing can shake you." Dixie licked Kya's face as I repeated the last of the message. "She says, '*Kya, the road ahead of you is straight and true. Do not waver, have no fear, and nothing can stop you. Though there is shadow along the way, I see it end in glory. May you finish as you have started. Farewell.*' And farewell from me too," I added, wishing now that I had Dixie's way with words, and I knew, if Kya didn't, the significance of the fact that Dixie had used her name.

"I'll leave you alone now," Kya said, a thickness in her voice. "I'd better be getting back, and you've got magic portals to get to." She turned and hurried back into the castle, pausing once in the gate to turn and wave. I waved back.

When she was gone, I sat, propping my back against the castle wall. Dixie stood very still beside me, and I reached for my throat. From beneath the surcoat of a Castle Bliss guard I drew the diamond, and it flashed in the late sunlight, making the whole world around me seem dim and colorless beside it. I held it tight, calm inside, waiting to see what it would show me and braced for the mental pain. If I had missed any part of this mission, it would show me.

I knew immediately that something was different this time. The random reflections of light didn't rearrange themselves into understandable pictures conveying a message. Instead, they seemed to stretch out to me, the broad beams of colored light shooting past me on every side and all around. It made me feel the size of a bedbug. I could see nothing of Bliss anymore, only the brilliant colors of the diamond's light. I couldn't feel Dixie next to me, and come to think of it, I couldn't even feel the ground anymore either. I was floating, caught in a shaft of rainbow light, sucked along into… nothingness. I knew nothing, saw nothing, felt nothing – was nothing. My mind drifted, losing itself as if in sleep.

CHAPTER XIII

"Who are you?"

I opened my eyes, feeling a little sick and disoriented, as though someone had picked me up, spun me around upside down a few dozen times, and then catapulted me through a Jell-O wall. Thankfully, it wasn't nearly as bad as it usually was. I found myself staring into the pale face of a young man. Nature had given him a smaller-than-average build, but he had clearly not let that stop him from anything. He had dark hair that hung down partly into his eyes – very piercing eyes they were too, as if they had stars buried in them. He was so distinctive it wasn't a great feat of memory to figure out that I didn't know him. Why did he want to know who I was?

"What?" I asked faintly, not knowing what else to say and shrinking away a bit.

"I asked who you were." His voice wasn't high or deep, and was so quiet that I felt he must never have raised his voice ever before in his life. I wasn't at all sure I trusted him; he seemed too poised, like the kind of person you can never catch off balance and always landed on his feet. He dropped into a cross-legged position on the ground, waiting for and clearly expecting my answer.

I supposed I could tell him. I didn't really see any reason to withhold it. I would save the withholding for the important things like the diamond and Dixie. Dixie! Where was she? I sat up abruptly, which was a bad idea. All the blood rushed to my head and my vision swam.

"Easy there, spitfire," the stranger said. The idea of anyone calling me a spitfire was laughable. If my family knew I had been called that, they would never forget it, and they wouldn't let me forget it either. I shifted my eyes cautiously, peering around for any sign of my best dog friend. It was gray and misty, and hard to see anything that wasn't within ten feet of me clearly, but eventually I spotted her, a patch of black and white on the hard-packed gray-brown dirt. She was curled in a ball, apparently asleep. Okay, so we were safe and in one piece in the next world with a new mission. But I needed this stranger to go away so I could look in the diamond and find out what it was.

I looked back at him. He was patiently waiting, as if he had all the time in the world. Then, I looked around.

I was on a hill, and several other hills cropped up in the mist around me. The ground was gray-brown dirt studded with large boulders and the occasional tree that looked to be the stunted cousins of baobabs. I knew this place. I knew it far, far too well. A strange feeling rose up in my stomach, and my heart felt like it was airborne. It had only been one year ago that I had stood here, on the Barren Hills, battling a dozen bandits… I'd abandoned that story, that world. I'd left Secret behind to build something worse, something darker and eviler and harder to beat. Secret was too easy, too predictable, what with it being basically a world of wizardry and warfare, of good kings and evil stewards, or good stewards and evil kings. I'd wanted more… And now I was back. Secret's practically rainless years, its mild winter – I was as certain as I could be by the gray-clouded sky and chilly wind that's what time of year it was – its grays and browns and muted greens, were all unmistakable. After all, I'd made this world. It's not surprising I'd recognize it.

"Maybe six hours," the stranger announced. Startled, I remembered he was there. *Six hours for what? Was he crazy, perhaps?*

"What are you talking about?" I snapped.

"Six hours until it's time to panic if we haven't left this place. So I suggest we hurry up. You were telling me your name… Kind of taking you a while."

I glared at him. "Call me Alex," I told him, hoping to shut him up and make him leave.

He didn't. "Just Alex? Not Alexa or Alexandra or Alexandrannamaria or whatever?" His face showed no sign that he was joking, and I was insulted. Sure, there were many different names that Alex could be a nickname for, but he didn't have to make fun of it.

"My full name is Alexandria, if it really matters, but you will be pleased to call me just Alex," I said with all the curtness I could cram into my voice. He had better not dare to call me anything else or I'd —

"Okay, Lexi, we're finally making some progress. So how old are you?"

"Hey, what is this, the inquisition? What's *your* name, anyway?" I asked, getting testy. At least between my headache and frustration I hadn't much room left over for fear. Much.

He gave a strange half-smile, hesitated, and said, "Lynx."

Okay, now that has the prize for weirdest name I've heard yet, I thought. *But he does kind of look catlike. He has a bit of that pleased-with-himself expression, anyway.*

"I'll tell you how old I am if you tell me what in the universe you think you're doing and what you want with me." I wasn't sure if "what on Earth" was exactly appropriate in another world, and emphasizing my words with "universe" sounded stronger and more forceful anyway.

"Actually," he glanced over his shoulder and leaned closer to whisper dramatically, "I'm on the run — being chased, you know. Assassins. They want my blood, and not without reason. That's why we have six hours, at most, before they catch up. So there I was, trooping along, abandoned by my Camden escort, and then I saw a flash of light that couldn't've been lightning but might be wizardry. So I crept up here, to the spot I thought it had come from, and shazam, there you were, and the dog too, flat out cold. I thought perhaps the wizards were up to something with you, and so I hung around for your story." He smiled, pleased with himself, and sat back. "I don't want anything with you," he added, then hesitated, frowning slightly. "Or do I? What is it? Why you?"

I stretched my foot out and poked Dixie in her sleep. I wanted her listening to this conversation. I knew he *said* he didn't want anything with us, but that last part had sounded a little ominous. I thought he sounded like he knew something, some secret perhaps, and it might be important for us to know. Also, I didn't want to deal with him alone, especially not in my condition. His "shazam" had alarmed me a little, too. It seemed out of place with his mild-mannered Secret citizen persona, what with his tunic and leggings and his high leather boots. I was slightly relieved to notice no visible weapons, but it wasn't a total comfort. There was something here I didn't exactly like, especially when I couldn't understand it. It frightened me.

"I'm twelve years old," I admitted reluctantly. He had answered me, and deserved his promised answer in return. As Dixie stretched, yawned, and shook herself, I rapidly filled her in.

"Well, that makes me six years older than you. Were the wizards pulling some stunt or was it something else?" Lynx glanced behind him again, as if he were genuinely suspicious of being followed.

"You can call it wizardry," I told him, making it clear that I was not going to answer him outright. "And if I know anything, you had best be going. Those assassins *smell* their way to a kill. You won't shake them yet. Try swimming."

"Are you serious?" He raised his eyebrows as his eyes traveled to the overcast sky. "In the dead of winter, you want me to go swimming?" He stood, tossing his dark hair out of his eyes. "I will keep on the move, though, rest assured. And if I know anything either, you had best move too. Try swimming," he said carelessly, and bounded down the slope of the hill.

CHAPTER XIV

I breathed an inward sigh of relief, glad that he had finally gone and left us alone, but it was short-lived. *"What are you doing? Don't you see? We have to go after him. I'm pretty sure he's important, and I don't think he's the treacherous type. The assassins are after him, so isn't that a good sign? Or are they good guys?"*

Never! They're evil, but few. I'd like to learn how things stand in this world now, but I'm not sure I like or trust him, and I need to look in the diamond to find out what our mission is in this world. I did not like the direction Dixie's mind was going.

"Oh, right! Tell you what, I'll go keep track of him, won't let him go far and won't let him snoop, and you look in the diamond and see what you can see."

Before I could argue or point out that looking in the diamond would majorly cripple me mentally and even a little physically and that that might not be the best idea under the circumstances, she was gone. I hesitated. Who knew when a good time would come? Dixie would look after me.

Not very reassured, I sighed and fished out the diamond. I noticed gratefully that in this world, I was much more appropriately dressed for adventure, with a long-sleeved gray-brown tunic that fell to my knees, loose pants beneath it, and sturdy leather boots. Much more practical. I also had a sword, and in my imaginings, I could use it with utmost cunning and skill, but since it wouldn't be simply my imagination using the sword, and I had never learned fencing in real life, I doubted it would be of much use to me.

I had looked in the diamond three times already, but still the awe and fascination were no less as the colors danced before my eyes. It started out with only images like before, and the very first thing I saw was Lynx's face, and I knew the diamond was telling me that this was the unexpected place I had found help in this world. *Definitely unexpected,* I thought dryly as doubt crept into my mind. *I'm not so sure he's a good idea. I don't really trust him, and I need to trust the people who'll help me.* Lynx was already fading, replaced by the face of another man, taller, broad, with light brown hair and laughing eyes. His face was almost stern but not grim. He looked like a natural leader, someone who put you at your ease and made you feel like he, and you by extension since you would follow him into anything, could cope with anything that the course of life or an enemy's schemes could throw at him. I liked the face; it had a noble look, kingly, in fact. That was when I heard the first words.

"Where is the true heir of Camden, the kingdom once so strong and noble? To what lows it has fallen, destroyed by Jodeh's hand. Right the kingdom, help the world. Repair the succession laws, strengthen Camden's future."

Whoever Jodeh was, I assumed he had something to do with the Fortress (the Camden equivalent of Castle Bliss) since its image took center stage at that line.

The words paused as dark, furtive shadows, masked, wearing all black, and armed with poisoned darts crawled across my vision. Assassins. They were kamikaze in philosophy – if you die, take as many with you as you can; life is nothing. More words came...

"The assassins' legion is strong and deadly, the serpent poised to strike and destroy. They must end forever. Wizards also walk dark paths, abusing the high powers. Rules and accountability birth justice and right. Begin the change."

Okay, so I knew the "high powers" was magic, and with that line I had seen the Wizard's Tryst, the place where they gathered at the beginning of each new year to meet. This was winter now, and I was pretty sure by the feel of the weather it was the right time for the Tryst. Maybe that would be a good place to start.

"Beneath the lake the hope of Secret lies, yet not in the water's embrace. Jeduthiam's blade must be taken up, wielded by the true heir. Only then can true peace, victory and change be won."

I saw a sword of unmatched perfection, and though I was no swordsman, I knew this was a blade among blades. I could almost feel it in my hand, its balance, its whispering swoosh as it sliced the air, its strength not only of steel but also of magic. It felt almost like a part of me. It was somehow connected with the Lake the voice had spoken of, and as those lines flowed through my head the only thing I saw was a smooth stone chamber. Identifying the lake shouldn't be *too* hard, as I didn't have many to choose from. The only unmoving bodies of water in Secret were the Five Lakes (far away in Rhindon), the Fiery Glacier up in the Wilds (the Secret version of "unincorporated county"), and the Great Lagoon, located somewhere in the Jungle (a region of legend and terror). The light and color faded and I fell back, gasping for breath.

The blood drummed in my head as usual, and I dug my knuckles into my temples, desperate for relief. The physical pain was much less than it had been before, which was a little surprising since the mental pain didn't seem to be improving hardly at all. Then, disconcerted, I realized why: I felt less connected with my Secret body than I had in Bliss, even at the end. I felt how I imagined it would feel if I were to suddenly have my hand chopped off – I could see the hand, I would know it was *supposed* to belong to my body, but I would no longer be connected with it. Lying on the ground, I felt almost as though I could sink into it and disappear forever, but I felt the cold solidness beneath me. It was a lot like feeling something in a dream. The physical pain was probably still there; I just couldn't feel it hardly at all.

Gradually, my headache began to ebb and, blinking, I found I could bring the boulders and trees and sky into focus. I got to my feet and considered the diamond's message as I stumbled after Dixie and Lynx.

By all the frustrations of pi, Dixie's right: I have to work with this Lynx, at least for a little while, I thought with some irritation. As for our mission, the whole "where is the heir" and his needing Jeduthiam's blade, well, that must be part of it. I thought the man with the laughing eyes I'd seen in the stone was the heir guy, and that amazing sword must be Jeduthiam's blade. There always had been trouble with assassins, but this was the first I'd heard of a "legion" of them. Maybe they were increasing, since the message had warned they were strong and deadly "a serpent poised to strike and destroy." Wizards, too, had always abused the high powers, and that was also nothing new.

That was about all of what I knew and could guess, other than what seemed fairly apparent from the message ("hey, go destroy this, end that, find this mystery sword and missing guy, and fix that other thing! Save the world! Cake!"). There was more than one lake in this world, and figuring out which one was *the* one would a doozy of a task.

As for Jeduthiam's blade, it struck a chord of memory in my mind, and I thought it was part of a long-ago legend in my imagined adventures, but I wasn't sure. I could start with that to sort of break the ice with Lynx.

I bumbled awkwardly into a boulder and righted myself, grateful that no one was seeing me walking like a drunk person. I was struck by the impression of my own physical smallness. In Bliss, I had been tall, fragile as a twig, but strong. Here I was at least less twiggy, being of a tough build, no longer of a goddess-like height but instead about five feet tall. I felt fairly strong physically, but it wasn't the Herculean strength I'd had in Bliss. More like what might be expected from someone my size who was really, really fit. Though it was more realistic, I felt sure I'd miss it sometime when I just wasn't quite strong enough. My confidence, never good to begin with, was at a low ebb.

Dixie, where are you and that dude we're stalking? I found some things out. I gave her a nutshell download, everything I had seen and all that I guessed from it, outlining the facts we had still to fill in.

"Great! Come on, we're down at the bottom of the hill. He's deciding how and if to cross this river thing, and he keeps hesitating and looking back up the hill. Quick, before he makes up his mind and leaves!"

"Quick" was not in my vocabulary at the moment. I staggered and stumbled down the slope colliding with the occasional tree and only just managing to keep my balance. What I really needed was more time to rest and collect myself, not charge after someone who was supposed to help me. Oh, yeah. That'd be a jewel of a conversation: "hey, I magically know that you're supposed to help me, like it or not. And yes, I don't like it. And no, I don't trust you." Perfect.

I became aware of a dark shape like a shadow wavering in the mist ahead and the sound of flowing water. The shape got rapidly clearer and more distinct and, trying to act as naturally as I could, I marched down the slope to stand beside Lynx.

He turned to face me, not appearing at all surprised to see me, with an annoying look of catlike self-satisfaction. "So you've come to the same conclusion," he remarked.

"Being?" I asked as crisply as I could manage while trying to steady the spinning world.

"That our paths are bound together… in this world." Something about the way he said the last three words gave me the feeling that he meant them the same way I might mean them, not an offhand comment or a reference to the afterlife or anything. Who *was* he?

I grunted. "I guess…" *Unfortunately*, I thought. Eyeing the river, I guessed from it where I was and that if I followed the direction it flowed I'd reach the Old Way (which was basically a jumped-up Roman road). Confident in my course, I spun on my heel to follow it north. The world tipped, the sky suddenly became the ground and the river rushed towards me as my heart lodged in my throat. I couldn't even scream in panic.

A cold chill tingled against my arm and the world froze, then righted itself. The icy claw gripping my arm warmed, fitting itself into the recognizable sensation of a hand, warm and alive, against my skin. I blinked the world back into focus as the lightheadedness ebbed, and turned as Lynx released me.

He gave me a slight smile. "I thought we established we didn't want to go swimming in the dead of winter. You're kind of young to be full sheets."

My cheeks reddened as I realized what he was saying. "I'm twelve years old!" I yelled. "And underage! I'm not drunk, just dizzy." I rubbed my arms, disconcerted by the cold prickling I'd felt before Lynx caught me, and I wondered if it was because of me becoming a ghost. If I had actually started to leave my body.

He shrugged and stepped away, apparently either convinced I was drunk and denying it or not caring enough to ask about the real reason.

Still unnerved, I searched desperately for a way to change the subject. "Why are you here?" I asked at last. "Where are you going?" I spread my feet, trying to right my tilting gyroscope. I need a bit more time before trying to charge off again.

Lynx sighed, seeming a little relieved and impatient at the same time. "I told you, I was chased out of the Wilds by assassins. I took an Old Way shortcut all the way across Camden because I needed to get to the Barren Hills. I tried to gain refuge in the Fortress until the assassins gave up, but they sent me packing like a criminal to the border, escort and all."

"That's the Camdens for you. They're very suspicious of strangers." So he wasn't a Camden. Rhindon then? I looked at him doubtfully. Rhindons were known for their bronze skin, swarthy build, and dark hair. Well, he had dark hair, but… yeah, no.

Lynx shot a quick glance at me, and I could swear he was gauging how much to tell me… or how much I'd believe. "I came to meet someone I knew would be here. Where we're heading is up to you."

"I'm on my way to the Wizard Tryst," I said, mentally confirming with my plan Dixie first. I would go there, and if Lynx was going to come, fine. If so, he could know whatever he wanted, except about the diamond and Dixie's and my ability to communicate. Of course, he might figure that out on his own like Kya had.

"So you were the wizard doing stunts up on that hill." He didn't seem particularly perturbed that he might have just signed up for traveling with a wizard, and I'll admit, it was tempting to not disillusion him. But if he was to get involved, he deserved the truth. Well, except the part about the diamond.

"No. I'm going there to spy."

CHAPTER XV

Without a word, Lynx turned and began walking along the river in the direction I'd tried to head earlier. Dixie trotted after him, leaving me standing on the bank, very confused. "*Well? You coming?*" Dixie called.

I hurried to catch up. *I thought he was abandoning us. It's no joke to mess with wizards, and the Falls of Elnoth is not a place you want to end up in a fight at. That's where the Tryst takes place.*

"*I'm telling you, you don't need to worry about him. He had some understanding or knowledge kind of thing just like you have with the diamond. He came to meet us, remember? He knew we would be here, and it's his job to stick with us and help us with our mission. He knows that.*"

I walked beside Dixie a pace behind Lynx, musing over what she had said. I hadn't figured out as she had that when he said he came to meet "someone" he had meant us. Riddler! Or did he have something he wanted to keep a secret, just as I wished to keep the diamond a secret, and being vague was his means of doing it? Perhaps he had his own diamond… I would've given a lot just then to know *how* he had "known" we would be in the Barren Hills.

I had to stop less and less frequently as we went on, and the headache and dizziness finally passed as dark dimmed my surroundings. The river had dwindled to a stream, then a brook, and was now hardly more than a trickle. The night air was freezing cold, even with my decreased sensations, and I envied Dixie's fluffy coat. At least the mist was gone and the sky was clear overhead. There were some things to be grateful for. Small things.

"Here we are." Lynx stopped at the edge of a raised, well-worn dirt track. He tossed his hair out of his eyes and looked very pleased with himself. The hills had been rolling themselves flat, and now they gave way to what I thought was the east Old Message Way. This was a long-disused route for taking messages throughout the various parts of the Camden kingdom, from outpost to outpost, and to and from the Fortress (which was, of course, right in the exact center of the kingdom). The Old Message Way, or Old Way as most called it, ran in a rough square around the border of the kingdom and crossed it in an X, uniting Camden with a road that messages or soldiers could travel on with incredible speed and ease. Travelers still used it at times, as Lynx had, and as we would to maximize our speed. Being tailed by assassins was no joke, and with our pace, I felt certain they were gaining, though none of us mentioned them.

I regarded the road for a moment, trying to dredge up a memory itching at the back of my mind. "Left," I said in triumph at last.

Lynx raised his eyebrows. "Left is a little counter intuitive," he observed.

"No, we're going to the nearest Way Station first," I said impatiently. "We might find something there to help us, like cloaks, for example." I rubbed my arms, trying to warm them.

"Oh. Fine then." He for his part didn't seem affected by the cold. "I don't suppose there's much chance of a map there."

We scrambled up onto the road and headed south, the hills on our left. "Maybe. It's been unmanned for a long time. Some people do use it as a rest stop, like soldiers I think, which is why I hope for cloaks. But we won't be able to get provisions there. I'm sure any food that might have been left is spoiled. Probably a fifty-fifty chance on the map, but we shouldn't need one. I know the way anywhere we need to go."

Lynx passed a glance to me and cocked his head, but didn't say anything. "I assume we're taking the Old Way straight over the Jaws and into the Wilds to get to this Tryst of yours."

The Jaws, the name locals called the only pass from Camden into the Wilds above, went over the bandit infested mountain range known as the Incisors. I wondered if that was what he was worried about, and I was a little relieved that he knew the slang. He seemed so… unversed in other ways, it was puzzling. Maybe he'd lived in a cave all his life and was just now picking things up, but something still niggled out of place in my mind. Determinedly, I ignored it.

"Yeah, it's the quickest way," I said, my teeth clacking together.

"The Falls of Elnoth aren't too far beyond the Jaws, and going around the Incisors would take more time than I can afford. With assassins after us, that's not a resource at our disposal. Also, it means we'd be in the Wilds for the least amount of time possible, which is good, and as far away from the assassins' territory as one can be in the Wilds, which is even better. The worst we have to fear on that pass is just a few hundred bandits, not a legion-full of assassins, and once beyond the mountains, we'll be closer than any bandit would want to get to the Haunted Palace of the Ancient King, and that'll be an umbrella of protection for us – sort of." It occurred to me that I had begun saying "we." I winced. I still thought of myself and Dixie as separate from Lynx in the grouping.

CHAPTER XVI

Apparently my trip plan hadn't been enough to satisfy Lynx. "And I don't suppose you've planned further than that." He sounded almost disinterested, and I had begun to notice that he almost never asked a direct question. He phrased it in a statement that encouraged elaboration but didn't require it. It was partly annoying, partly relieving.

"Not yet," I admitted a little defensively. "But that's because it all depends on what I learn at the Tryst. Or," I added pointedly, "You might be able to shed some light on some of my problems."

Lynx didn't answer, instead running his eyes over the passing landscape around us, perhaps hunting for black-clad figures stalking under cover of darkness. Finally, I just threw my questions at him.

"Okay, Mr. Stoic, so what I want to know is how things stand in Camden. What's up with the king and the heir, who is Jodeh, and what in long division is Jeduthiam's blade?"

"What in long division?" Lynx looked both perplexed and amused. I could almost feel Dixie rolling her eyes.

"Well, it fits, doesn't it?" I demanded. "When you do a long division problem, there's so many numbers and steps that you could've made a mistake anywhere. And by the time you get to the end, it's like a great big riddle trying to find what you did wrong. But what about my questions?"

Lynx shrugged, but I sensed he was laughing up his sleeve at me and my habit of using mathematical expletives. "I'll tell you everything I've learned. I'll even make it simple, as a bonus." *Learned? What does he mean? Who is he?* "The king is dead, and has been for like twenty years.

71

Not sure on the exact timeline. People don't talk about him or the prince. Jodeh is the steward. I met him myself at the Fortress actually. I've no idea exactly who or where the heir is, but I gather it's a very touchy subject. I've only heard brief allusions to his existence. When I try and ask, everyone shuts up and looks scared to death. And I have no clue what 'in long division' Jedidiah's blade is."

"Jeduthiam," I corrected. Okay, so something was seriously fishy about this dude. In fact, I was flat out scared. He didn't even know for sure how long ago the king died, and he said things like "heard" and "gathered". If someone were to ask me what the president's wife's name was and how I knew, I could answer the first question, but I would never be able to tell how. He knew so little! How could he know so little? He sounded like a shady character from distant parts trying to catch up on local news. And he didn't stop to ask why I wanted to know – he probably thought I was another fellow shady type – and seemed to just trust me that I'd do the right thing with his information. And that was exactly it: he trusted me, but I didn't trust him, and I wasn't happy that he *did* trust me.

I put on a burst of speed and pulled ahead, wanting to run, run so far and so fast that my plaguing troubles couldn't catch me up. I put my hand to the diamond underneath my tunic, groping for reassurance in its solid touch. I was a fast runner, and running always made me feel better, giving me the time and space needed to regain control of myself. Also, when I'm physically worn out, any feeling, whether happiness, fear, or curiosity, is weakened and dulled. I glanced over my shoulder. Dixie was trotting, head low to the ground, beside Lynx, who had increased his stride without breaking into a run. Apparently neither cared about catching up with me. They knew I'd have to slow down eventually, and maintaining their speed would bring them level with me then. I did stop to let them catch up, deciding to save my energy in case I needed to make a desperate escape from a treacherous villain later, and meanwhile pump him for more information.

"What is Jodeh like?" I asked, stomping along to keep the blood flowing in the cold night and not so much as glancing sideways at him as I spoke.

Lynx gave a small snort. "Sly as a fox, cold as an arctic winter, and slimy as a wet toad. Oh, and did I mention, he is king in all but name in Camden, very much to everyone's annoyance."

Mentally I began ticking off a list. "Dwayne and Durahir, Curtis and Turin, Klondel and Lukus… Oh boy, here we go again. Nothing is new under the sun, especially under this sun."

"What are you talking about?" Lynx asked, actually allowing himself the indignity of a question. Maybe his catlike persona was less impenetrable than I had thought.

"Kings and stewards of history. Durahir, Turin, and Lukus were all kings at different times in Camden. Dwayne, Curtis, and Klondel were treacherous stewards who betrayed them. Dwayne and Curtis both worked behind the kings' backs while they ruled, but Klondel's story is the more interesting because he was steward while the true heir was missing entirely. He had a puppet king on the throne, sure, but everyone knew he wasn't the true ruler and he didn't do the ruling anyway. Klondel was the power behind the throne, and it took a great upheaval by a small band lead by his niece and nephews before he was deposed and the heir sat on the throne."

"How do you know this?" he asked, again permitting himself a question.

I glared at him. "I just do. And any of your average Camdens would know it too." That shut him up. Dixie seemed blissfully ignorant of the conversation above her head, but I received the sudden mental message she sent me.

"I think that Way Station is ahead. The smells are faint, but they're nothing like the other smells I've been picking up. It smells like old wood for one thing. But we can't stay there long; those assassins who were chasing our friend are getting awful close."

Thanks, Dixie. You're like the only reason I'm still in one piece. "We're almost there," I announced, then wished I hadn't. I had no particular reason to know, and it'd make Lynx wonder…

"So you 'just know' this, too," Lynx observed.

I chose silence as my best refuge, and he didn't press. It was probably his persistent incuriousness that stopped me from parting ways with him a while ago. He just picked up on too much. I shivered, but not from cold. Whatever Lynx was, a reassuring traveling companion was not it. I missed Kya and her dogged determination, her unbeatable spirit, her certainty that we'd find a way to succeed. Lynx seemed to be coldly philosophical; whatever happened would happen, and he wasn't going to paint it in rainbows and unicorns if it was coming up snake eyes. I wanted the rainbows and unicorns, even just a little.

There it was, up ahead of us. Dilapidated, sagging in places, but still standing as a mark of where two roads met and where so many people over the centuries had found rest and shelter. I felt a rush of relief seeing it, not because I was especially hungry (surprisingly, I realized I wasn't really at all) or tired (which I was, but that seemed like a minor detail). The strain of the road, fear of assassins behind us, and my guarded conversations with Lynx had taken their toll on me. The Way Station symbolized an end to all that, at least for a bit.

I hung back a bit when we came to the door, half expecting an ambush of black-clad assassins to leap out to shoot us down with their poison darts. But when I did push the door open, nobody was inside. With a bit of exploring, I found a stash of hay and oats, obviously for horses, but we obviously didn't have any with us. Still, the oats weren't entirely useless. I also found a stack of old neatly folded cloaks, which I instantly swooped on and rescued one.

Dixie curled up in the middle of the room and went straight to sleep. I ate a handful of oats dry – owning horses can do strange things to your eating habits – and that more than satisfied my non-hunger. I supposed this losing-feeling wasn't without its advantages. Not feeling hunger pangs would mean I wouldn't need to tote rations around with me.

I lay down beside Dixie, wrapping my cloak around me. I'd just rest a little, I told myself. We couldn't stop; we had to keep ahead of the assassins. I realized that Lynx was nowhere to be seen in the little one-room Way Station. I struggled to remember him leaving. He had stood, watching me in my search and helping occasionally, but never seeming to do much. He hadn't wanted a cloak, hadn't eaten a bite, and now he was gone.

I couldn't sleep. The assassins were hot on our tail, following Lynx's smell right to here. We couldn't wait for him to come back from wherever he was. We had to keep on the move. My mind conjured scenarios to explain Lynx's absence: him leading the assassins to us; him betraying us evil wizards who wouldn't want their Tryst spied on; him simply deserting us. As my mind teetered on sleep, the images got more dramatic and terrifying: me lying helpless and asleep beside Dixie, and him creeping in and stabbing us in our sleep. Then he was cutting my hair off and shouting: "Wake up, Lexi! The assassins are upon you!"

CHAPTER XLII

I shoved away the bizarrely disturbing Lynx/Delilah vs. Alex/ Samson nightmare as the door squeaked open. I sat up, groping at my side, trying awkwardly to draw my sword, blinking the sleep frantically from my eyes. It didn't matter, thankfully, or at least I thought not at first. Lynx stood in the doorway, framed against a paling sky outside. He had a faint smile of satisfaction on his face, but it quickly vanished when he read the suspicion in mine.

"Where were you?" I demanded.

"Chill, Lexi. I was leading the assassins on a wild goose chase. I had to throw them somehow. We can't hope to race them all the way to your Falls of Elnoth."

"Will you give the poor guy a break, Alex?" Dixie exclaimed as she stretched herself. *"I told you, he's just fine. He has secrets, but so do we. You can't be distrustful of everyone and everything or you'll never have any friends and hardly a life at all."*

I'm just cautious, that's all, I retorted, somewhat hurt. *You have to admit he hasn't exactly lent himself to trust, has he?*

"Have we?"

Dixie's lightning-fast counter took me aback a bit. I considered this seriously for the first time, arriving at the surprising conclusion that no, I had been stiffer and more guarded than was strictly necessary (particularly considering that he had come with a letter of recommendation from the diamond, which was basically like from the Phoenix himself). It was actually *him* who had been open and honest with me, but it had only made me more suspicious.

"Just do me a favor, will you? Trust him for today, and take everything in

the best possible way. Give him the benefit of the doubt. Tonight, see what you think. Okeydokey?"

Fine. In Bliss, I had been stunned by Dixie's brilliance both in strategy and in understanding other people. Here in Secret, I was beginning worry about her judgements. I cringed inwardly at the thought of just trusting Lynx unconditionally, and the thought of what might happen if it was misplaced inspired a shudder of fear. But I owed it to Dixie to give him a chance.

"So you're saying we won't have to worry about the assassins from now on?" I asked, getting up and rearranging tunic and hair into a more presentable state.

Lynx shrugged and propped himself against the doorway. "Depends on who you are. Those particular assassins probably won't bother us again, not if we make good time, but there are tons of others waiting in the Wilds. Don't worry about them if you want, but they're definitely still a threat."

The words of the diamond's message rang in my ears: *The assassins' legion is strong and deadly, the serpent poised to strike and destroy.* I hugged my arms. I didn't need the message to tell me to steer clear of them.

"Are you coming?"

I nodded and followed him out silently.

The first few hours passed in total silence. I couldn't help keeping a furtive eye out for our black-clad pursuers, but Dixie reassured me that it wasn't necessary. She could catch no fresh scent of them following us. We kept a fast pace, me sometimes running, sometimes walking, Dixie trotted at her ground-eating lope, and Lynx walked with his long strides, never falling behind, never taking the lead. Finally, it was Lynx who broke the silence around noon. We hadn't once stopped, except to drink from streams we passed, and had made, as far as I could estimate, pretty good progress.

"So... don't want to get all 'give me your life story' here, but usually by now I've learned a bit more about who I'm working with. I guess everybody else is a little more chatty. Anyway, I'm curious to know more."

"You talk like you do this a lot," I noticed.

He shrugged, not looking at me. "I do. It's kind of my job."

I waited for him to elaborate, but he didn't. "You're asking me to tell you about myself? Do you realize how little *I* know about *you*?" I thought at first it was anger bubbling in my stomach, but then I realized it was resentment. Of course, I didn't care. I didn't give a hoot about Lynx. Not one. Not a single one.

He gave me a lopsided grin at that. "You'd be surprised how very few people point that out. I'm... complicated. I can tell you more in time, maybe." He paused, squinting ahead at the Old Way, at nothing at all. "I'm just curious, that's all."

"Why do you even care?" I asked. Even I could hear the bitter tone in my voice. I didn't care about this, of course.

"Good question." I looked up as a note of my own bitterness was mirrored back. "After all, I'm just a heartless sidekick you want to follow you like a pet and help you when you need me."

"I never said that!"

He shrugged. "Could've fooled me."

I blew out a breath. "Look... I just – it's just that – well, so I come from another world." My heart sped up at the thought of actually revealing who I was. But somehow, I couldn't help it. "It's called Earth."

Lynx shot me a funny smile. "Yeah, I know it. Been there before." I wondered what he meant by that, but it was clear from his tone that he wouldn't explain.

"Oh," I said. "Well, I come from Texas, from a place called Timberwood Ranch not far out of Austin. I'm not native born Texan, though. We moved down from the Northwest a few years ago when my dad inherited the ranch. I still miss Portland sometimes. A lot actually. But Elliot loves it. He's my brother. Of course, he was only six when we moved, so he doesn't remember it so well anyway. I've always been so annoyed by him, you know, but now I'd give almost anything to see him again." I was rambling on, almost more to myself than to Lynx. "He's a good kid, except for the times he massacred my dolls or ruined the last of my cheerios for his glue-and-food castle. Or the time he peppered my toothbrush."

"He peppered your toothbrush?" Lynx sounded intrigued. "That is one ingenious kid."

"Well, I peppered his first, and then he took revenge," I admitted. "Hey, wait!" I protested, processing the last part of what he'd said. "Don't sound so excited. Peppered toothbrushes are *not fun!*"

Lynx shrugged. "Sounds like you deserved it, though."

I snorted. "I read about it in a book, and then after he dropped my favorite flashlight in a puddle of water and ruined it, I decided to try it as pay back."

Lynx shook his head a little, and out of the corner of my eye, I saw he was grinning. It suddenly occurred to me to wonder why I was talking about this. I asked myself again, *why did he care?*

"Anyway," I said quickly, exchanging my tone for one that clearly said *this conversation is ending*, "so I made up these worlds in my head to have imaginary adventures in. Now, you probably won't believe me, but turns out those worlds are actually... real. At least, two of them are. And both kinda messed up. So I had to fix them. First Bliss, and now Secret."

"Ah. So you're a Mastermind."

I blinked at him. The word sounded awfully familiar. "What do you mean?"

"A Mastermind," he repeated, as if the word alone should explain everything. Then I remembered where I'd last heard it. The Phoenix had called me a Mastermind at the end of our conversation. "Someone who creates worlds. Not too surprising, though. I help a lot of Masterminds. I –" he cut himself off.

"You what?" I prompted. He didn't answer. I stopped short, the late morning sun glaring in my eyes as I turned to face him. He ignored me and kept walking, so I put out my arm to stop him. He stopped quicker than a criminal who spotted a cop and pulled away. "You what?" I pressed again. He wasn't going to get away with me talking so much about my own past and then clamming up about anything personal to him.

He looked down at me, as if trying to decide how much to tell me. "I'm a Mastermind too." Without another word, he turned and continued along the Old Way, heading straight for the Jaws. I followed, lost in thought and memory. By unspoken agreement, neither of us pressed for more details. The last conversation had been a little too nerve-wracking and come too close to my secrets. And maybe his too, who knew?

We pressed on through the night, until I was almost stumbling with exhaustion, but I refused to make camp beside the road. There would be time enough for that in the Wilds and wherever else my road led.

Finally, as the sun lightened the sky to my right, warning of the sunrise, we reached the northeastern Way Station and the border of Camden. It stood at the foot of the Jaws, or Pass of Death, the pass between two mountains in the Incisors range, which was outside the borders of Camden and a haunt of bandits. They were too superstitious and too sensible to hang out in the Wilds, but the mountains afforded a perfect lair and woe betide the intrepid traveler who dared to pass beneath their noses into the Wilds. Only the wizards passed back and forth without serious difficulty. No one, not even a bandit, would dare to mess with a wizard.

Dixie's voice piped up in my head. *"Um, so just wondering, Alex: do you have any plans, like for how we're going to cross the pass, or for how we're going to spy on this Wizards' Tryst?"*

The pass is the hard part. I've actually spied around a few Trysts before, and it's, well, I suppose you could say I designed it to be easily infiltrated.

"The gateway to the Wilds. And a few friends to pick daisies with on our picnic," Lynx said, looking up at the pass, climbing high above us.

"Thanks. Your encouraging words are inspiring hope in my faltering heart," I said irritably. "I do have a bit of a plan, believe it or not, but I'm going to try and catch a little sleep before I go picking daisies."

"Go on then. I'll keep watch. If I see anything, I'll give a shout, and then you can wake up before we die."

"I'm flattered." I stepped into the Way Station, bitterly tired, and sagged to the ground.

Dixie's thought slid into my consciousness. *"Look, I know you're real tired Alex, but just one more question. What do you think about Lynx now?"*

I groaned. I was too tired to talk, even in my mind, but I did despite myself. *I see what you mean. I mean, he has secrets obviously, and he's Mr. Mysterious and all that, but I feel like he's on our side no matter what. I think he knows as well as I do from the diamond that this job needs both of us to succeed.*

"I think so too, Alex. I think so too. I know he drives you crazy, but then, we all drive each other crazy sometimes. What matters is that you're in it together. I'm here for you, Alex, and you have to be there for your friends."

That was the last thing I remember processing before I fell asleep, but it stuck with me, and I never forgot it.

I'm lying in the dust, groaning with pain, trying to call out for Mom, Dad, Elliot, anyone who can help me. All my bones feel crushed to pieces. I try to open my eyes, to see the Texas sky, but when I do, I see nothing. I'm blind, dying out here alone with a broken promise – a "maybe next time" to my only brother – I will never have the chance to keep. Poor Elliot! Why did I never take him riding? Why was I never a better sister?

I'm afraid, more afraid than I've ever let myself be before back home. I can see my fear now. It's like an enormous slimy monster, stooping over me, creeping up behind my blind eyes through my fog of pain. I know him; it's the fear of failure, of my own inadequacy, of what might happen if I venture too far from the realm of what I know I can do.

I'm riding on Starr, and Elliot is riding ahead of me, laughing with pleasure. The horse stumbles on a tree root, Elliot flies from the saddle, his helmet disappears at the last second, and he crashes into a tree. I leap from Starr's back and run to him where he's lying unconscious on the ground. I'm crying and crying, because there's nothing I can do. I know Elliot is dying. Then he opens his eyes, but they're not his. They are bright, laughing, brown eyes, deep and wise. I've seen those eyes before, but where?

"Oh, Alex!" he cries. "You should see! Oh, you should so see! It's so breathtaking it could kill you. You should see!"

"I can't see! I'm blind, I can't see! I can't see!" I awoke, startled by my own desperate sobs. Dixie was licking my face frantically, nosing me into wakefulness. I sat up shakily, reaching out my trembling hands to scratch her ears, taking comfort from the solidity of the black and white fur feathering beneath my fingers. I wondered if Dixie had seen my nightmare, but if she had, she didn't say anything.

I stopped my stroking and held out my hands in front of me, staring hard at them. They looked solid, not transparent as I had almost expected. I clapped them together and dimly sensed the impact, though it didn't sting like a hard clap normally would. It made a solid sound though, and they didn't pass through each other like I imagined ghost hands would. Was I or was I not dead in Texas yet? How could I do this? A ghost can't perform dangerous missions. How long did I have until I was all-the-way ghost? I was slowly dying. And I had to finish before I died.

CHAPTER XVIII

I was shaken by my dream, and it hadn't helped that I felt less existent than ever. When I came out of the Way Station into the late morning sunlight, Lynx was standing, arms crossed, with his back to me. I wondered if he had slept at all –for all appearances he'd been standing there the whole time – and I knew he hadn't eaten a bite since I had met him. How could he survive? Some people. I felt sick, and not at all like explaining an idea of mine to someone who would probably make dry remarks about it, but I pulled myself together as well as I could.

"Okay, so I have a plan," I said, my voice still a little croaky from sleep.

"Good morning, sleepyhead." He turned around with that teasing half-smile, but his expression quickly changed. "Are you feeling all right? You look awful."

"Thanks for the compliment, but I just had bad dreams, that's all." I didn't want to admit or have to explain about me becoming less there. When he started being able to see through me would be soon enough for explanations.

"So here's the big idea," I said. "Wizards don't go to the Tryst all done up. They look just like ordinary people, like they do all the other days of the year. We're going to pretend to be wizards. If any bandit tries to stop us, I'll scare them off with a few threats and a pretense at spells. Follow my cue."

"So they won't bat an eyelash at the dog…" He sounded unconvinced.

I blinked. What was he talking about? "I don't understand."

"Her." Lynx indicated Dixie, leaning into the strong breeze sniffing the air with glee. "I mean, she's definitely not a wizard."

"Oh, you mean Dixie! I think they won't bother her if she's with us."

"Right. Here we go. When in doubt, wave your hands and yell gibberish."

I rolled my eyes at myself. Lynx knew my clichés. No dragons with treasure hoards here, but gesticulating and garbling unintelligible words most certainly were.

The trail was steep, and if any winter rains had fallen in the past few weeks, it would have been impassable. Thankfully, after my young days in the America's wet Northwest, I had made this world practically devoid of rain, and snow only came for a few weeks in the peak of winter. If the farmers wanted water for their crops, they would just have to haul it from the rivers or divert it into irrigation trenches. As it was, it was like a difficult hike, my second hike total to be precise.

I had been going to warn Dixie not to bark and Lynx not to talk so as not to draw bandits to us, but I soon saw that this wasn't necessary. Neither of us was talkative to begin with, and we needed all our breath for getting up to the top of the pass. The air was thinning, and I knew we couldn't stop for a rest at the top. We had to go while the going was good.

The trail wound back and forth up the gap between the two huge mountains. I wondered whether we would make it over before the sun set. I was beginning to actually doubt the accuracy of the pass's name when just at the summit, as I turned to look back at how far up I was, Dixie fired a thought into me.

"They're here, and in full force too!"

How many? I asked anxiously.

"Uh… at least fifty or so. They're on either side of us according to my nose, but I don't think they're on the trail yet. I guess they want to be sure we're not wizards before they risk it."

I saw my chance to convince the bandits that I was truly a wizard. I drew myself up to my full five-foot height, thinking how much more impressive it would have been if I was the seven-foot-tall self I had been in Bliss. Tossing my long dark hair, I cast what I thought was a piercing glance to left and right up the mountainsides.

"If my advice is worth anything to you," I called airily, "I suggest you think twice before daring to mess with me. I won't mind nuking your guts like bacon if you do, and you, I think, would mind very much if I did. Go, before I blast you all to cinders!" I rolled my eyes dramatically. "The nerve of some people."

Lynx was running his eyes surreptitiously along the mountains rising above on either side of us. He didn't say anything then, but he raised his eyebrows and glanced at me.

Are they gone? I asked Dixie. She didn't answer for a minute.

"I think most of them are moving off. I can still pick up the scent of a few of them, most likely left to watch us, but the others are getting fainter. Either they're laying an ambush farther along the road or they're leaving."

Thanks, Dixie girl. What would I do without you? "Oh, well, you can sit there and gawk if you want. But you'd better not try anything," I made mystic motion with my hands, "or I will zap you into a negative."

Lynx rolled his eyes. We pushed on down the slope and made better time downhill. Still, the sun was all but gone by the time the ground leveled out ahead. I tossed around the idea of camping, here on the fringes of the Wilds, but I didn't like it since it was so close to the bandits, especially when we had just had a close call with them.

I suggested a rest before going on, and Lynx agreed. While we sat, catching our lost breath, Dixie paced sniffing, whimpering, hurrying from one place to another, twitching her ears to listen.

"You know, I should probably warn you..." Lynx began quietly, almost sounding uncertain, but Dixie's thought cut him off, screaming a warning in my mind.

"They're coming! They're sneaking down to ambush us now!"

"Hold that thought!" I hissed at him, leaping to my feet and whirling around, searching desperately in the gathering dark for a sign of the bandits. I could see nothing, but I had far greater faith in Dixie's nose and ears than in my own eyes.

How many? Run or fight?

"Same as before. I think we'll have to run."

"They're coming for us," I whispered urgently. "We have to move now."

"It's not like we can fight," he remarked, getting up. "Where to?"

I thought for a moment, wasting precious seconds as I forced myself to make a calculated decision. The bandits feared the Haunted Palace of the Ancient King like the plague, but who could say what other horrors lived there? There might be things worse than bandits. It was a little out of our way too, but it wasn't too far to the Falls of

Elnoth. The closer we got to them, the more the bandits would be inclined to turn back. We might be able to reach it in one night.

"To the falls," I decided.

"It's dark. Might not be easy to find the way."

"No, but I can do it. It's pretty squarely northwest of the foot of this pass."

"Don't worry if you lose sight of me," he added. "If we're separated, I'll meet you at the falls."

I always considered myself to be a pretty good runner, and as a child had been the fastest in relay races, but I stuck mostly to sprints. This was all-out running, and I discovered that I was the slowest in the party. Dixie of course had four legs and I knew she was faster than me, but this was the first time I saw Lynx break into a run. Whether it was because he was older or that one of the secrets he was hiding was that he had superpowers, he was a good deal faster than I was. His feet didn't seem to touch the ground as he ran. I was hard put to keep up, gasping, struggling along in a body that didn't feel a part of me at all, often hearing noises behind me (though whether I imagined them or not, I'm not sure). I had no idea if I was maintaining my direction properly, but there did seem to be a sort of track, and I followed that, quickly losing the strength to even think of blazing my own way.

The night seemed to last forever. Time became a meaningless blur. I didn't notice when I lost sight of Lynx ahead. Glancing over my shoulder once, I could have sworn I saw dark figures hurrying along behind me.

"Keep going! They're dropping off. Before long we'll lose them altogether!" Dixie flung encouragement back to me as my stamina wavered. I had a stitch in both sides now, so at least they matched. Then, after an age more of endless half-running (which in reality was often more like drunken staggering), *"I can hear water shouting ahead! Let's go!"*

I couldn't see Dixie in the darkness, but I knew she was somewhere ahead of me. Occasionally, between the sound of my own ragged breath and thundering footfalls, I heard her slobbery panting floating back to me. Vegetation brushed its leaves against me now, big trees with leaves like dandelions by the feel, and the smell of damp growth filled my nostrils. Sure enough, I could hear the roar of water now, constant and continuous, hardly changing in volume as it plunged from a great height to rocks below. I staggered to a halt near where I sensed the edge was, and then quickly backed up. In this dark, it would be only too easy to accidentally slip off. Dixie's wet nose and tongue nudged under my hand, and I collapsed in a wrecked and exhausted heap at the foot of one of the trees, wondering vaguely why so much of my life in the past few days seemed to consist of endless running and walking.

CHAPTER XIX

Whether I passed out or fell asleep is impossible to tell. When I woke up, my first thought was, *Dixie can't go in with me! No wizard would ever bring a dog to the Tryst. I'll have to go alone.*

Groggily, I surveyed my surroundings in daylight. The waterfall was a beautiful raging streak of white and rainbows. Heather grew in banks along either side of the river, and somewhere in that mass was a secret entrance to the cave halls where the Wizards' Tryst was held. I couldn't remember the exact location.

Dixie, you'll have to stay out of sight in case anyone comes. When I find my way in, you can't follow. Wait for me out here, and if Lynx comes along, direct him to where I went in, okay?

"*Are you sure I can't come?*" Dixie pleaded, looking mournfully at me with those irresistible brown eyes.

I had to deny her a second time. *The last thing I want to do is leave you behind, Dixie girl. But it would put us both in danger if you came. Wizards keep to themselves like hermits, and I doubt any of them would have a dog at all, much less bring one. It'll be hard enough keeping them from being suspicious if they so much as guess that Lynx and I are traveling companions. They might look like ordinary people, but they're not, and they don't usually have friends, not even other wizards. At least, all that was true as of my day. Keep your eyes and ears open, and you might find out something useful.* I scratched her ears, trying not to imagine that this was a last goodbye, trying not to wonder if I would die before I saw her again.

"*Okay, Alex. I guess you know what you're talking about.*" I wished I did. I sensed that there was something beyond the norm in this world, beyond what I was used to here. Sure, there had always been assassins, but going freely on the shortcut of the Old Way all the way across Camden itself? They would never have dared in my day. And of course, it was expected that wizards would misuse their magic, they always had (which was part of why I was here now in the first place), but could there be something extraordinary in it now? It too had been significant enough to be mentioned in the diamond's message. What all was up in this world? I hoped the Tryst could give me some insight.

I pulled myself into the low branches of the tree I'd slept at the foot of, and Dixie disappeared among the other trees and brush along the track. I waited, scanning the heather for any sign of where a secret door might be or any activity. I was a hundred percent certain this was the time of year for the Tryst, so where was everyone? And where was Lynx?

I heard the wizard before I saw him. He was muttering to himself things like "Bolgadesh vandoh bennerhiem," and "poedock loss enock sheevonday", and other disjointed unintelligible words and phrases. A few words glimmered in faint half-memory in my mind, and I guessed they were fragments of one of my old favorite spells for wizards to use. There he was, a Rhindon if ever there was one, completely average in every possible way except his magic. He stopped at the end of the track, whistling softly as he poked about in the heather. Stepping what I thought was terrifyingly close to the edge, he gripped a chunk and jerked it up, folding it back on itself just long enough to let out an "ah!" and vanish inside, pulling it back behind him. Where a moment before there had been an opening, there was now only heather, waving gently in the cold wind.

I climbed stiffly down from the tree, my tight muscles refusing to work properly. *Goodbye, Dixie. I'll be back in a day at the latest if all goes well and I'm not caught.* Then I gripped the heather and dragged it back, groaning with the effort pulling at my poor overworked muscles. A minute later, I was inside.

The interior was lit by torches, showing a long dark tunnel. I followed this until it ended in a choice of ways: right or left. Oh boy. Things were getting spicy right off the bat. I couldn't remember which way to go. Somewhere near the entrance there was a closet sort of cave that housed "formal robes" as the wizards called them, used only at the Tryst. These were long brown robes that hung almost to the floor with wide sleeves that all but covered their hands, and had a cowl at the back. Wearing one of them I would be virtually hidden, like a turtle in its shell, only my features visible in torchlight, and no one would ask any awkward questions. I wanted to go right, so I did, and soon came to an oak door in the wall. Opening it tentatively, I found what I had hoped for – the robes. Ditching my cloak, I quickly took one down from a stack, unfolded it, and wriggled in. I breathed a sigh of relief. I was as safe as I could be here. Now I just had to act like a wizard, keep my mouth shut and my ears open, and learn as much as possible.

I did fortunately remember that the closet for the robes was on the same wing as the Great Hall, which was where I was heading. I hoped to hang out with the wizards who had already gathered and do some sniffing around, picking up what pieces of information I could that Lynx had not been able to fill me in on. I didn't expect that they could tell me, or that their opinion would be anything I could rely on, about the functionality of the Camden royal succession laws. Still, they might know a thing or two about Jeduthiam's blade and the missing heir. Wizards had ways of finding stuff out like that.

I passed a couple of robed wizards in the hall, headed for the apartments on the other wing, and I nodded in greeting. They never gave me a second glance. So far, so good. How long would my luck hold?

The hall I was in emptied out without warning into the Great Hall, blazing with torches and a huge fire at one end to beat back the winter chill. Brown-robed men milled around, drinking fragrant wine and talking softly among themselves. I saw a few women among them, but not enough to make me quite as comfortable as I would have liked. I wandered over to the fire, wondering how one began poking around for information in such a situation as this. If I was caught, I was as good as dead.

I panicked. Lynx! I was surprised that he hadn't beaten us to the falls, and I had left Dixie to direct him when he came to the entrance, but after that he would be lost. He didn't know about the Great Hall or the robes in the closet. As casually as I could, I went to the door again, having been there only a few minutes. I kept my head low, hoping there was nothing conspicuous about me that might be remembered later. As I approached the door, a wizard passing me give me a piercing glance. I could make out little of his face in the cowl, but I saw the eyes. Dark, penetrating, as though they had stars buried in them, eyes that made you shiver.

I stopped short. How could he be here, in disguise and all? Slowly

I spun my head around. He was leaning against the wall, taking the room in. He did not seem interested in me at all, but I recognized his stance. I went all shaky, relief flooding me. Obviously, since I didn't really trust or like him, it was just because we were obligated to be mission partners that I cared that he was safe. I scowled ferociously at my feet as I circled as nonchalantly as I could and returned to stand beside him. All I had to do was pretend he was a stranger. Easier said than done.

"Devilry at work if there ever was," he muttered. His eyes flashed and I wondered what he was talking about.

"How long have you been here?" I asked, trying not to sound too indignant.

"Since some time last night or early this morning."

"But how did you know what to do?"

"I've done this before," he said briefly. "Look, we can talk later, but soon we'll start to draw attention."

"Divide and conquer," I breathed so the group of wizards debating ten feet away wouldn't hear. "You see what you can find out about the heir, and I'll do some digging on Jeduthiam's blade."

"This may not be the best idea." Lynx was chuckling quietly at my foolhardiness.

"I know, but it's all I can think to do. You already seem to know what's going wrong with the wizards, and we'll keep listening for details too. We need to fill in the gaps."

He gave me a curious look, as if I was going crazy. Then I realized I had begun talking as though he knew all I had learned from the diamond. He didn't. All he knew was I had asked him the same weird questions I was now wanting answers for from here. I could guess what he was thinking. "Why that? Why now?" I didn't answer his unasked questions, though. I just shook my head.

"I'll explain later." I sauntered over to the wine barrel on tap. Trying to act like I thought any other wizard might, I decided I'd look more convincing with a tankard of wine in hand. I picked up an empty glass tankard and filled it. As wizard-Lynx passed by, he caught my eye and grinned.

"At it again? This isn't really the time to be going full sheets to the wind and falling into rivers."

I glared murderously at his back as he walked away. Any other time and I could have argued back, insisting that I hadn't been drunk, explained the truth, something. Here, now, though, he could tease me with impunity, knowing I couldn't argue back. It had been what he'd intended, of course. I forced myself to forget about it, knowing I needed to focus on the job at hand. Lounging against the table, I stood, clutching my tankard of untouched wine, watching the crowd.

CHAPTER XX

"Greetings," a voice said at my elbow. I turned, nearly sloshing the wine all over myself, and saw a brown-robed man a full head taller than I was looking down at me.

"Greetings to you too," I said warily. I had to act the guarded but coldly friendly wizard while wheedling out bits of information from him, or whoever else I might strike up a conversation with. I desperately wished now that there had been some sort of "how to" book I could have checked out at the library on this: "How to Wring Information from Suspicious People Without Giving Away Your Identity as a Spy," written by an ex-FBI guy. Something like that.

"You are young and weary. May I be so bold as to inquire as to how long you have practiced the high powers?"

"Perhaps." I swallowed, feeling like a complete idiot. I was bungling this, I was sure. "Not long, but long enough for somewhat of usefulness. I had a run-in with bandits last night. They regretted it, but it has left me sorely weary." This was my best attempt at cryptic pompousness.

"Ah. Would you then like to refresh yourself in the apartments for worn wizards on the left wing? I would escort you there if you wish." His manner was gracious, but I didn't think I liked him in the least. I sensed the coiled serpent inside him, and I imagined that in his voice I heard the echo of a sibilant hiss.

"That is kind of you," I replied icily. "But such wine as this does wonders for reviving the soul." To demonstrate, I took a draft of the wine. I had never tasted alcohol of any kind before, and had always heard the praises of its rich fruitiness sung by those who had. The sudden bitter musty taste of old grape gone wrong burned on my tongue and I choked. With difficulty, I masked my gag reflex and gulped it down with as close to a look of pleasure as I could contort my face into at that moment. All the same, I was grateful for the concealing cowl.

"You may call me Xerxes," he said. "I have practiced the high powers for more than a score of years, and have recently discovered the connection to the lost art of the shadowlands, what some give the uncouth term of sorcery. I tutor interested juniors of the high powers in this art, and if you are interested, I would be delighted to teach you too, if you can afford my price."

"Really?" I tried to hide my shock. A wizard, working with sorcery, and using the high powers to do it? The idea was too absurd, too awful, to believe, and yet this wizard, Xerxes, had declared it to me himself! "I always heard that the shadowland arts brought a curse on those who tried to use them." I knew that was the legend according to my stories, but I had never addressed whether it was true or not. I felt like kicking myself now.

"That is the old lie, told to bind us from our full usefulness. With this new power I hold, I could – well, I could do great things, and if you learn from me and aid me, you will not be forgotten. I have a handful of students already, and ask them if you doubt my word. I do not make idle promises, and no evil has befallen any of us yet." He smiled, and his teeth flashed white in his hood. "Do what you like, but I give you an opportunity that is available only to a lucky few."

I squinted calculatingly. "You said you had a handful of students already. There aren't that many wizards, so you must be almost king-of-the-hill here."

"No, Artemis has several followers." Xerxes ground his teeth, jerking his head in the direction of a slight, dark wizard talking to a group of other brown-robes. "He stole my seeds of research and branched out on his own. Then there's another group, call themselves the Remnant, and they don't take up with either of us. They stick staunchly to the old ways, trapped in the past, and they don't like to associate with us or look like they're so much as thinking about joining." He shook his head. "Blockheads like them are what tie us to the old-fashioned and the clumsy. They hold back progress. But forgive me, I preach to the choir, do I not?"

I hesitated. Should I lead him along any further? I was possibly too far to back out. "Perhaps," I said mysteriously, "I do not take sides easily, but I may be inclined to join you. We shall see."

"Yes, we *shall* see." Xerxes gave me a long look, turned, and slid away, off to seek new prey. I watched his departing back and wondered just what exactly I had gotten myself into.

My goal now was to find out all I could about Jeduthiam's blade and then get out while there was still time. It seemed that every day that passed left me more ghostlike than the last, and I still had one more world to help, according to what the Phoenix had said. If my guess was right, I'd need all the time I had and more to get through that one.

I targeted the wizard Xerxes had indicated as Artemis, intending to drop a few comments, eke out a morsel or two of information, maybe incite the feud between the factions and instigate a quarrel, and make myself scarce.

As I approached Artemis, I gradually became aware that he was studying me acutely, though to all appearances he was shifting his gaze constantly from follower to follower as he answered their many questions. He seemed capable of listening attentively to an inquiry and giving an intelligent and meaningful answer while keeping an eye on me and a lookout for other possibly interested wizards, and also watching those belonging to the other sects. There was no doubt I was in the presence of a great man, and if he had not turned his talent to evil, who knew what kind of mighty legend he might have become. But here he was, using his gifts for sorcery. Sorcery! I shuddered.

As I got closer, I began listening intently, and was delighted to hear they were discussing the differences and intricacies of myth, legend, and the Old Laws (the laws imposed on the first wizards for all generations after dictating how magic should be used, under what circumstances, and where all the lines were drawn between lawful powers and sorcery). I should be able to make it bridge into my questions about Jeduthiam's blade, since I was fairly sure that it was part of an old legend, if I only played the cards right. I stopped on the outer fringe of the circle of huddled wizards, but the instant I did, Artemis broke off mid-sentence and looked at me. His dark eyes seemed disconcertingly to pierce right into mine.

"What do you want?" he asked. "You spoke with Xerxes concerning his Neoterics. Do you now expect to turn around and join us?"

"We didn't talk much," I said carefully. My heart was hammering in my throat. "This is the first I've really heard of any of this, and I want to get a better understanding before I take sides with anyone. I must confess I am an extremely suspicious person, and don't take sides on anything easily. I want to know what both sides have to say. May I please listen?"

Oops. I shouldn't have added that last part. I was fine up until then, but in my nervous state, I was, in a sense, too gracious. Wizards didn't ask, they just did. The "may I please" was old-fashioned and overly-polite here, especially added to the timid way I said it. I might as well have walked in wearing a bright red tunic. Actually, maybe a tee shirt.

Artemis gave me another piercing look. His hangers-on waited in breathless silence to hear his verdict on me. I was surprised when he smiled, but it was a smile that did not shine out of his eyes. It was stuck on his lips as if it was painted there. "Stay then, little magic girl. Learn somewhat while you can. We are very open to expanding, we Freedomists." He shifted his gaze to another young wizard. "You asked about whether the Ancient King really was a wizard or not."

I bit my tongue hard. I had come so close to blurting, "of course not!" before I remembered that I had no reason to know for certain any more than the wizard who'd asked had, nor was it anywhere near my place to speak. I would've blown the whole thing then and there.

"I have done extensive research on the myths and legends surrounding the Ancient King, his domain, the Haunted Palace, and his fabled sword. In my investigation I did discover the answer to your question. Most intriguingly, he was by several accounts a wizard, but he kept the fact a secret for many a long, long year. My sources I cite as a certain journal of his son, the first king of Camden, and a record of one small but violent battle written by his sword thane. They are the main ones at least, and both declare that he made use of the high powers both in battle and at other times of desperate need. Hilkiah of old also once said something of the kind, before he went mad and spoke of the things people now take for prophecies."

Liar! I thought, but I couldn't say. He was good at it, though. If I hadn't personally known the king and happened to know with absolutely for sure that he had no wizardly powers, I might have been fooled myself. By aligning the Ancient King with the wizards (and having the connection supposedly discovered by him), he had made a strategic power play. It would earn the attention of many wizards, and perhaps their respect and loyalty. And he'd managed to smack-talk Hilkiah and his prophecies into the bargain. It was enough to drive me mad. And I could say exactly nothing.

As I waited for an opportunity to broach my question, a thought ran into my head. *"Um, so Alex? Hey, sorry to interrupt if I am, but... nothing's going on out here. But these two wizards met outside the little Tryst place thingy, and one of the guys mentioned that he'd tried to concoct a spell that would let him spy on the steward dude at the Fortress. He couldn't get one to work, by the way, but he said that he really wanted to, and then the other guy said that yeah, doing that would give them a treasure trove of information and might unlock a way to overthrow Camden entirely."*

What! The wizards want to overthrow Camden? I forgot momentarily about Artemis and the other wizards. This felt so much more important.

"Oh no, I don't think so. He just said it casually, like it wasn't super important, and the other dude said 'leave that can of worms well enough alone', and they dropped it. But so I was just thinking, the steward wouldn't think much about a dog, would he? I could go poke around there, see if I can find out anything useful that will help us to kick the steward off his throne when the time comes. 'Course, I'd rather not leave you, but I just thought..."

Nah, it's a good idea, Dixie, I forced myself to say. It was, but I desperately didn't want her to go off on her own. Who knew when and how we might be able to meet back up? *Go ahead.*

"I'll come if you need me, just let me know! I'll come back like the wind!"

Thanks, Dixie, you're the best! Somehow though, I didn't think that if I needed her, she would be able to cross all the distance from the Fortress to me in time. But I didn't say that. At times like this, we had to make sacrifices, however painful.

CHAPTER XXI

Tuning back into the conversation, I wondered what had been going on while I was not paying attention. Artemis was monologuing, in answer to a question I'd missed, about the Ancient King's palace (whether it really was haunted or not) and his sword (whether the Ancient King and his sword was indeed the king in the story of Jeduthiam's blade or not). I almost hit the stone roof of the cave. That was it! Of course! King Jed, who had ruled the world from his wonderful palace on the little island that saw most of my adventures here, the Ancient King, one of my first friends, half-forgotten in the mists of imaginary time, was King Jeduthiam whose sword was crafted by smiths of power. That sword, the inexorable sword, the flashing sword I'd seen in the diamond, the blade that could never be dinted or dimmed, the sword that if its wielder wielded it for what was right and just and true would never betray him or land a false stroke, was the hope of Secret. Whose hand would wield it now?

"Why are you so stricken?" Artemis's words cut into my thoughts. I glanced up to see him eyeing me shrewdly.

"I'm just fine," I managed, but I was not able to fully put on the icy façade I had with Xerxes. In fact, my whole false persona of a cold, detached, and very wary junior wizard was slipping dangerously. I was caught in the crossfire between two striving factions, I was fish bait pretending to be a Parana, I was a twitch-nosed rabbit munching peacefully, waiting to be shot; I had to get out, and fast.

"You'll excuse my saying so, but I request for the sake of the safety of the Freedomists that you leave us now. Do not return to us unless you wish to join us. We cannot afford to have anyone else thieving our ideas as Xerxes did. Go." His voice was cold yet somehow almost pleasant as he dismissed me.

Without a word, I turned, nodding in farewell to the group at large, and tried not to bolt away. Across the room, I took a deep, steadying breath and looked back over my shoulder at the huddle of wizards around Artemis like brown-robed football players around a magical patriarch of a coach. I was very shaken up, and almost lost the grip on my tankard of wine, still full, which felt like no more than a prop in my hand. I had to get out! One thing I still needed to know was where Jeduthiam had left his sword. Which was kind of important. I remembered he hid it before his death so that the wrong person shouldn't get it, but where was it? *That* I couldn't remember and I felt like punching myself for forgetting the most important part.

"I wouldn't take up with them," a new voice said behind me.

I turned, trying to control my trembling, and my frightened eyes met those of an old woman. Her skin was like brown paper, slightly crinkled in places, making her more beautiful. Her hair was pure white like snow and neatly braided, her eyes were like deep brown wells of wisdom, and though she was small in size, I instantly had the feeling that she was tough inside. Her manner was gentle, but if anyone messed with her, she seemed able to handle it.

She smiled, making more little creases. "Do you know who they are?" she asked.

"They say they're some sort of Freedomists," I said. "I just got kicked out from their confab, or I might have learned more. That group," I gestured toward the cluster of wizards now gathered around Xerxes, "calls themselves the Neoterics, I think, or something like that."

"Yes, they are the cults that darken our midst, shadow us with the curses doomed upon their kind, tear us up with strife, and bring the word wizard into bad repute." She regarded me with a sad look in her eyes. "But are you not among their number yourself?"

"Oh no!" I took a step back and almost splashed the wine a second time. "I'm not one of anything. I'm just, well, here. I don't belong to any group at all. Are you one of the, ah —" I struggled to remember what Xerxes had called them.

"Remnant. I am the wife of their leader. We stand by the Old Laws handed down to us. We believe that no so-called superior knowledge or supposedly new discovery justifies in any way a deviation from the Old Laws. They served generations of wizards before us, and they can serve us just as well too. It is our opinion that, in the light of the curses set over the heads of any who break the Old Laws, even should these prove hollow, it is on the whole wiser to follow what is known to be safe and true than to risk life, limb, morality, and soul over a possibility of greater power in our short lives. But forgive me, I am so sorry. I expound my position to you who have not inquired. What a state things have gotten into here!"

"That's all right," I told her. "I'm very much interested in your side too. You see, I think the Old Laws could use a little adjustment myself, but not in the direction they want to take. I think they ought to be more guided. Of all positions, I think yours is the most right. I want to encourage you... not to give up." I felt awkward saying this, keenly conscious of our age difference, but I felt I had to or I would burst from not. I'd heard too much junk from the other factions to keep my mouth shut any longer. "Um, and as a little heads up, times of change are on the wind," – fine print: *oh, yeah, I'm bringing them* – "and no one will get away with sorcery again. Oh, and you might want to separate yourselves from these others while you still can; maybe leave the Tryst now or something. Hopefully, we'll meet sometime later," I added.

"In the happier hour of which you speak, I hope," she said, giving me another crinkly-eyed smile.

I nodded, turning to find Lynx and leave, but then remembered one more question. I turned back. "Do you know where Jeduthiam's blade was hidden?"

She shrugged. "Nobody knows. Don't you remember Hilkiah's prophecy, the one that says it will be discovered when the time is right for the heir of Secret to come forth, wielding it with justice to set all to rights? I guess when the time comes he'll just know or something. There is much speculation, but that is not my preferred forte."

"Thank you," I said, my insides flopping about in a dreadful way. "My memory on that score is a bit... faded."

Glancing around the Great Hall, I saw the two groups around Xerxes and Artemis, and another smaller group in an out of the way corner to which the old woman I had spoken to was returning. Aside from them, the room was deserted, and among none of the groups of robed wizards could I spot Lynx. They must nearly all be gathered in here, judging by the numbers, so where was he? Had he gone back outside? I walked quickly to the door, conscious of, like, every eye in the room watching my back. I paused in the doorway as my eyes adjusted to the dimmer light of the passageway.

A figure stepped away from the wall ahead of me, gesturing silently for me to follow. "Lynx!" I gasped, relief flooding me as I recognized him. "We need to go! Where have you been?"

Vaguely I was aware of the thundering silence rippling out behind me. He didn't stop for a minute to answer my question. That eerie icy chill raced over my skin as he pushed me ahead of him, down the passage and out the entrance. Now I could hear shouts, angry cries, and the sound of pursuit. I pushed through the guarding spray of heather and burst out into the red blaze of a sunset evening. I whirled, facing the way I'd come just as Lynx sprang out behind me, already having shed his robe, and crouched like a cat ready to pounce. It was Artemis himself who emerged from the hole next. At that moment, I surprised myself more than anyone as I leapt forward, filled with sudden anger and indignation at this man. With all the strength I had, I smashed my tankard of wine down on his head. It shattered, and he crumpled back down the hole senseless. The shards of glass sparkled on the heather, beckoning for grasping hands to test their edges.

I was now weaponless, except for the clunky sword under my robe, and that was of no use to me. I saw no weapons on Lynx, and I wondered what he had planned to fight with.

"Let's go," he said briefly. Apparently nothing. Not fighting was best, I decided. I followed as he struck off due east in the direction of the jungle rather than heading straight to the pass. I wondered why but had no wish to talk at that moment.

CHAPTER XXII

"You shouldn't have said my name," he said at last, breaking the deep silence. We were hurrying along at a good trot. I was not feeling up for running again yet, not unless we had to (which we probably would, but the longer I could put it off, the better).

"Why not? You didn't tell me not to. I say your name all the time." A familiar disoriented confusion crept over me, as though someone was tilting my world and asking why I couldn't see straight. Why couldn't they see why I couldn't see straight?

"Didn't I?" Lynx reflected for a minute, and then a strange light came into his eyes. "No I didn't. You see, they know me, and not exactly in a friendly way, you know what I mean?" He glanced sideways at me, but I had no breath to spare by now for unnecessary speech. I nodded. "I have secrets, as I'm sure you've noticed," he continued. I nodded again. I felt a tinge of hope. Maybe he was going to shed some light on them, but – "I can't tell it to you." Too bad. "At least, not yet, not all. But I will tell you this much: I visit worlds. There are many, far more than I have ever been to, and I've lost track of those. I've been here before, long enough to make enemies of several of those guys – Xerxes, Artemis, and some of the tag-alongs of theirs, and others too. That's how they knew me, which was why I made myself scarce as soon as possible. I go to various worlds and help people do things, occasionally with the Mastermind themselves, though that's more unusual. You are the third one so far."

"And you're a Mastermind too," I panted, remembering what he'd told me on the way here.

He nodded. "That's what started…everything." He tossed his hair out of his eyes, searching the horizon for some memory. When he spoke, his voice was unusually quiet, vulnerable. "I made twelve worlds. I didn't know they were real, but still… I didn't think it mattered, if I was just imagining them, even with so much…willful darkness. Half of them died. The other half…"

"Yeah, I think I know that story," I said. *Twelve!* I was impressed with the sheer creativity that would have required. "This is one of my" – I cleared my throat, feeling suddenly very guppy – "three worlds. Basically, I was sent here to 'create change' and set the worlds straight. I think I'm beginning to understand why, and why me. I made these worlds, so it's up to me to fix my mistakes. I mean, I *created* darkness; I wanted it, in a way. I didn't realize it was wrong."

I stopped, surprised I'd said so much. His glance was quick, the smile even quicker, but I knew what they said: *We know. We share that story. And… thank you.* I was glad I'd opened up, and I knew this moment had been very important, had helped the change I was striving for in me. And my sharing had nothing to do with a sudden feeling of sympathy, that we had more in common than I first realized. Nothing at all, of course.

"Where are we heading now?" I asked him, shifting the topic to tamer waters.

"The Jungle. Last place I want to go, but it's the only place here we have a chance of hiding in."

"Are you crazy? It's full of wild animals that'd eat us as soon as look at us! Why not the Haunted Palace at least?"

"Because the wizards don't fear it like the bandits do, and it's too small to hide in forever. It would be way too easy to get cornered or trapped. It really would be crazy to try to go back to Camden over the Jaws, so we'll head for the Jungle. We just need to hide out there long enough to throw them off the search."

"We don't have that kind of time," I muttered, thinking of my fading. "We can't wait or hide out."

He gave me a puzzled look, and I realized I hadn't explained about my ghostliness since I wasn't see-through yet. He didn't ask about it, though. "We'll figure something out." He paused, checking over his shoulder.

"How long until they're after us?" I asked anxiously, noticing the gesture.

He tilted his head, then shrugged. "Could be a while. Depends on how thorough they decide to be. Artemis' followers will for sure insist on reviving him before they set out to chase us. If we're lucky, that will cause a lot of argument and conflict between the factions, which will buy us more time. If we're incredibly unlucky, they'll realize they can't catch us on their own and get all of the Wilds to help."

"The assassins and bandits would never help them." I shook my head. "Certainly not both of them at once."

"If anyone could unite them, wizards could. And wizards madder than hornets just might try."

"For spying on the Tryst?" I said skeptically. "I doubt it'll be that big of a deal."

"No," Lynx agreed. "But after last time, they'll want my blood, and I wouldn't be too surprised if they went to great lengths to get it."

"Why?" I asked, simultaneously nervous and curious about what he could possibly have done to make them that angry.

"Let's save that for story time around the campfire."

I paused, catching my breath. I didn't care if all the Wilds were after us at that moment. My robe was tripping me up so that I could barely go more than five steps without nearly face-planting myself. I jerked it off and flopped onto the ground. I also needed a second to do some hard thinking in as close to peace as I could get. We needed a definite plan of action, but that depended on what I could remember.

"I don't suppose we have a clear plan yet," Lynx observed, as though he had read my thoughts.

"Give me a second. I have to get the facts straight. The heir is a big question mark – we know nothing and no one will talk."

Lynx shook his head. "Couldn't get anything on him from the wizards, either."

"Figures. On the Camden front, we have a corrupt steward rampaging evil through it, and he might have nobles on his side – he and the guys who follow him must be deposed. The Ancient King, Jeduthiam, hid his sword somewhere, and I have to remember where it is and get it. Then I have to find the heir and give it to him. The wizards are split into three factions: those who cling to the Old Laws, and two opposed groups who believe in deviating as wackily as possible from them. They will have to be set straight. The assassins have grown to practically an army compared to what they were, and are a very dangerous threat to the world, so they have to be destroyed, just like in the days of the Ancient King, only more thoroughly. I also have to 'right the kingdom' and 'repair the succession laws' or some such. There." Now he knew all the details of the mission. The only things I had withheld were the diamond and Dixie's and my ability to communicate.

"Is that all?" Lynx sounded disappointed, but when I shot him a suspicious glance, he looked impressed. "Well, I suppose we start by finding the sword, then the heir, and then he can take care of the assassins, wizards, and treacherous nobles."

"Right." I sighed, feeling more overwhelmed than ever. "Just that. Find the sword that I can't remember where it is, and an heir whose existence everyone ignores, and all the while being chased by wizards, and probably bandits and assassins too. Let me think for a minute."

I rolled over and burrowed under my arms. So long ago! I was like eight when I imagined that story, and here I was, four years later, trying to recall a little fact about a sword in an imaginary adventure. I was having difficulty focusing – Lynx was too quiet and I missed Dixie. My mind kept reverting to what I'd seen in the diamond, and the image of an enormous still lake flung itself at me again and again with the line "beneath the Lake the hope of Secret lies" ringing in my head. Next thing I knew I was sitting up straight, shouting, "The Lagoon! It's under the Lagoon!" Dusk was in the sky, but now I had a destination.

Lynx looked perplexed. "The Great Lagoon in the Jungle? How do you plan to get it, then?"

"Yeah, that one. The Ancient King was the only one who ever ventured into the Jungle, and he made friends with the animals by the Great Lagoon, don't you remember?" Of course he couldn't, but I was too excited at the moment to be thinking clearly. "When he was old, he returned once more to say goodbye, and he hid the sword then. It'll be simple enough to get it back. I just have to find the entrance."

"Care to elaborate a little more?" He looked almost amused at my animation.

"About what?" I was slightly nonplussed.

"What entrance to where, and how do you plan to get *to* the Great Lagoon without being lost or eaten first?" Lynx was standing now with his back to me, using the last few remains of daylight to orient himself in the direction of the place where the Incisors met the Jungle. "I assume you plan to leave for it now?"

"Oh yes, of course!" I exclaimed, scrambling hastily to my feet. Naturally, walking more was the last thing I wanted to do ever again, but the thought of angry wizards on our tail and all the while me getting more ghostly did wonders in motivation. Plus, I knew where to go now, even if it was as good as a death sentence.

"The point is," I explained as we quick-marched in as straight a line as possible over the rolling rocky landscape of the east of the Wilds, "is that we have to think of ourselves as reliving the time of the Ancient King. In his day, there were thousands of assassins, and they threatened to rampage across this whole island thing and tyrannize it under their iron thumbs. The wizards were then, just like now, the only ones who could stand against them, but they were few. When they got bigger and more powerful, they organized themselves, Tryst and all, under the Old Laws. The problem: they didn't have clear enough laws and no grand poohbah to keep them in line. So that's got to change. The Ancient King started on the right track, but we have to finish it. So not just cripple but completely destroy the assassins, and not allow them to become a thing again. The Old Laws will need to be clarified and the wizards given a leader to keep their use of the high powers honest. As I said, he started with good ideas; he befriended the wild animals, so we should too. The Wilds and the Jungle should be tamed and not allowed to be Outlaw Central anymore."

"How does this help us get the sword without being eaten?" Lynx reminded me of my real point.

"Oh yeah, that. Since we're finishing what he started, it makes sense to pick up where he left off, doesn't it? The last important thing he did was hide his sword. Where?" I paused for dramatic effect, unable to resist. "In the Chamber of the Guardians, beneath, and I don't mean in, the Great Lagoon. And in order to get there in one piece, we'll befriend the wild animals, and get the wolves to guide us just like they did for King Jed himself. I don't think a war is exactly avoidable at this point, and we might be able to get the wolves and other wild creatures to help us. We'll need all the help we can get." I crossed my arms, hoping to look far more confident than I felt, but then discovered that trotting with one's arms folded greatly increases the risk of falling, and quickly uncrossed them.

"Your confidence is reassuring," Lynx said thoughtfully. "I guess we'll see in time how well founded it is." This frightened me dreadfully, but he seemed unperturbed. I guess he was just used to adventures.

We kept on hard all through the night. Sometime before morning we struck the tail of the Incisors and they stuttered to an end in the fringes of the Jungle. This was what I had hoped for. If we followed along the skirts of the mountain range, it would bring us into the Jungle, and after a short distance cutting straight through from there, we would be at the Great Lagoon itself. The Jungle was in sight, and my heart pounded with anticipation. Would my plan work? How did one befriend a wild animal exactly? Would the Guardians allow me to take the sword, supposing we even got that far? Dixie might have been of help, but she was far away on another task. Lynx, I observed, never took great trouble to encourage others with him in dark circumstances. He simply accepted them philosophically and dealt with the problems, expecting others to do the same.

We were almost there, but once in the Jungle, what would happen? I was soon to find out, but not quite yet. The trees had not so much as cast their shade on our faces when disaster decided it hadn't seen enough of our faces.

CHAPTER XXIII

Lynx vanished. No flash, no sound, no warning at all. One moment he was there, real as 2 x 2, and next, there was simply nothing at all. He was gone, just like that.

I wanted to scream. I wanted to faint and not wake up until I was out of this horrible world, with any luck at all back on Earth. I wanted to find Lynx, even a body that would indicate normal means, but there was nothing at all to be seen of him, not so much as a hair. What wizard, what devilry, could do this? It was simply impossible. Never, ever, in all my reading or imaginary run-ins with magic or sorcery had something like this happened. Mechanics in magic, yes, they were there, and any spell or magical mischief came with a flash and a bang, or at least some sort of signal to say "I am a magic spell! Fear me!"

I sagged against a boulder and slid to the ground. Why now, of all times? I had never been more alone. On the brink of deadly danger, without Dixie, without even Lynx's company and no way to get either of them back. I refused to admit it, not fully even to myself, but I missed Lynx. I hated the thought of never seeing him again, thinking that his time for helping me had passed forever.

I held my vaguely non-present hand up before my eyes and stared at it. How long until I puffed out like that? How long until I was no better than a wraith, wafted on the breeze, powerless to accomplish my missions and unable to return home?

"What now?" I murmured aloud. "Go on alone? How can I? I'm not a hero by a long shot." The words sounded familiar as the slipped off my tongue. Had I said it before? Probably. It was true enough. Then I remembered one time at least: in that bright, green world talking to the Phoenix himself. And then I remembered his answer.

"You must choose: will you serve fear, or let it serve you?"

I cracked my knuckles. "Okay, fear, time to serve me." I remembered everything I'd been through up till now, all the fear I'd felt, everything I'd done despite it. *Fearlessness is no virtue,* he had said. *Courage in the face of fear is.* I stared my fear in the face. "I feel you," I said aloud. "You are telling me that what I'm going to do is dangerous, which is true, so thanks for the heads up. But I'm going to do it anyway, which means your job is to sit down and put yourself to work giving me energy to get this done. I will not serve you."

I stood up, taking a deep breath. Then, before my determination could waver, I squeezed my eyes shut, turned my head aside, and plunged into the Jungle. Maybe not exactly a heroic display of courage, but it was all I had to give.

Sticky is the only good word to describe the atmosphere of the Jungle. The light is dim and greenish from falling through so many leaves, vines are tangled everywhere, and underbrush clogs the spaces between the smooth-barked trees. I knew that at that moment any number of poisonous snakes, prowling tigers, venomous insects, and all manner of nasty creatures could be stalking me and I would be oblivious. I wouldn't know it was there until it killed me. *One step farther, don't think about back, keep going deeper, too much relies on you now...* I advanced slowly inward, into the heart of my fear.

So alone, the wind rustled in the tree boughs. *Hopeless,* moaned the vines as they swayed. *Get out, get out, get out!* was the pounding of my heart. *Serve me!* I demanded back. Bit by bit, the Jungle was swallowing me. I had to maintain control of myself, of my fear that wanted to rule me, or I might as well not have come at all.

As I stumbled through the snarls of growth, clutching desperately at the shredding vestiges of what I had hoped might be considered the seeds of courage, I remembered a line from a long-forgotten song. It was simple enough, for I'd only been eight when I had composed what I thought a grand sonnet, but it was something to reach for and hold on to. I tried to remember the rest of the words and the tune, and softly, I started to sing.

The time is dark
The foes are here
There is no spark
In all this drear

107

Come friend, come foe
I'll still keep on
No threat of woe
Can stop my dawn

Yet still I hope
To see the day
And no more grope
This jungle way

Come life, come death
I'll do what's right
No fatal breath
Can end my fight

We seek the light
And freedom's song
We'll see the sight
Of all fear gone

Come tears, come joy
I'll no more roam
No earthly ploy
Can ward off home

It was from one of my first imaginary adventures in Secret. I was reminded of it at this time most likely because I had made it up as a song from the Ancient King's childhood, and he was supposed to have sung it as he found his way to the Great Lagoon. I had been so proud of my minstrel skills that I wrote it down, memorized it, and sang it often to myself when I was alone. Gradually I'd grown out of it as I got older, but I found I still remembered the words, and the tune was the same for every verse. I sang it through once tentatively, and then a second time, gaining more confidence and striding a little more purposefully into the Jungle. If I got eaten, I got eaten, and there was nothing I could do about it, especially not by oozing forward at a pace a snail could beat.

I was wrapping around to "come friend, come foe", when I thought

I heard a wild accompaniment in the shadows of the foliage. I paused, listening hard. Nothing. I took it up again, and the chorus came again, slightly stronger, coming from both sides of me. As I entered the third verse, trembling now despite my best efforts, my unseen accompaniers swelled in powerful voice. It was almost like the untamed howling on a moonlit night in the country, but this was serenading, harmonious, following me note for note, always in perfect time, and I thought I caught words in the howls. It was the voices of wolves, no doubt about it. I was being invisibly escorted and choired by a pack of wolves.

I can recall very little of the long minutes, or possibly hours, after that. I'm pretty sure I kept singing, but thinking back on it, it's surprising to think that I could have kept it together enough. At any rate, I remember the moment that I burst from the grasp of the Jungle onto the narrow sandy beach of a huge, still lake, improperly named a lagoon (it was entirely fresh and nowhere near the sea), scratched, scraped, and in a state of fearful exhaustion. I turned, breathing hard, staring wildly back the way I'd come. *Lynx was right after all,* I thought. *I was stupid to hope I could make friends with wild animals. I'll never get the sword now. I knew I would fail.* Tears of fear and loneliness, of failure to be what I needed to be, stung my eyes. I squeezed them shut and sank to the ground. When the wolves got here, they could eat me. There was nothing in me left to fight.

Dixie, I don't know if you're paying attention, but I'm going to die. Thanks for being such a good friend. Goodbye.

As if I had conjured her, a wet nose touched my face. I squeaked in fright and my eyes popped open. There, large as life, gray like the Barrens, majestic as any mountain, was a wolf. He peered at me solemnly through dark eyes.

"Who be you, young stranger, who sangs ye old lostish songs of yore ago?" he rumbled. His speech was less than strictly grammatical, and he had my habit of improvising his own spin on an existing word to make his own one tailored for the particular occasion. Somehow, it was comforting in a way.

"I am Alex," I said faintly. "I knew the Ancient King." I supposed that was true enough, though definitions like this were always a fine line for me to judge.

"I seeith." He backed off a step, allowing me to sit up. I saw many members of a huge pack jammed onto the beach, thirty at the least, probably more, but I had no time to count or properly estimate. "Tell

I, pleases you, what bringed you here to the Water?"

I didn't see any harm in telling him. "I'm looking for the Chamber of the Guardians. I need Jeduthiam's blade. The time of those old prophecies Hilkiah made is finally here, at least, I'm pretty sure. Seriously major trouble is havocking the world outside this Jungle." I could remember a little of the prophecies, but not enough to be totally confident.

"That we know alreadily," the wolf snarled, though I didn't think his anger was directed at me. "Warrage is on the wing. It cannot touch us'ns here, but it will sweepith through the kinglands out there. Then we shall have troublings." A rumble of growls rolled among the pack, but they maintained a studied silence. It was, apparently, extremely rude to interrupt the chief while he was conversing.

"It certainly won't completely ignore you," I agreed. "That was why," my heart pounded, and I wondered if this was the right time. *Oh well, now or never. It's not like you've got time to waste.* "I also intended to seek for help from the Jungle, from those here who would volunteer, to help the new king."

The wolf seemed to frown. "Who be he? Rhindon be far offish, and I know of no king or heirling in Camden."

For a wolf of the Jungle, he was well-informed with the outside world. "He is the lost heir of Camden. I don't know where he is, but I'm trying to track him down, since if I get this sword I'll need to give it to him. I happen to know – you'll forgive me sir, but I can't reveal my sources – that only by him wielding Jeduthiam's blade can true peace, victory and change be won," I said, quoting the diamond. "As for me, I'm only a sort of backstage aid, prepping everything behind the scenes. He is the real hope of Secret."

The wolf cocked his head several times, as if digesting the information and stewing over what to do. "Forgive I, but let me have wordage with my trusty advisors." He turned away, his long tail streaming like a banner behind him in the breeze. Several other wolves clustered around him, and I couldn't understand their speech as they conferred together for several long minutes. The weariness of my sleepless night was just catching up with me again when he turned back.

"King's friend," he announced, bobbing his head at me in a formal way. "The legendary of the Ancient King has been passed down over long yearing from our ancestors, and we know of you from them. Your song from yore ago told us of your presentage, and it is our desiry to do what you wish. But we will not hunt where the moon does not shine; that saying, we won't do without knowledges, and we cannot help you without being sure of you. So I lay this testage before you: find the Chamber of the Guardians, and if you come back with the sword, we will take that as the Guardians' approvingness of you and your honestiness. If you fail to return, or fail to return with the sword, we will seeith you as no friend. Be we agreed?"

"We are agreed," I gulped, trying to swallow the golf ball lump in my throat. I was really in for it now. The wolves all drew back into the fringes of the Jungle, some still visible, leaving the beach clear for me to see and find the secret entrance into the Chamber of the Guardians.

CHAPTER XXIV

From where I sat, legs now crossed beneath me, I could see the entire rim of the lake. Somewhere, there was an entrance to a secret chamber, and in that chamber was a sword of legends, and on that sword rested all my hopes. But where? It wasn't an underwater entrance, I knew that, not just from my memory but from the diamond's message. Maybe the diamond would tell me? But it didn't work like that, just handing me the coordinates, and I didn't think I'd get any more out of a second look in this world – I'd made it through the whole vision the first time. Anyway, I couldn't afford the mental impact now. So where? It was all dependent on the old cranium again. I blinked rapidly, trying to recall the way I'd pictured it when I invented the story and overlay it with how I could see it. The sun was nearly straight ahead of me, glittering on the smooth surface of the lake.

In my mind's eye, I saw an old man stride out of the Jungle behind me. He stroked the fur of a wolf that paced beside him. I saw him break off what he was saying and send the wolf back into the Jungle. Then he drew out his sword. It shone in the late evening sunlight, flashing red like fire, the blade among blades I'd seen in the diamond. He stood still, erect, then swept his gaze around the lagoon and beach. I could almost feel them pass over me. He stepped backwards to a small rock protruding from the sand under the shade of the trees.

Slowly, trying hard not to break my concentration and lose the picture in my mind, I got up. I stepped backward and sideways. Then a little farther back. My foot struck a rock, and I knew without looking it was the right one. I saw the man in my mind's eye turn toward the sun so that it shone straight in his eyes. Then he strode forward, pressed a protruding tree root with his foot, tugged hard on a dangling vine, and the roots of the tree splayed, opening wide a mouth into darkness. The man vanished. I stood, blinking in bright sunlight. Turning, I angled myself so that the sun glared into my eyes. It was hard to see now, but I couldn't see that distinctive tree root protruding from the ground anywhere near. Maybe the tree had fallen, or maybe the root itself had been buried over the years. Much might have changed.

Then it hit me like a clap of thunder, laughing with Elliot's voice. "Alex, you muddled the points of the compass again! I told you, east is where the sun *rises*, not where the sun *is*." How many times had he said that? Too many to count. Orbiting around the stone, I faced the opposite direction, hoping my back was as close to directly towards the sun as possible. It didn't really matter. Now that I was facing the right direction, I spotted the root instantly.

In sudden relief I ran to it, pressed my foot on it as the king had, groped for the vine which was still hanging down from the branches overhead and tugged. Nothing happened. The vine didn't give in my hand and the roots remained as solid and immovable as ever. I was only twelve, and pretty small for that... I stepped with both feet onto the root, feeling it shift slightly underneath my weight, and gripping the vine tight, I dropped to a crouch over the root.

This time it worked. The vine jerked down several feet into my hands, the roots at the base of the tree spread, and I tumbled backwards onto the soft sand. The dark hole loomed before me. Next hurdle, the Guardians. Who could say what they would make of me? I wondered if they were even still alive.

I stepped down into the hole and landed hard in a twisting and rapidly descending tunnel. The walls on either side pressed in around me, brushing my hands as I hurried along, trying not to think about any of this, or let myself feel the growing fear in me. Earth beneath my feet, stone on either side and above, and who knew what was ahead.

I was almost sobbing from exhaustion, but I knew I couldn't stop. I had to keep going, with no light at the end of the tunnel – literally. My feet refused to take another step, but somehow I managed to force them, again, and again, and again. I started to hum the tune of the old song I'd sung in the Jungle that had drawn the wolves in an effort to keep my spirits up and the fear down and to keep me going. I didn't have the energy to sing. Without warning, the sound of a dozen other silvery voices, pure as the voices of stars, echoed up the tunnel. A moment later, I stumbled into a large, circular room, completely empty and with only the one entrance. Around me, coming from nowhere as it seemed, the voices sang now in full song, unseen voices that had no bodies.

I shouldn't have been surprised. I had known about the Guardians, had talked about the Guardians, but the fact was I hadn't *expected* Guardians. They had first been instituted to guard this place (or more to the point, the sword that it kept) who knew how many hundreds of years ago, so by all rights, they should be dead or gone away. Yet here they were, and at their old tricks too, to frighten off unsuspecting intruders. There was in reality a space between the wall I was looking at and the real wall, and here the Guardians took up their position whenever someone entered to scare them off if they weren't legitimate. In this wall, surreptitious slits were hidden, and sound emanated in a spooky way from the gleeful Guardians.

I was startled, but they didn't frighten me. Probably because I knew the source and cause of the supposedly frightening thing. As it was, my attention was almost entirely taken up with the sword that shone gently on a large rectangular table in the center of the room. I knew it. I walked slowly towards it, the moment pulsing in me. I stopped in front of the table. There it was –the legendary blade of King Jeduthiam. Reverently, feeling slightly like a grave robber in Tut's tomb, I reached for the hilt. I would never, in all my life, forget this moment. The voices of the Guardians broke off as though cut by a knife. In absolute silence, my fingers closed around the hilt. I lifted it from the table. I was holding a legend, holding both history and future in my hand.

Drawing the sword in the sheath at my hip clumsily, I felt the difference. The one felt like a child's plaything compared with the other. It was an awkward, bulky, hack-and-slash weapon, while the other was light, ideally balanced, almost alive in my hand. I sheathed Jeduthiam's blade in my own sheath, and it fit reasonably well. I placed my most-definitely-not legendary, completely unmagical sword on the table. Let it stay there until Jeduthiam's blade returned, I thought. I turned to go.

My path was blocked by about fifteen small personages, wispy in build, at least two feet shorter than me. Every face was set and stern, every hand held a white flickering orb, the last defense to strike down sword thieves. I had come face to face with the Guardians, last elves of the twilight hour.

"Who are you, and what do you intend?" asked the man I guessed to be their leader. He stood a little in front of the others, and his voice was clear like the chimes of a silver bell, but it was stern and uncompromising. I wondered how exactly I could explain myself.

"My name is Alexandria Bell. I am the Mastermind who made this world," those words felt strange on my tongue, "and was a friend of the Ancient King Jeduthiam a heap long time ago. This sword," I touched the hilt of the blade at my hip, "I take to the heir, hopefully, who is the one foretold to wield it in Secret's darkest hour. P. S. You would kind of basically end this world if you try and stop me from taking this and fulfilling the prophecy. Um, but you don't have to stand by and watch me walk out of here with a legend at my side," I added hastily, seeing the grim look of doubt on the leader elf's face and the slight raising of his hand that held the flickering orb. If only one of those hit me I would be dead.

"What are you asking, then?" he demanded, taking a step closer. The Guardians behind him did the same.

I tried to keep my cool and not freak out entirely. "Maybe you can come with me," I suggested hopefully. "We'll need help. There'll probably be a war – if I can find the heir – when he takes his stand and rights the kingdom and the world and all that. You could stop hiding from people and come fight, come help the king to save the world."

"Do tell us, Mastermind," he said, slightly less sternly, "why we should believe you?"

It was the inevitable question. I had no answer for it. Trying to hold my head high all the same, I answered, "Because the Phoenix sent me. I don't have a better answer, but if you kill me now or stop my mission, we'll fail. This world will fall into darkness, which is exactly what I was sent here to prevent. I need your help, and the help of everyone who doesn't serve the darkness. I have to give this sword to the heir and set the prophecies in motion. That's what the Phoenix sent me here for. That's all I have to say." I bit my lip, wondering if they would kill me or just kick me out without the sword. It didn't really matter that much. I was dying anyway, either by Guardians, wolves, or fading, and it only changed the timeline. But the matter of the third world tickled my mind. If I died in this world, it would be doomed. I had to survive and keep going for its sake.

A rustle passed among the elves, as though a silent signal had been given, and all the glowing white balls disappeared. The leader elf took another step forward, but now his pose was less threatening. He was smiling, in fact. He held out his hand for me to shake.

"My name is Keliel, and I am seventh in descent from Hilkiah, first leader of the Guardians whom you no doubt knew."

My eyes widened as I shook his hand. "Not *the* Hilkiah, the one who aided the Ancient King all those years ago in his war against the assassins and everybody, established the first Guardians, and made the prophecies? Not *that* Hilkiah!"

"Yes of course. Quite the *déjà vu*, don't you think? Here we are, you and I, about to see repeated those same times again in our lives, if all goes well."

"Actually, I'm hoping to see them completed, if all goes well," I muttered. "The tricky bit is finding the heir himself without getting caught."

"True enough," he laughed, gesturing to his elves. "But come, let us leave this place. We will not be needed here for some time yet, and we shall have business elsewhere. I will call upon my friends and rouse the Jungle to your aid."

"Thank you so much, sir," I said as I followed the elves up the tunnel. "The wolves are waiting outside to see if I come out alive or not. They will help me if they know you're on my side. My biggest problem at the moment," I admitted after a pause, "is where the heir is. It's now all up to him, and up to me to find him."

CHAPTER XXV

"I don't know how much I can help you there," Keliel said. "But the depth of sight my ancestors possessed does not wholly fail me. Of this much I am sure: he is on this island, for as a king would not desert his country, so even a hounded boy would not leave farther than the nearest sanctuary. But of this I am also sure: he is not in Camden itself, and I don't think in Rhindon either. It would be too easy for those enemies of his who have wanted him dead for so long to track him there. He is nowhere within the borders of my influence, restricted exclusively to the Jungle here. Therefore, that leaves one logical, if extensive, location: the Wilds. I believe that it is there you will find him, or rumor of him."

"The question is," I said in frustration, "how exactly I'm supposed to look for him there. The place is teeming with assassins who'd stick me full of poison darts as soon as look at me, the wizards are ruffled and out for my blood, and if I bump into any bandits, they'll be clamoring over who gets to hack my head off for my tricks on them. I couldn't go a half-mile into the Wilds without scores of different enemies swooping on me like vultures, and my friends are gone now, so I'm alone. How can I hope to find someone there when I don't know where to start looking?"

We trudged on and up in silence for a while. Then Keliel spoke so suddenly I jumped. "Men and means may fail, but the Phoenix never does. If he sent you to do this, then I believe it is possible for you to do it. You must hold on to your courage, and keep on trying. If you give this your best, everything in you that you have to give, then you have nothing to regret. No one can ask for more than your very best, your all. I don't dispute the odds, but you have what it takes to succeed, if you don't give up. I can tell you this, and it might help you in your search. The heir's name is Jedidiah.''

We emerged into bright, midmorning sunlight, and it, combined with this startling statement and my sleep deprivation, dizzied me. Up till now, no one had known anything about the heir, no one would talk about him, and certainly I'd never gotten a name. But from Keliel, leader of the Guardians, who had most likely never left the shadows of the Jungle, I had gained this small bit of information, and it encouraged me.

"One more question please," I said, blinking against the sun. "What do you mean by the enemies who wanted him dead since he was a boy? This is the first I've heard of any of this. All I know is the king is dead and the heir is missing. Who are they?''

"I thought you knew." He gave me a long, thoughtful look, then nodded. "I'll tell you. Jodeh, steward of Camden, and four of his closest officials. They hold prominent positions in the kingdom, advisors to the steward, fawners, puppets who do his bidding. All the dangerous people, one-time nobles and such, have been kept neatly out of the way and from any dangerous activities. Paralyzed in their positions, or dead, in a few cases.''

"No!" I gasped, shocked.

"Oh yes. There's little I could do, if it were my business, and less that they and the other faithful ones can do, not until the steward is deposed. That is why the heir must come forth soon, before his kingdom his utterly ruined.''

I rubbed my face with my hands. There were so many vital things that hung on me. How could I do this?

"Rest now," Keliel told me. "Your weariness shines in your eyes, and when you awake I will be arranging everything already.''

I slumped to the ground, not caring where I lay as long as I could sleep. I wished Dixie were there with me, and I wondered what had happened to Lynx and why it hadn't happened to me. Despite the forward steps I was making – I had Jeduthiam's blade at my side, gotten the friendship of the wolves and engaged the Guardians to raise an army for the heir – I felt more alone and discouraged than ever. What use would an army be without the heir to lead them and wield Jeduthiam's blade? How could I search for him alone in the Wilds? Fear, ever the enemy of action, crept into my heart, squeezing at the little seeds of courage there.

As the blanket of sleep wrapped me up, I murmured softly to

myself, "I have to. There's no choice. Do it or die."

Darkness. A world I know too well. Harlan, my last and most recent creation, an incarnation of darkness and evil itself. A world that defines the absence of light, of hope. I hover above it in space, staring at the raw evil I made. Overwhelming horror and guilt wash through me, ripping at my soul. It is killing me, but I don't fight it. Shame tells me I deserve to die for doing this.

"There is always hope. Even in the darkest night, there is always hope for a sunrise," the Phoenix had said, but I know instinctively that because of how I created this world, what I had created it to be, I had methodically blocked out all chance, all hope of sunrise. On purpose. My fault. My darkness. It's too late for Harlan.

I fall to my knees in the nothingness of space, sobbing uncontrollably. I don't want this to be real, but I know it is. I did this, I created this darkness, it came from me, and not by accident either. Have I gone too far? Am I too full of darkness to be beyond hope of a sunrise in me?

I see the Goths raging throughout Harlan, reveling in their barbaric pagan rituals, mocking light and life.

"No!" I scream. "Please, don't let me become that! Don't let the darkness have me! I'll choose the light. Just not this. I know this is my darkness…" My voice breaks. I'm looking at the darkest parts of myself, given flesh and blood and a physical life, because I had let it. "I – I'm sorry. I'm so, so sorry. I can't – I'm not – I'm sorry."

It's better that I die. Then I won't be able to create such deliberate evil ever again. The universe will be a better place without me in it.

Light bursts from a point beyond the spinning world of Harlan. I look up, but my eyes can't handle how bright it is. It sweeps straight for us, me and that world of utter darkness, devouring the dark. It cannot stand against the light. My eyes burn and water, but an incredible peace and power together wash over and through me. Then my eyes can see the light. I can look straight at it now. A terrible, beautiful joy and fear fill me, a feeling I've felt before and don't ever want to end.

Harlan is gone. I'm surrounded only by the light. Peace. Forgiveness. A new beginning. A door to a new life if I choose to take it. Gratitude I can't begin to find words for fills me, and I stand, ready to step through into the change. A change in myself, in who I am. Me, but so much more all at once. I smile, and in the light fire around me I see a shape flash. A fiery bird. A Phoenix.

A roaring fills my ears as I move forward, and a disembodied voice announces: "Stupid alarm clock. Sorry about that." And everything disappears.

I blinked my eyes open, struggling to get my bearings after the dream. It was so strong, so potent, reality felt like a shadow beside it. The dream had been the real reality. The sun was about the same position in the sky as it had been when I fell asleep, if maybe a bit lower and on the other side.

Lynx was sitting with his back to a tree a few feet away, tracing his fingers through the sand. He looked uncomfortable, an expression so foreign to him it was a little startling. At the sight of him, safe and sound and just *sitting* there, all my anxiety and worry instantly flared into irritation. I snatched the nearest pebble and threw it at him, and he nimbly dodged it.

"Don't *ever* do that to me again!" I yelled. "You totally freaked me out. Do you realize how spooky that was? What happened?" Naturally, it wouldn't have bothered me that much to never see him again; I didn't really like or trust him, right?

"Look, I'm sorry." He twisted and met my angry gaze. "I really am. I didn't mean to do that at all. In fact, I was going to warn you that something like that might happen a few nights ago, when the bandits chased us, remember? I never got far enough and then I forgot I hadn't told you. I'm sorry. It just happens sometimes."

I let my breath out unsteadily and clasped my arms around my knees. "Okay. But what happened? People don't go poof every day."

Lynx looked away. "I think you deserve the truth."

"Gee, thanks," I said sarcastically. "I'm truly flattered."

"No, it's just that... I don't normally tell people." I remembered how I'd wondered if he had his own diamond, and thought of how I'd been warned to keep it secret if at all possible. Maybe that was what he was getting at. I wished I hadn't said anything. "Anyway, so the long and the short of it is that I'm a Dream Walker."

"A who?" I asked, not sure I'd heard right.

"A Dream Walker," Lynx repeated. He had a habit of repeating things people asked about, as if in some bizarre way he expected repetition to explain things for him. "Someone who travels to other worlds – real worlds – when they sleep, to help people do things and stuff. A lot of Masterminds wind up being Dream Walkers too, like me."

I remembered the last part of my dream. "Did you say something about an alarm clock? Or did I dream that?"

Lynx ran a hand through his wild dark hair. "Oh yeah, I did. Time is funny when you're Dream Walking; it isn't predictable between the waking world and the time you spend Dream Walking. Normally I can sense when I'm close to waking up, and I find a convenient way to slip out of the dream, like I did on the way to the Wizard Tryst. But this morning I had a dentist appointment at early o'clock and had to set an alarm. Of course, it went off right at the Jungle and yanked me out of the dream without warning."

I laughed. I couldn't help it. Lynx, the mysterious enigmatic friend who was helping me find a way to bring a magical sword to a lost heir and destroy a host of evil wizards and assassins, had a dentist appointment. It was so ordinary it sounded crazy. He smiled a little too. "So, this Dream Walking gig... How does that work? I mean, are you here to help me, or do you just roam from world to world looking for interesting things to do, or what?"

He shrugged. "Some of both. I do roam a lot in between specific missions, but sometimes I'm sent to help a certain person, like you. I was told that if I went to the Barren Hills I'd meet someone there, which I did." He rubbed his hands together. "I have to say, this beats imaginary adventures in my worlds. This is like the real thing, you know. I mean, it's my job and all, being a Dream Walker, but it's pretty much the coolest. Adventure, excitement, chases, thrills and chills... just doesn't pay the bills. Only drawback."

"You're nuts," I said. "I prefer to be able to control the adventure."

He shook his head, getting to his feet. "Yeah well, not for long. Once you get used to this, going back just isn't the same. Trust me, I know. But seriously, Lexi, your friend there says you have Jericho's blade, so we should get a move on. Enough dawdling."

"It's Alex, and it's Jeduthiam's blade," I insisted, part of me knowing I was only encouraging him. "For once, can't you get it right?"

Lynx grinned and shook his head. "Not once, Lexi."

I rolled my eyes, giving up. I got to my feet, not exactly feeling rested but better able to continue on my inevitable road. When I turned, I saw Keliel approaching, obviously the "friend there" Lynx had referred to. He looked fairly pleased with himself.

"The game has started and the pieces are in motion," he said cryptically, rubbing his hands together as if he were trying to discover how much friction he could create between them. "The Jungle is aroused and is gathering to this spot. I sent swift messages to Rhindon, and they will join us, though they will be hours late to massing, however fast they march. I also sent messages to those I know to be faithful in Camden, and they are gathering an army of trustworthy warriors with that vigor men have when their blood is up. They should arrive sometime after sunset, since I dispatched the messengers the minute we joined you, as one might say. Battle is in the wind; the only question is whether the armies to fight it will be in time."

"The battle will follow us, I'm sure," I said darkly. "And we will be in the Wilds searching for the heir with little hope of success, but not for lack of effort… let's hope," I added more softly. It would take a lot of hope against my small courage (which was running out), and there was none of Dixie's there to ride on as I had in Bliss.

"We can hope," Lynx interjected. "But hoping isn't doing. Are you ready, Lexi?"

I sighed. "As ready as I'll ever be. And thank you," I added, turning to Keliel. "I'm pretty much in your debt." I couldn't help thinking how much my family would like to meet the friends I was making, and especially people like Keliel would make my mom laugh, and like Kya, who she would say was a sweet little spitfire. In sudden wistfulness and loss, I plunged into the Jungle, heading as straight as I could for the Wilds.

Apparently, my course was a little more north than I'd intended, and when at last I blundered out of the tangle of Jungle, the Incisors were purple and steep on the left, farther away than I had meant. I was scratched, bedraggled, and tired again already, but Lynx, following behind me, was to all appearances unscathed by his trip into the Jungle.

I snorted at him. "Next time you can go in front." His continual imperviousness was getting a bit annoying.

"We don't know there's going to be a next time," he pointed out. "What's our course?"

"Don't know. Not to the Falls of Elnoth, that's for sure. I'm as certain as I can be that the heir is not there."

"No, he isn't," Lynx agreed. "No one can remain in hiding there for too long. You saw how quickly we got discovered, and with their magic, no disguise is impenetrable forever. So assuming he's alive, he's not there."

"Awesome! We've eliminated one tiny little spot in these vast Wilds. We're making devastating progress." I always got sarcastic when I was nervous, and at this point my nerves were at a fevered pitch.

"I don't think we should start in or near the Grand Chasm either," he continued, ignoring my comments. "The assassins have their main hideout and headquarters there, and I've been there myself too – that's how come I was being chased out of here – and I don't think he is, or would be, there."

"Also a stunning beginning!" I exclaimed. "That's on the other side of the Wilds, so just getting there would be ticklish, especially if we wanted to get there *alive*, so it probably would not make a good *starting* place. Any other insights?"

"Actually I do have one more." His thoughtful tone was replaced by an almost mischievous one. "I see moving things below those mountains to the south."

"What!" I whirled, looking at the little mountains at the end of the Incisors range. I was sure I could see something moving too, not as far away as they looked, and anyway, I'd learned in the past few days that Lynx's eyes were much sharper than mine.

"Oh yes. Some of them are hodge-podge patches of color – nothing distinguishing or unique about them, but I could swear some of them are wearing all brown; brown robes to be precise." I gasped at his cool manner as he narrated the details to me. "The bulk of them though," he said, turning away with a frightening look on his face, "are wearing all black, if my eyes aren't lying to me."

CHAPTER XXVI

Lynx had been right. The wizards had united the Wilds against us for our blood.

Without another word, we both broke into a run. There was no question of course or direction now. Aside from back, which would get us nowhere and I steadfastly refused to think about, we had only one hope in all of the Wilds: the Haunted Palace of the Ancient King.

Lynx was apparently thinking the same thing. "I suppose we'll find out just how superstitious that lot is behind us."

I had no breath to spare for talk, but it was my thought too. It was common knowledge that the bandits refused to go within sight of the Haunted Palace because it was said to be haunted. They believed bad luck would fall upon anyone who so much as glimpsed the majestic palace that was said to be built of gold and glass, and to have never cracked or fallen or sagged in all the hundreds of years since the Ancient King dwelt there. As for assassins, no one knew for sure what they thought about anything – most people who so much as saw them usually ended up dead – but it was rumored that they too were extremely superstitious. The wizards, for their part, held a refined contempt for everything and everyone. It was them who would be our great fear, even if we could outrun our hunters all the way to the Haunted Palace.

It was only a couple of hours distance at the clip we were going to where I knew the palace to be. We had the start on them too, as I was pretty sure we had spotted them first. We had, after all, only just come out of the Jungle and they were still tracing our tracks into it. The real question was whether we would have the greater endurance or be able to keep enough ahead to be out of range for poison darts or magic blasts. We had to get there, we had to get there, we had to... My mind beat out the cadence with my pounding feet, my heart beating double time to the same pace. I ran, head down, all attempt at anything like good form long ago sacrificed. I was still going, and that was all I could manage.

Shouts behind us. Whizzing of darts. A pulse of magic that struck my back but seemed to pass right through me.

"They want to take us alive," Lynx said, slowing to keep pace with me. "*If* that's any comfort to you. We aren't going to make it."

"Thanks, Captain Sunshine," I wheezed. "Why are they shooting, then?"

"It's stun darts. They'll just knock us out. And the wizards are trying to paralyze us." He gave a grim smile. "But we happen to be immune."

I staggered to a stop, propping my hands on my knees as I spared a few seconds of breath. "What? Why?"

"Because of... who we are. Dream Walker benefits. You're close enough. Look, we can have this fascinating conversation later. We need to figure out what we're going to do."

I looked hopelessly back at the pursuers, practically on top of us now. "So this is it? I've got no idea of what we can do."

"Let me think," Lynx began, and then we were surrounded.

It quickly became apparent why they wanted us alive. They had, it seemed, made some deal among themselves that whoever managed to catch us would get to kill us. The problem: they had *all* caught us. Angry words were thrown about as each of the different groups clamored for our blood. Meanwhile, several members of the factions worked together to disarm me (which wasn't hard; thankfully they didn't realize the significance of the sword I carried), and tie us to a tree, back-to-back with the tree between us. They did it very thoroughly too, so that I could barely wiggle my fingers. A bandit drew Jeduthiam's blade from my sheath.

"Nice sword," he remarked. "Imagine the irony when it takes off your head." He raised it as if to chop off my head, but a wizard barked a rebuke – and apparently a spell – at him, and the sword dropped from his limp hand. Gingerly, he picked it up again and stuck it in the ground a few feet in front of me with a wicked laugh. "Drool over your freedom, pretty lass!" he cackled and wandered off.

It seemed that everyone had agreed to an impromptu court session. Pseudo-lawyer after pseudo-lawyer stood up and delivered a lecture on why our heads belonged to his group.

"Why aren't they just killing us?" I asked in an undertone. "Why not just kill us and fight over it afterwards?"

"They're too smart for that," Lynx whispered back. "It's equal chances that either the wizards or the assassins would win if it came to a fight; the wizards are more powerful, but there's like four times more assassins. Neither will want to get in a fight if they can help it. They'll try 'diplomacy'."

"Peachy," I muttered. I rested my head against the tree and tuned it out.

After a minute, Lynx chuckled humorlessly. "Well, sounds like you've got the bandits on your bad side, I've majorly ticked off the assassins, and the wizards seriously want us both."

"Okay, campfire story time," I demanded in a low voice. "How did you tick off the assassins? And you mentioned before about the wizards too. What did you do?" It was more to take my mind from our predicament than anything else.

"The assassins? Just a little raid, really," Lynx said, and from his tone I knew immediately the catlike self-satisfied expression on his face. "I burned most of their supplies of poison darts, dumped their spare barrels of poison down their wells, and sabotaged a good portion of their buildings, causing them to collapse."

I gaped. Such a thing hadn't been dared in... basically forever, and I didn't have a clue how he'd pulled it off. But I didn't doubt for a moment that it was true. "No wonder they followed you through Camden," I said at last.

"As for the wizards... I kind of blew up the entrance to their Tryst the last time I escaped. They had to rebuild, like, half of it. That was the straw that broke the camel's back for me with them."

"Wow." Even there, expecting to die at any moment, I couldn't help but be impressed. This guy had serious talent. Top of the list? Making epic enemies.

Lynx was silent for a long moment. I realized that the court session was getting more and more heated, and also going nowhere productive. The sun had set and in a short time the army Keliel had called would be assembled and ready to march. I needed to find the heir, like, yesterday, and here I was, stuck tied to a tree, while all my enemies argued about who got to kill me. It was pretty pathetic.

"I've got an idea," Lynx muttered. "Bear with me."

"*Hey, Alex, you listening? I've found out bunches, simply bunches here. Are you ready to hear my report or should I just come straight to join you?*"

Uh… Currently we're trying to escape from, like, all our enemies at once. They've got us prisoner. So no, not yet. But go ahead and join us — we're heading for the Haunted Palace of the Ancient King if we get free. Hurry if you can!

"*All right!*" she whooped in my mind. "*I am come-ing!*"

"This suspense is killing me," Lynx moaned theatrically, loud enough for the court to hear.

"I know," I agreed, trying to follow his lead. I banged my head dramatically against the tree for emphasis and winced at the pain, less sharp than it might have been, what with my dulled senses.

"Just do it already, guys," he shouted, surprising me. I'd never heard him shout yet. "If the suspense kills me, you won't get to. Just duel for it or something. Fighting is always better than talking." He snorted. "More *to the point.*"

I choked on a laugh at that. That was about the exact opposite to Lynx's philosophy. His was: "Why fight when you can talk your way out?" The bandits, however, seemed to think it was a good idea, and the assassins began thoughtfully tapping their dart guns against their palms, eyeing the wizards and bandits distrustfully.

"Fine, fine!" a wizard I recognized as Artemis barked. I hoped he had a nice headache. "We'll each choose a representative to duel for our group for the right to the lives — or deaths — of these prisoners." He clearly planned to be the wizards' representative and was confident of winning.

A brawny bandit and a silent, black-clad assassin were quickly elected, but not without argument. As the others quickly crowded together to watch the duel and the parties began calling advice and encouragement to their representatives, I seized my chance.

"Now what?" I muttered nervously. "Hurry up with the plan, will you? Did they happen to miss a dagger on you, by chance?"

"Shh!" Lynx paused, seeming to gauge the duel that was just beginning. As the three duelers clashed, roars erupted from the crowd. The ropes around me went suddenly slack. I tried to fling them off, but they still circled completely around me and the tree. Lynx appeared in front of me, a faint outline in the dusk. He grinned.

"What are you, a contortionist?" I gasped, trying to calm my heartrate from the spike the shock had given it.

"Later," he breathed. "Come on."

I squeezed back into the tree, letting the ropes drop around my ankles, and stepping free, I yanked Jeduthiam's blade from the ground and slid it into my sheath. As quietly as we could, we crept away.

"It won't take them long," Lynx remarked quietly.

"No, it won't." I sighed moodily. "Guess we should run again. I'm getting really sick of running."

Each minute of the next hour seemed to last for an hour itself. I strained my ears for any sound of anyone following us, my nerves stretching further and further the longer I heard nothing. A stitch gripped at both of my sides, and a bungee ran from my stomach to my knees, jerking it down with every step. I gasped for breath in uneven spurts, occasionally falling onto all fours when I couldn't run anymore in a very dignified and heroic manner. Somehow, driven by the fear of pursuit (yay fear for serving me finally!), I always managed to find my feet again and somehow keep going.

"Thickets close ahead!" Lynx called back to me. I dragged my head up and saw with a tinge of renewed hope the almost-forest cluster of trees and bushes sprawling across the path ahead that I knew surrounded the palace. A little ways into the woods there would be a small river, diverted in two, encircling the palace with a running moat. And there would be a palace huger, more intricate and more labyrinthine than any palace ever before designed. It would be our refuge. In there, we could hide, and the chances of anyone finding us, at least for a while, would be very small.

CHAPTER XXVII

Gasping, staggering with exhaustion, I hauled myself step by step beneath the trees. I saw Lynx standing at the edge of the river that ran on either side of the palace, and then I saw the palace itself. Even in the dark, lit only with scattered moonlight, it sparkled and glimmered like some otherworldly gem. The gold glinted faintly where it accented the walls of glass, which were not transparent and seemed to be made of millions of tiny chips of glass fused together in a sheet stronger than iron. It took my breath away to actually see it before my eyes. It was at least as big as the White House in perimeter, but it rose more than four times as high. There was nothing like it on Earth in size and beauty, and the years had passed it by untouched.

I stood for a full minute, staring in awe, and if I hadn't been so hopelessly out of breath, I would have forgotten to breathe. Then I remembered the thousand or more pursuers who were no doubt on our tail would not have slowed. With the assassins to track us and the wizards to drive them under the shadow of fear of the Haunted Palace, we couldn't stop now, not by a long shot. We were far from safe.

"Come on, let's go," I panted, my breath still not wholly regained.

"We can't hide in here for long," Lynx said. "Just a while to try and throw them off our trail. We can't let ourselves be cornered."

I nodded in agreement, exhausted at the thought of running without hope of being able to stop. "I need a breather. This is as good a place as it gets. Let's head in."

"I don't see a drawbridge, but the gate's right there." Lynx pointed to the gate, which was across and a little to one side of the place where we stood.

"It's been pulled up," I pointed out. "If we're going to cross we'll have to –" I paused and glanced sideways. At the same instant we both said, "Try swimming." Remembering our first encounter in this world, we somehow managed a laugh. I grinned, reflecting that now… we were friends. Okay, okay, even I would admit it.

"Well, Geronimo!" I cried, leaping from the bank. The water was shockingly cold. The wind was instantaneously gone from me, I could feel my diaphragm and lungs constricting, and the shivering that had already taken control of my body made any sort of stroke feeble and nearly ineffective. I'm not quite sure how I got to the other side. Thankfully it wasn't too broad of a moat, and I think it was almost more of me being washed up on the opposite bank than due to any swimming attempts on my part. I rolled up, wondering vaguely through the ice in my bones and mind whether the water would freeze on me. I lay curled in a ball until I had recovered enough mobility to sit up and look around. Lynx was just stepping from the river, or was it off the river, I wondered crazily. He seemed scarcely touched by the water, and still less by the cold. With a little shake, the drops sprang off of him and there he was, dry as an old bone.

He grinned. "Shall we head inside?"

"How?" I asked in sudden horror. "It'll be locked for sure." I hadn't thought of that.

"We could try the gate for a start, just for giggles and grins." He shrugged. "I mean, I don't think it's likely since the drawbridge is up, but it's worth a shot."

I nodded and dragged my wet frigid self to my feet and along the strip of gray-brown dirt on the palace's perimeter. "Maybe the ghosts will let us in."

"Doubtful," Lynx mused. "I don't believe a ghost would be able to open anything, since they're disembodied and all that."

I shivered, not just from cold but from the talk of ghosts and disembodiment. How long until that was me, who wouldn't be able to open anything since I had no tangible body?

I halted in front of the massive gold gate, almost too cold to be much good. I glanced over my shoulder at Lynx.

"Go on," he said. "We don't have all the time in this world to spare." I knew that better than he did.

I raised my hand and knocked. It was stupid maybe, but it was such an ingrained habit that it felt violating to open the gate or try the latch without first knocking. I wasn't prepared for the loud, booming, almost musical sound that echoed inside when I did. I jumped.

"Sorry." Reaching out, I gingerly wrapped my numb fingers around the latch and pulled. Nothing happened.

"Harder," Lynx urged. Then I heard the sound I'd been dreading: the sound of the hunters behind us, the arch enemies who had banded together in a common cause of destroying us. They had come.

With all my weight and strength, I jerked on the latch. Still nothing happened. Then, as a thought struck me and in a last desperate attempt, I lifted the latch and threw myself against the gate. It gave way unresistingly and I burst into a wide foyer.

Pearly white light was all around me, as if I'd stepped into the moon itself. Stairways branched off of the foyer both up and down, glimpses of other levels and rooms of equal beauty could be caught through wide doorways. The railings were gold, the stairs glass, of the same sparkling fused chips style as the walls and floors. Everywhere was the light-catching chiseled glass, accented artfully with gold inlay and framing. I stood stock still as Lynx leapt in after me, only moving to close the gate (or front door, looking at it from this side) behind me. I ignored the sounds from outside, wanting to just stand and stare.

"Come on! We have to get farther in," Lynx said in a whisper, but his voice magnified, echoing through the palace.

I nodded and began to climb slowly up the nearest stair, careful not to touch the rail. I wouldn't dare print that shining spotless surface. The stairs wound up and in, and looking back, I could see the door we had come in a good way below.

"This would be the kind of palace I would have if I were a king," I whispered.

"Perhaps we should move faster and save admiring the scenery until later," Lynx said. "Those guys won't be too far behind us, and with their numbers they could easily get a tree or two or five down to cross on. And *they* won't be stopping to gawk at pretty sights."

That got me going. Hurrying in fear, expecting the door below to burst open at any moment, I hauled myself up the stairs two at a time. The door disappeared around a bend in the stair, and rounding the second bend after that I came suddenly face to face, not with a ghost, but with a man.

He was about thirtyish years old, tall, broad, almost stern-faced. He eyes sparked with the authority of a natural leader. I recognized him, though of course, he couldn't recognize me. I had seen him in the diamond on my first day in this world. Instantly I went from hope level zero to level seventy-eight.

"Who are you that dare to enter this place?" he asked crisply. "What brings you here?"

"I – my name is – that is, we're here for –" My wits were scattered completely, and I stood on the stair, one foot hovering, my mouth flapping like an idiot and nothing sensible coming out. At last I managed to pull myself together. "Sir, I am Alex and this," I drew out the sword that was sheathed at my side and presented it hilt-first, "is Jeduthiam's blade. In the name of the Ancient King, I ask for your help. The time of the old prophecies' fulfillment has come. Take this sword and wield it to victory for your kingdom and for Secret."

"That blade," he said, looking searchingly at me, "can only be wielded by the one foretold. Who am I?"

It didn't sound like an actual question, in that he didn't seem uncertain of his own identity. It was almost more of a challenge, a dare for me to proclaim who he was and his destiny. I took it.

"You are Jedidiah, true heir and King of Camden, and the one of whom Hilkiah the elf spoke when declared that in Secret's darkest hour, the true heir would come forward to free the world with this sword. You are the last hope of Secret, and this is the moment – and I mean literally *the* moment, you know, what with the bandits and wizards and assassins on your doorstep and all – to act, or all will fail. Take it, sire, and may it bring you to victory and all that good time stuff."

He studied me a minute, and then, half-smiling, he took the sword from me. "Touché, my young maiden; you have named me aright. A fight awaits beyond the gate, and to it I shall descend." He whistled sharply over his shoulder, and the rumor of feet echoed from the depths of the palace. "But who is your friend?" he asked.

I turned and saw Lynx standing on the stair below, looking on with interest. "Oh, that's Lynx. He's been helping me, and –"

The gate down below and just out of sight crashed in with the flash-bang of a magic blast and the roar of many voices.

CHAPTER XXVIII

A score or so of men ran down the stairs ahead, drawn swords in hand.

"Stephen, take these two to the Inner Sanctum. The rest of you, follow me!" Jedidiah called.

"There's an army that'll be coming on their tail, hopefully," I interrupted. "Our friends. We can always hide out and wait for their arrival."

"Then perhaps this will not be a losing fight." He nodded to a slight young man in the rear. "Don't let either of them be seen on the way, Stephen."

Dixie! I hollered mentally. *Find the army of wolves and elves and men and lead them to the Haunted Palace of the Ancient King. I've found the heir and this is where the battle is. And it's kind of happening right now, so tell them to hurry.*

"You got it, Alex! I can smell 'em already. We won't take long, so just hold on. I'll see you soon!"

Thanks, girl, I thought with a sigh of relief. *You rock.*

Stephen waved for us to follow him back up the stairs. I had never quite grasped how vast the interior of the palace was. There were too many passageways, stairs, foyers, chambers, halls, and rooms of various kinds to count. I was dizzy from the confusion of it, and though we only scrambled after Stephen for less than ten minutes I was entirely lost and turned around. He seemed to know exactly where he was and where he was going, though.

We came to a place where the wall of a room ahead was curved, not just slightly for effect as it was in many other places in the palace, but it was clear that the entire room was perfectly round. The walls were made of solid gold, hard as titanium. It was the heart of the palace – the Inner Sanctum. No door was visible in the wall, and the

133

passageway we had come from ended in a narrow circular hall that ran around the outside of the wall of the Inner Sanctum. Peering to either side along it, I could see no door anywhere.

"How do we get in?" I asked nervously, half-expecting assassins to spring from behind and attack us.

For answer, Stephen walked across to the gold wall, raised his hand, and knocked. A door appeared where there certainly had not been one visible before about a foot away. It swung outwards, and a woman stood there. Stephen gestured us forward, and I stepped hesitantly through the gold door. Lynx followed more slowly, looking back and frowning in deep thought.

"Mira, these are guests who must not be seen," Stephen told the woman. There were three other women in the Inner Sanctum besides the one named Mira who had opened the door. Other than them, there was a stack of neatly folded blankets, a stash of provisions, and nothing else. Turning to me, Stephen said, "I will return when the battle is over to guide you and your friend back out. Mira will look after you meanwhile." He spun on his heel and raced off.

"Don't keep a man from a fight when his blood is up," I observed, but I thought I understood. With a king like that, it'd be hard not to follow him. The gold door closed and vanished, no trace of it remaining on the inside either. The women remained clustered together, sometimes whispering, sometimes sunk in tense silence.

I huddled in a ball by myself on one side, feeling very alone. Where was Dixie now? I had done all I could in my mission, but now it was out of my hands, and that didn't guarantee I was successful. What if the king and his small guard were hunted down and killed before the army could get here? That would be the end of all hope for this world. What if we were found in the Inner Sanctum? *But I'm dying anyway. What does it really matter?* I stood, lifted my foot, placed it on the ground again deliberately. I felt a vague twinge that might have been coming from my foot region, but I couldn't be sure. I held out my hands, staring hard. Did they look real? Something... something was off about my body. I was in a body, but only able to sense and touch and be like a dream body – almost not at all. I was fading to a ghost of my former self. At least, that was the best explanation I could come up with to explain what was happening to me.

I looked up suddenly from my self-scrutiny, aware that Lynx was speaking rapidly to the woman named Mira.

"No," she answered him, shaking her head. "The Sanctum itself is our only real protection and it is a good one. We each carry long daggers in case of some unexpected need, but this room is virtually inaccessible save if it is opened from within. We have no need for further defenses, nor could any be spared." So he must have been asking about the defenses of this room. Why? Was he thinking of making a sortie? That thought horrified me, and I edged closer, all but intruding on their conversation.

"There are assassins out there. Perhaps you are familiar with the fact that they smell their way to their victims. I am certain that they are close on our trail, following the scent of Lexi and myself to *this very room*. Since they are in partnership with wizards," he spoke with careful emphasis, "I have *no* doubt they will find a way in."

Eerie nervousness shivered through me. "But what can we do?" I protested, breaking in without planning to.

"That's what I was asking." Lynx's gaze flicked toward me.

"We can do nothing," Mira said, and her face had a terribly calm look in it, like someone who expects to die but isn't afraid of it. "We can only wait and see what time will bring." I found this statement very glum and dark indeed.

"Can't we?" Lynx seemed to be conversing with himself. "It could be tried. Perhaps – well, time will show, truly enough."

I wondered what he was talking about. Mira was right – there was nothing to be done. What kind of harebrained idea could he have? Straightening, he walked to the wall. It was hard to be sure, but I didn't think it was where the door had opened.

"What are you doing?" I asked, puzzled.

"Going to give them something to think about." He took a deep breath and closed his eyes. As if someone had adjusted the focus on a lens, his mysteriousness and almost unearthliness came into sharp clarity, in the forefront of my attention. It was so striking at that moment that I took a step back. A second later my shock and fear were instantly multiplied as he stepped forward, not into the wall, but right through it.

I gave a little squeak. I couldn't help it. I don't think anyone who watched another human step clean through a wall of solid gold as if it wasn't there *could* help it. It was beyond all words. I felt suddenly dizzy and sat down. *This is a dream, this time it really is a dream, it has to be. Just like the time I dreamed that I was blind and Elliot was dying. It has to be like that this time. Good old Elliot. He never stepped through walls. If only I could see them all again, just one more time. Even if I can't go back forever, just one minute there to say goodbye and to tell them I love them.*

Mira cleared her throat. "Kindly, would you enlighten us, young lady?"

I looked up, mind still reeling with shock, at Mira standing before me. The other three women had shrunk back, and simply stared aghast at the place where Lynx had gone.

"What do you mean?"

"How it is that your friend is not a friend of the wizards yet possesses some of the high powers? Or so I must guess, judging by this… exploit."

"Oh." I wondered what I should say, since I had no answer myself. *You have to be there for your friends.* Dixie was right. My jaw tightened and I straightened. "Okay, first of all, Lynx is not a wizard. Second of all, it wouldn't make a huge difference if he was. Not all wizards are evil or misled or anything, just most. A few still follow the Old Ways. Thirdly, if you only listen to one thing I say, make it this: Lynx has been a good friend to me and has stuck by me through thick and thin. You see," I went on quickly, seeing that some of them wanted to interrupt, "I needed to basically do the impossible, from finding Jeduthiam's blade to bringing it to your king, and he helped *make* that possible, even though he didn't have to. He didn't need to stick by me and help me through, but he did. So wizard or not, he's helping your king. Isn't that good enough for now?"

Exhausted and out of words, I flung myself down on the floor, not bothering to grab one of the blankets. For a while I wandered in a state somewhere between waking and dreamland, thinking of Texas and my family. I felt guilty, realizing how caught up I'd been in finishing my missions, so much so that I hadn't thought about them in a while. Of course, I was pushing so hard to get through my missions, not just because I was becoming a ghost the longer I went, but also because I couldn't go home until I finished them. At least, I was pretty sure that was how it worked. Also, especially after my last dream, I was haunted by the thought of fixing what I had done, creating change to make up for and heal my creating darkness. I wanted to go home, more than anything I wanted that, but somehow, simultaneously, I *needed* to take care of my worlds. Remembering my dream, I pushed back my fear; the fear that my third and last world mission would be in my own third and latest world, Harlan. The pattern was too clear. I wasn't *that* stupid. But I had been stupid enough to make Harlan in the first place… My mind teetered into sleep.

After drifting in and out of a doze, I eventually gave up. In that golden cell, it was impossible to tell how much time exactly had passed, and dim echoes of fighting still reached us occasionally through the walls, so it couldn't have been too long. I was sitting up with my back against the wall, watching the others trying to sleep in makeshift blanket pallets, when Lynx ghosted through the wall again a few feet away, a characteristic pleased-with-himself look on his face. He tossed the hair out of his eyes and grinned.

"You should've seen it," he whispered. "It was quite the chase: all those black assassin dudes and a few pompous wizards all in tow. Priceless."

"Assassins *and* wizards? How did you avoid being blasted to a cinder or poisoned like a fly?" I asked in shock. As far as I knew, it was virtually impossible for anyone to be seriously chased by either wizards or assassins and come back alive. If they were intent on killing you, they would do it.

"If a wall can't stop me, I don't suppose poisoned barbs will," he said cryptically. "And anyway, I told you before, you and I are immune to magic." I imagined angry, hornet-like assassins blowing out dart after dart after a strange elusive shape, continually frustrated in their attempts as the darts passed clean through the figure without so much as slowing him down, and wizards vainly hurling magical bolts of lightning that might as well be striking air.

"So you knew what you were doing the whole time?" I demanded.

He glanced at the possibly-dozing women across from me and bent down to whisper in my ear. "Perks of being a Dream Walker. I'm basically intangible. Why else do you think I do so little and keep back?" He swung his hand at the wall and it passed right through and back in again. If he'd had a blade of any kind, he would have chopped my head off, but I felt nothing, only a prickling cold as his hand passed through my head. He might as well have been air. My mind flashed back at the feeling to when I'd first met him and I'd nearly blacked out and toppled into the river. I'd thought it was my own ghostliness that had chilled my skin, but it had been him. "There are times when I am more tangible," he explained. "When I really concentrate. But I —" He stopped, stepping through the wall again, and I could make out muffled voices. I tried not to feel creeped out by finding out my friend was basically a ghost. If I'd known that at the beginning, I didn't think I would've let him help us, diamond or no diamond.

The thought of the diamond was a comforting one. I needed comfort and reassurance at that moment. I'd just take it out and look at it, to reassure myself. I'd be quick. Turning my back on the other women so they couldn't glimpse it, I took it out, staring at its marvelous depths. I felt better. The diamond reminded me of the Phoenix, and that brought its own comfort. It also reminded me of all I'd been through already, reminded me of Dixie and Kya and Queen Vida, reminded me of the dragon we'd brought down. Everything had seemed hopeless then, too. I breathed out a sigh, and moved to tuck it back under my tunic. The moment was shattered as Lynx stepped back through the wall and came face to face with me, the diamond between us.

I was caught with my most precious secret.

CHAPTER XXIX

With a jerk of surprise, I leapt backwards at least four feet. Hastily, I thrust the diamond under my shirt, out of sight, but most definitely not out of either of our minds. Lynx's face was unreadable. He just stood absolutely still, looking at me as though for an explanation for the diamond and my behavior. I stood, frozen with the guilt of a criminal caught in the act, with no explanation forthcoming. There was simply nothing to say.

At last, Lynx broke the intense silence. "Well?" he asked, raising his eyebrows in question. "Is this secret open for discussion?"

I whipped my head around to look at the others behind me. Some were stirring, muttering in either sleep or the dim beginnings of wakefulness. Others looked ready to wake soon. I shook my head abruptly. "Not here. Not now. Ask me later. All I can say is," I added, desperate as a sudden thought came into my head, "I have this by right and I'm not a thief."

Lynx looked about to say something, but it was Mira's voice that spoke. "How goes the battle?" she asked, unintentionally breaking off an extremely awkward and uncomfortable situation, though I knew it was only a delay.

Lynx shrugged. "Varied." The women were sitting up, pulling themselves together after a restless sleep. Mira moved forward, as pulled together as if she had never laid down to rest at all, and I gave ground eagerly. "It remains to be seen who will have the final victory," Lynx added. "But the army of Camdens and Rhindons, along with a quantity of fierce animals, has reinforced the king, and I think the palace might be encircled by them, but I'm not sure. I only saw a part of the ring outside, but I guess they go all the way around. Inside, the palace is full of men and animals hunting each other, so while in one place the enemy is retreating and losing, in another it's the king's men who are hard-pressed. It'll be a bear of a project to finish this business, and worse to clean it up."

"Don't," I muttered. I was already feeling queasy.

"Is there aught we can do?" Mira asked anxiously.

"Stand by and be ready to help the wounded when everything's over. Heaven knows we need healers… Can you let Lexi out?" Lynx asked as an afterthought.

"For Euclid's sake, call me Alex for once!" I interjected. "And why do you want me out there?" The last place I wanted to be was out in that battlefield.

"You need to see the king and explain everything to him briefly. About the wizards and assassins and Camden – everything you told me. Also, Dixie's out there somewhere just about going off her head to get to you. Will you open the door, Mira?"

She hesitated. "Stephen said neither of you were to be seen. Are you sure your message to the king cannot wait? He is in a fight, after all."

"My news from Dixie quite possibly cannot wait," I told her, though I wasn't so sure about that. Frankly I was desperate to see her again and hearing that she was out there changed my mind about staying in the Inner Sanctum. "Also, the king really should be told as much as possible as soon as possible."

"Then I must ask you to close your eyes. We allow no one who is not one of us – if you know what I mean – to see how this door opens." I nodded and obediently closed my eyes. I heard a soft swish, a muffled groan of hinges, and then Mira's voice pierced my blindness. "You may look now. I will close the door behind you. If you need to reenter, knock four times on the wall and I will open it again." I thanked her and darted out before I could second-guess myself.

"Up these stairs." Lynx pointed past me to a stairway. "I left the king on a landing there and he meant to linger, if he could, for you to catch up. I'm going to try to connect the army, and if I see your dog I'll send her there if I can, though I don't know what you meant by your 'news' from her."

"Thanks," I said, turning away and dashing up the stairs before he could press this question further. One of my two secrets was enough for one person, and he already knew about the diamond.

It was impossible to ignore the signs of war that scarred the palace as I ran up and around the curving stair. Blood marred the beauty of the gold and glass of the palace. A stained and dropped blade lay in my path and I edged gingerly around it. Over the rail, worse things that I tried as hard as I could *not* to see could be glimpsed. I was already losing my sense of direction when I wrapped around a bend and came out onto a landing. Two men stood there, seeming undecided about something. One I recognized as the king, and behind him, elevated close to normal height by his position on a stair, was Keliel. He had been speaking but broke off as I stumbled out on the sudden level of the landing.

"Oh, and there she is herself," he added. "Alexandria, this is King Jed."

"We have met already," the king said. "Your friend tells me you have valuable information for me now."

I struggled to pull my thoughts together. "Yes, I do." Rapidly I outlined the basics of my mission and what I had to do and how and why I had done what I'd done. I mentally paged Dixie, groping for her report. As I was finishing, she finally answered, and I translated her thoughts to the king.

"The steward, Jodeh, is a treacherous cockroach, as you probably know." *Why "cockroach", Dixie?* "He's king in all but name in Camden, but the weak link in his power is that it requires force. Anything contrary to the laws and customs of the kingdom takes armed men to execute, and the people are living in a state of part rebellion, part tyrannized fear. In investigating, I've found the root, aside from the steward himself, comes from the four lords who stick to him: Lord Kendal, Lord Erik, Lord Timothy, and Lord Fallow. If these five were out of the picture, the matter would be relatively easy to restore the kingdom to its old state and honor. Under them, though, the whole kingdom has a knife to its throat. I suggest an open confrontation of Jodeh and the lords in front of the people. That seems like the best way to catch him out from what I've learned."

"He is *a cockroach. What do you think about my info?"*

You learned an amazing amount, I thought back in admiration, *and I trust your judgement about how to handle the situation. But where are you, girl?*

"How did you learn all this and gain such an understanding of

141

the steward's nature?" the king asked. "My spies have been trying for many long years to worm their way in so close on his counsels, but in all these years we've never succeeded."

Claws clicked on the stairs ahead and a black and white train barreled into me, licking and frisking with tired enthusiasm. When she was a little calmer and I had regained my balance, I scratched her ear as she sat panting beside me. I smiled. "People take dogs for granted. It's simple enough when you're as sharp *and* as adorably cute as Dixie here."

Further conversation was cut short. I noticed Dixie moving and sniffing uneasily, and then a contingent of bandits together with a small force of wizards rushed up the stairs I had ascended minutes before, blocking my way back.

"*Run, Alex!*" Dixie's thought blasted into my head, and without thinking I leapt for the far stairs and raced up, adrenaline pumping in my veins. I forgot my weariness and even my nervousness in one surge of action powered by fear (See? Fear decided to help me again. Good boy). Never before had I run so fast up a stair, up and around until I was long past tired and dizzy. Dixie shot past me and her barking howl rang in the palace.

It was now my turn for the cat-and-mouse game. I had no idea where I was going and at the moment I didn't care. If there was a way, then I would take it. Running, never knowing the path ahead or where I might encounter a dead end and be cornered, seldom quite sure whether I was still being followed. Now stopping from sheer inability to go on, gasping in precious breaths, now running on. Pounding footfalls behind me. Staggering on. Forever. Why could I never stop running? Where had Dixie gone? Why was I always so alone at the worst times?

I charged into a wide chamber that had apparently been a bedroom suite of some kind. Panic etched every detail in my mind as seconds stretched long enough for me to take them all in. Everything remained in it, perfectly intact, the bed still made, the wood as new as if it were freshly carved, and it all gave the impression of the palace inhabitants having simply moved out, taking their possessions with them and leaving it waiting for the next tenant. The smallest decorative pillow was slightly crooked.

I ran into what must have at another time been a closet. No way out. I whirled on my heel, dashing for the door. I had lost precious seconds. Shouts. Cries of "that's her! Get the girl!" coming from the passage. I was too late! I saw the brown of a wizard's robe through the door. There was no escape that way, and as I cast one last frantic glance around the room, I saw there was no other way out. I had only one chance, and I took it swiftly.

Time slowed. I made a dive for the bed, dropping on the floor beside it and rolling under. I could see through the crack and out into the hall, see the boots of the men as they raced by. Some ran past the door like I'd hoped, but not all. Two wizards stalked in and ran their eyes around the room. Heavens, it was glass and gold – there was no way in any world under any sun they could find a trace of me unless they found my actual self. But the wizards could sense things, things eyes might miss.

"Stay!" one called to the men who had run on. "She is here."

With those cold words, the crowd in the room increased, and methodically they began to search. They were swift and efficient, not wasting time but not rushing things. They knew they had me cornered, and it was only a matter of time. They would find me. I could count the seconds left of my life down to zero. It was over.

"You're in that room, aren't you, Alex? We're right out here waiting for you. We'll turn this trap around. Blast out and we'll have them in a pincer." What was Dixie talking about? There was no sound other than vague rumors of battle far off and the sounds the searchers were making in this room. I trembled inwardly at Dixie's easy order to "blast out". She clearly either had an exaggerated idea of my speed and ability, or was seriously underestimating the wizards and bandits. I wouldn't get halfway to the door.

I gritted my teeth. Now was the time to prove myself. *Courage, Alex. I know you don't have much but it doesn't matter. You have to do what you have to do, and fear can't stop you. Just go!* Talking about being brave in the face of fear is easy enough when you're sitting comfortably at home or analyzing the actions of a character in a book, and at any other time I might have taken the idea for granted. Actually doing something as daring as what Dixie wanted me to do was entirely different. My heart pounded with fear, sharpening my senses, slowing the seconds as in one movement I rolled free of the bed on the door side, sprang to my feet, ducked instinctively as a responding blade sliced the air where my neck had been an instant before, and bolted top speed out the door.

Angry roars. Men rushing to follow. For a fractured second I was aware of a few armed men and dozens of wolves on either hand, poised to strike at the first enemy who showed his pathetic face. The next instant I crashed into the artful gold stair rail. The speed of my charge from the door was crucial to my escape from the room, but was altogether too much for the short distance from door to rail. It was entirely insufficient to stop me. One minute I was on solid ground and the next moment I was flipping over it, a hundred feet in the air over a drop to a first floor gallery.

CHAPTER XXX

I reacted instinctively, saving my life. I don't actually remember doing it, but somehow I flung my arms out and caught the rail. One hand slipped free and I twisted, dangling awkwardly.

It would've been impossible had my crash into the rail not destroyed most of my momentum. Even as it was, my arm felt practically wrenched from its socket as I hung there for what seemed like hours, staring wildly down in blind terror. It was only a matter of time until I lost my grip and plunged to my death below. I had to do something! *Think, Alex!* With all the strength I had, I pulled myself up, no more than a foot or so, not enough by a long shot to get me back over, but I managed to get my other hand back onto the rail. A bloody battle was raging in front of me, snarling wolves leaping on men, knocking them to the ground, swordsmen hacking away at each other. No one saw me or realized my predicament in the heat and rush of the battle, and Dixie – where was she? Then I caught a flickering glimpse of her barking, nipping at a man that seemed to be on our side, and had she been speaking intelligible words I was sure they would be flailing abuse and urging.

"Hang on, Alex! Please, just hang on! I'm doing all I can – just don't let go!"

I – I can't! I'm slipping! I'm going to fall!

"Slide!"

The single word exploded in my head. Confused by panic, I was in no state to think clearly. Staring down the long circuitous stairway that connected eventually to the floor below me and at the rail I clenched, I somehow grasped what she meant in a blinding flash. My hands were sticky with sweat. They would get me nowhere. Rocking my grip farther around the rail, I pinched the sleeve of my tunic between the heel of my hand and the rail. Easing my grip back a touch, struggling with all my might to keep from losing my hold entirely, I grasped the rail now with my sleeve ends between most of my hands and the rail.

Already I was sliding sideways down the rail, my fingers holding me to it and preventing a fall. I gained speed, whirling around bends, my legs swinging free wildly, whiplashing back and forth as I wove down around the curving stair. Time was an instant from the beginning of my descent to the bottom, and yet every fraction of a second was crystal clear in passing. Now dangling from my hands, now half hugging the rail, never able to fully flip back over, hurtling down as I desperately tightened my grip, feeling the burning abrasion and soon-to-be blisters despite my almost nonexistent senses. The end, a swirling spiral of thinning gold, rushed toward me with blinding speed. I squeezed my eyes shut, bracing myself for the splitting impact, knowing that all I was doing was entirely insufficient.

I heard Lynx's voice, a shadow of its normal self, almost wailing somewhere above me, "Beware! Beware this day, O men! The prophecies come true, and when the sun has set our sleepless souls shall rest. This is the day of your doom! Beware!"

With the last "beware" I crashed into the rail end. My body jackknifed up into the stairs and supporting pillars. My hands tangled and caught in the spiral end, bending my left back painfully. The right gave a hideous rolling crunch, and pain roared in my bones. I groaned, flopping loose onto the floor. After a minute, I managed to struggle to my knees, head spinning, my right hand completely useless. Why were all those assassins huddled down, gazing up wide-eyed with fear? The few bandits who remained – and there weren't many – also cowered, moaning in despair. Only the wizards stood, stiff as stalks of dried reeds. With set faces, they slowly advanced, moving to the front, trying to gain further power from working together, clearly at a low ebb. Then I realized why.

Lynx had evoked their ghostly superstitions. His theatrical imitation of a ghost warning intruders would give even the only slightly superstitious goosebumps. And anyone, including myself (who had personally never quite believed in ghosts), would be spooked out of their senses by Lynx's pass-through-walls act. A perfect silence, taut as the moment in a race before the pistol blows, reigned in the whole palace.

"Now!" It was the pistol blowing, signaling the start of the race, and a deadly one at that. Wolves poured down from a dozen stairs, soldiers in two different uniforms and men in ordinary clothes raced out of every hall off the main gallery. Before the assassins realized it, they were suddenly engaged in close quarters hand to hand fighting, a range that rendered their darts virtually useless.

I stood slowly, watching in awe through a blur of pain as I saw how the wizards' powers had been so crippled in this epic battle. The king stood on the bottom step of a main stairway, Keliel and his elves forming a guard around him. He was directing the battle with subtle movements of his sword like a choir director with his baton, and from his vantage he had a perfect view. I saw Jeduthiam's blade raised, and it flickered with a brilliant light. Wizards, chanting, cast bolt after bolt of magic at the troops, but before any could fall it veered away, drawn in and splintered by the magical sword. It was a battle like no other, but I couldn't watch it. I stared for a moment, fascinated by the blade I had brought through dangers to this man, the missing heir. I wasn't sure what to do, or where Lynx and Dixie had gotten to, and I was in pain. Too much pain for being a ghost.

Then I saw her. I saw it all in horrible detail. Dixie bounded out of a side hall off a landing a few feet above the gallery and the stair where the king and the elves held their position. She didn't hesitate, but made a soaring leap and scrabbled at the rail for a second. I saw the wizards working at their spells, an instant away from flinging a blast at the army. I knew it would sheer off to be dissolved by the blade.

"Dixie!" I shrieked. Already I was diving forward under the path the magic bolt would take. Already I was launching upward, ignoring the dull throbbing pain in my right hand. Somehow, with the same blind instinct I had caught myself with a few minutes before, I slammed into her before she got within range of the bolt. We tumbled down together in a heap, the blast of magic passing in a white crackle less than a foot behind us. We stayed there on the floor near the foot of the stairs for several seconds, just being together, glad to be alive. We were both badly bruised, and the impact had half stunned Dixie. I was shaking and dizzy, but determined. We were sitting ducks like this. Rolling free, I slid her limp body across the glass floor, between the pillars under the stairs where they swept down to the floor, making a small sheltering place. I glanced over my shoulder at the battle. I could see few enemies still standing. They neither asked nor gave quarter, but they were now completely outmatched, soon to be brought down.

I blocked out the battle, the dying cries of men. I huddled in the shadow of the stairs with Dixie, in our own little bubble. I shrank my world to just us. I couldn't handle one more moment of it all. Pain, stress and exhaustion chained my consciousness, and dragged me down into darkness.

I only heard later of how the king's troops had driven the last of the enemies out onto the circle of waiting men and beasts. How the last assassin died, ending their kind once and for all. How the last few bandits surrendered, choosing to face the king's justice over certain death. And how Xerxes and Artemis and their followers had refused to stop fighting even at the very end when they knew they were doomed beyond doubt, throwing themselves at the king's troops until the last one was killed.

I have a dim memory of half-waking sometime later – it's really only Mira's face hovering in my vision that I remember – and drinking something horrid tasting from a flask she held. Then I went out like a light again and knew nothing until who knows how much later, when I woke in the homey comfort of a log cabin in winter. A fire roared in the hearth, the cabin had surprisingly little draft, and I was startled to see an old couple sitting at the smooth pinewood table with Mira and King Jed. A kettle and pot sat near the fire, contents unknown to me. On the table and obviously the center of conversation was the legendary sword of myths I'd had the honor to carry for a time – Jeduthiam's blade.

"The thing is," the old man was saying, "no one knows exactly who Jodeh's spies are, and you can't risk chancing it. A man hardly dares to so much as whisper a threat in the privacy of his own cottage, because he never knows who might hear and what they might tell. He lives side by side with his neighbors, but he can never be sure whether any of them are there to watch him or not. He can hardly plow his field without being watched and suspected.

"There was actually a rebellion some time ago, not too long after your father was murdered and you disappeared. And we thought things were bad then! It was too small, too young. Jodeh found out before we were prepared and snuffed it out – just like that. Ever since then his spies have been everywhere. We've been cornered into our own holes, cats prowling outside to pounce on any foolish mouse who so much as sticks a whisker out. Believe me, they've done it to more than one enterprising nobleman. He has no scruples. He's a slippery one, that Jodeh. Like a fox, but one that knows his own limits. If he gets wind of you before you strike, he'll either blot you out before you have a chance, or if he knows he's doomed to failure, he'll run, mark my words."

"I never liked him as a boy," the king remarked. "But I was too young then to be an accurate judge of character. And he certainly is the fox in evading counterspies. Mine couldn't get in for years, though we never stopped trying. But I think we have enough to act on at this point. You've lived among the people for many uncounted years, Ezra, and done a tidy bit of snooping considering circumstances. Do you think the people will be with me?"

"Oh yes, in general they most certainly will. Between you, and this sword, there will be no doubt in the minds of all those who still hold faithful," the old man answered. "Of course there are the few who are committed to Jodeh, but I think when you turn up, these two groups will be polarized and the line between them will become clearer. It will be easy enough to deal with them then."

"That was my thought and hope. Well, I see little reason for delay. If we may impose so much further on your hospitality as to eat a meal, we will then be off and —" The king was interrupted by a knock on the door. "Excuse me a moment. I believe that is my chief of the Counter Intelligence Agency."

CHAPTER XXXI

T he door revealed a grinning Keliel, who was instantly let in. He seated himself on the edge of the table, looking like a child beside the group there.

"I don't believe you've met my wife Mira, Keliel," the king said. "And this is Ezra and Camille, our good hosts. Now, what is your report?"

"We're identifying and tracking down Jodeh's spies, sire. They're a slimy bunch, but not too difficult for my elves to locate. We've already nailed a few, and I estimate we'll have the majority of them by tomorrow morning. But I have an interesting little possibility based off of the spies we've caught so far."

"What is that?" the king asked, leaning forward.

"I suspect these spies are convicts who were offered the opportunity to spy for the steward to duck the noose. My elves have not taken a man yet who is not such a one, though they seem reluctant to confess to my guess."

"Good work, Keliel. We'll wait on making our move until tomorrow morning then, and get everything we can from these spies of yours. You'll come, won't you?"

"My pleasure, sire," said the little elf with a bow. He departed like a wraith into the night.

The kettle began to sing, and Mira got up quickly. "Oh, there's my tea already. I hope the girl will be ready for it." She cast an anxious glance in my direction.

I honestly thought I was dreaming, everything I'd heard in the last few minutes seeming too crazy and far-fetched to be reality, so I watched in fascination, waiting to see when I would wake, as she filled a mug with steaming liquid and brought it over to where I lay on some kind of pallet. My head felt a little foggy, almost as if my brain were waterlogged, but aside from that I felt only tired. This being an almost-ghost business had its advantages.

Mira set the mug on the ground and felt my pulse. She smiled at me, seeing my eyes on her, and asked softly, "How do you feel?"

"I'm fine, I think," I answered. "I mean, unless I'm dreaming."

"You do not dream," she said, laughing. "If that is so, my treatments may be unnecessary, but I should still drink it anyway to be safe. You don't have a fever yet, but let's keep it that way."

I sat up awkwardly, discovering my broken hand had been put in a cast, and propping my back against the cabin wall, took the mug from her. It was better tasting than the last potion, but nothing I would have chosen by a long shot. As I sipped it, I got the story I was missing. After the battle, some of the freshest soldiers were sent into the Wilds to ensure that every last one of the bandits and assassins had been crushed. Messengers sent to the Wizards' Tryst, which was technically still convening, reported that only the members of the Remnant were to be found there. The wounded were tended by Mira and her friends and evacuated from the palace, while others began the cleanup process.

"It will be restored to its former grandeur in time, and become what it must once have been in the days of the Ancient King," Mira said with a wink. "But first we have more dirty work to do."

I had been among those who were moved from the palace and treated, Mira splinting my hand and giving sleeping draft to knock me out, as she said "you were as drained as a drunkard's flagon and needed some good rest". All the wounded unable to walk benefited from that one as well, so that they wouldn't feel the jolting journey. Then they had been discreetly distributed to various cottages and cabins in the remoter areas of Camden, to those who were willing to house and care for an injured warrior or two, or taken back home to Rhindon.

"And tomorrow," the king said, stretching, "we shall see what accounting that steward can give for his behavior. I wonder what story he hopes to concoct to satisfy me."

"Can I go too?" I asked, insides flip-flopping like a live fish. I desperately wanted to be there and see the diamond's message happening, and see this steward who had held the kingdom by the throat for perhaps twenty years, and also, I felt like I ought to go.

"It might get dangerous. Why is it that you wish to come?" the king asked.

I took a deep breath. "I am a Mastermind. I created this world years ago. I messed it up pretty badly too, but I'm doing my best to fix it now. The trouble Jodeh and his followers are causing are connected with me and what I have to do to fix this, I believe. So I want to go and make sure he's taken care of, if you know what I mean."

"So that's it," the king mused. "Your friend let on that there was more to you than was plain to see. If you're the Mastermind of this world… well, that explains much. If you wish to come, you may."

"Where *is* Lynx?" I asked suddenly. "And Dixie too? Where are they?"

"Your dog is being cared for by a kindly man not far from here," Mira explained. "He is experienced with animals and their medical needs and is caring for all the injured animals from the battle. She was not grievously hurt, only shaken, but he is keeping her for the night just in case. You will see her in the morning most likely. As for your friend Lynx, he is about somewhere, poking around. I think he plans to join us in the morning as well."

I relaxed in relief, though to tell the truth I wished Dixie was there with me, but my eyes were still heavy from the effects of the sleeping draft. As I settled down on the pallet, I thought of the horrible battle, and shuddered, glad it was over. I felt a pang at the thought of my business here being almost over. I'd have to say goodbye to King Jed, Mira, Keliel, and of course, Lynx. For the first time, I admitted to myself that I would miss him, annoying habits and all, but yes, miss him.

It was gray and early when I woke up the next morning, and chilly too. I vaguely wished I had a cloak again, but I was gradually ceasing to be aware of the cold. When I had first come to this world, it had been biting, and I could barely survive until the Way Station when I got the cloak. By now, I was dimly aware of an uncomfortableness in the air that made it impossible to be quite relaxed out of my cocoon of blankets, but not the unendurable ice it had been my first day. I had to admit, I was getting worried, actually, more than worried, about making it through this world *and* the next while still tangible enough to accomplish my mission. What if I faded too soon?

Forcing these thoughts, as dark as the sky overhead, from my mind, I stepped out of the cabin behind the king and queen with a farewell to our hosts and set off. We were joined minutes later by Dixie, revitalized like spring itself, and Lynx was not far behind her. Not much later we struck the shortcut and headed left on it. Subtly, as we walked steadily to the Fortress, men joined our ranks. Once, glancing casually over my shoulder, I almost jumped out of my skin (which was actually a very possible danger, what with going ghost and all) when I saw there must have been at least a few hundred following.

"Where did they come from?" I wondered aloud.

"Various villages and towns," Lynx answered. "That's part of what we were doing last night: secretly informing the people of the king's return. Just wait until we get to the Fortress. They'll be gathering there, and fairly nuts with anticipation now too, I guess."

"What do you mean, 'we'?" I asked.

"Your little elf friend and his gang," he said, chuckling to himself. "I was helping them out. Strange fellow, that one." *As if you have any room to talk,* I thought. "If all goes as planned, the steward and his friends will be virtually besieged with a mob of people asking questions and demanding answers. He won't be able to slip off prematurely."

"Good," I said in satisfaction.

The Fortress was a perfect square, made of perfectly squared dark gray-blue stone, with stark angles and cheerless ramparts. The gate was iron, and a sole tower of the same stone as the walls rose out of the middle inside. It was a somber sight. Compared with the palace of the Ancient King, it was a dungeon. Lynx was right – it was surrounded by hundreds and hundreds of men and women, yelling, banging on walls and gate, demanding for the steward to show his ugly face. The silence that fell was contagious as people caught sight of the king and the sword in his hand. Within one minute of our group joining the outskirts of the crowd, a hush reigned. The people parted the way, and the king, with Mira, Keliel, Lynx, Dixie, and me close on his heels, walked quickly to the gate. He didn't knock, but raising his voice, called over the wall.

"Jodeh! Come forth! The wheels of prophecy are grinding against you, and now you must answer for your deeds. Why do you hide like a rabbit in his den? What is it that you fear? The truth? Come forth, I say!" The silence was a presence hung like a storm over the place.

"He can't hide forever," I muttered.

"Oh no, and I don't think he'll want to," Lynx said. "He'll try and talk his way out of it, I'm sure." Sure enough, in a few moments, the gate creaked and groaned ponderously, easing slowly open. The people edged back a bit; for them, whenever that gate opened, it meant trouble. Their faces were flushed and expectant. They waited, breathless with suspense.

A small gray-haired man of about fifty stepped out, flanked by four nobles in fine dress. There was not a trace of anyone else to be seen in the Fortress past them. He was dressed surprisingly simply in a black tunic embroidered with a silver emblem of a graceful swan in the center – the sign of the royal Camden line, an insult in of itself on him – and silver on the hem and cuffs. A heavy silver chain was around his neck, but he wore no other sign of rank. I didn't like him. His face was harsh and etched, his expression could only be described as venomous, and though he was small, personality practically radiated from him, forceful as darkness itself. It was the strength of this personality I guessed that held his regime together. He was like a snake, poised and ready to strike out without warning.

I remembered my first impression of King Jed, when I had seen him in the diamond. I had seen in him a natural leader, someone who put you at your ease and made you feel like he could cope with anything that came his way, good or evil. I had liked the face – it was the face of a king. I saw them together now. The lion and the serpent, the true and the false, the honorable and the deceitful – the king and the traitor.

No, Jodeh was no match for this man, and I think he knew it. He held his poise well, you had to give him that, but I caught the occasional flicker of his eye, a nervous lick of the lips, a discreet clenching of the fists at his sides. Signs of worry, confirming in my mind that this man, Jodeh, steward of Camden, who had held sway over a small but sturdy honest kingdom with evil and lies, this man was afraid. On the one hand, he had his reputation – what little there was to it – and position at stake. On the other…what, exactly? His life? Quite possibly. Such a traitor as he deserved to die. Was his power over the kingdom so intoxicating that he would risk his neck to rebuff the king himself? Yikes! I didn't envy him.

CHAPTER XXXII

"What right have you to dictate my actions? What do you mean by coming in this manner to my gate?" he demanded, his voice haughty and almost oily.

I felt the people stir in anger, a barely audible murmur running through them, but they stilled as the king began to speak. "I am Jedidiah, son of King Zeroth whom you murdered with your own hand." Oh, a liar, traitor, *and* a murderer. Definitely begging for the old rope about the neck. "I am here to call you to account for your actions since my father's death and to this day."

Jodeh licked his lips, eyes sliding nervously from side to side. Clearly he knew the truth of the king's words and was in a funk. But I hadn't reckoned with the snakelike cunning of the man. "What proof have you of this?" he asked, a little too loudly. It came out almost like a squeaky hinge.

"Proof enough." The king swished Jeduthiam's blade from his sheath, holding the unmatched blade up for every eye to see. Then he raised his voice so that even those on the outskirts could hear. "This is Jeduthiam's blade, lost for years uncounted, hidden by the Ancient King before his death in a secret place to lie, watched over by the Guardians, until the time for the prophecies' fulfilment came. It is well known, is it not, that the one to wield it would be from the royal line of this kingdom?" Oh, right. I'd forgotten that part before.

"This sword was brought to me by this young lady, Alex, who was sent to find it, find me, and deliver it. She did so. In the recent battle, this blade shone again, and we triumphed. You know as well as I do that Jeduthiam's blade cannot be wielded by any for whom it is not intended, for it will not obey him but be his own undoing. So then, I ask you, who else could I be besides who I claim to be? How could I wield Jeduthiam's blade if I was not the heir of Camden?"

"You have yet to prove to me that it is Jeduthiam's blade, if such a myth is true," Jodeh challenged, but I noticed he was rubbing his palms as though they were sweaty. I was tempted to recommend Jodeh try and use it and decide for himself if it was Jeduthiam's blade, but didn't. "It is a good sword, that much I can see, but marching up here making wild claims founded on legend – how about a little reason? I don't have time for this." He made as if to go back into the Fortress.

"I'm not finished." Something in the king's tone made the steward stop, made us all stop. We froze, perfectly still, all of us, waiting for the king to speak. "Do not mock the prophesies, Jodeh," he said mildly. "They have a way of destroying those who get in their way. It is not a habit I recommend."

Jodeh swung back around. "Is that all you have to say?" he sneered. "Threaten me against disbelief in you with some mystical danger of a prophecy. You haven't proved anything to me yet, except that you're wasting my time."

"It is Jeduthiam's blade!" I declared suddenly. "I brought it from its secret hiding place myself. I aided the prophecies to come true, and it can be done again. Remember that the prophecy mentions you when it says that the snake who strikes at the lion will be crushed." (I had *loved* that line when I was little – so poetic) "I know for a fact that this is Jeduthiam's blade, and beware of doubt. It will destroy you." Startled at my own outburst, I subsided, adding under my breath, "I should know," and fell silent.

Jodeh regarded me, looking singularly unimpressed, almost disgusted, with me. "And how can you prove, assuming you did indeed find a special sword in a secret place, that it was that same sword you gave to this," he gestured to the king, "man?"

"I was with her," Lynx said quietly, "from the time she found it until she delivered it. She didn't once try to use it, not even when in great need. She knew better."

Jodeh turned his gaze on Lynx and sized him up too. "I've seen you before," he said. "You're that fellow named Sphinx who came here claiming that assassins were on your tail and asked for refuge." I was tempted to snicker. Sphinx. I'd have to remember that one.

"And you refused it. Yes, I remember. We had quite the chat about you and your work. And it's Lynx, by the way." I tried to envision that: Lynx coolly inciting the snake in his own den, bantering back and forth with him until the steward dismissed him in exasperation. Lynx was a tough nut to crack when it came to probing into secrets he wanted to keep, and I didn't think the steward would've gotten anywhere. I simply couldn't picture it.

"Until you can prove that this is a blade of that caliber and significance, I have no reason to believe you, nor any duty to submit to you," Jodeh said, turning back to the king.

"See? I told you he was a cockroach."

Yeah, but shh!

"Keliel," the king said, sheathing the sword but not taking his eyes off the steward, "what sword is this?" I noticed the four nobles had been slowly edging back and were now within the confines of the gate. If they were so inclined, they could dart in and slam the door on their unlucky steward.

Keliel moved to stand slightly apart from the group that faced the steward. "Allow me to introduce myself," he said to Jodeh with a formal little bow. "I am Keliel, son of Jadorel, son of Gabriel, son of Malachi, son of Berua, son of Kish, son of Caladen, son of Hilkiah. I am descended directly from Hilkiah himself, the one who spoke the prophecies of old. Since the Ancient King hid his sword, his loyal friend Hilkiah, and after him his descendants and those of his people, were entrusted with the task of watching over it to see that no thief took it and no harm came to it while the world waited for the time of the prophecies' fulfilment. So the elves of the twilight hour became the Guardians, and in the long uncounted years since the time of this man's and my ancestors, we have watched over it faithfully. It is Jeduthiam's blade, which has never left its secret hiding place from the day the Ancient King hid it there until we permitted this girl to take it. There can be no doubt."

Jodeh sneered. "So I'm supposed to accept the testimony of a few people who are all in league against me and turn over the kingdom to some imposter? No."

The murmur of anger was louder this time, climbing to a roar. The crowd lurched, as if they meant to fling themselves en masse upon the treacherous steward and wring his scrawny neck.

Whether it was this or the inner tension snapping in the man I don't know, but there was no warning for what he did next. He took a half step back, as if he meant to retreat within the safety of the Fortress, then in one movement, he drew his sword with a metallic slither and leapt at the king. Before the king could draw his sword, before Jodeh could cover half the distance between them, someone else was already acting. A flickering white orb flew out of nowhere, striking full on the silver swan. It exploded, flinging the steward backward several feet. He was dead before his body hit the ground.

CHAPTER XXXIII

So much had to happen, so much explaining and arranging and issuing orders, and so little for me to do after the steward died. I felt like a tree in the autumn, dried leaves tossed about all around me in a whirlwind gale of activity, but myself virtually unmoved. I spent most of the time sitting with Dixie on the rampart of the Fortress, legs dangling over the edge. We sat there, and simply *were*. We didn't need words as long as we were together. Lynx had vanished into thin air again, and who knew when he would be back.

It was late, long past when any sensible person would be in bed, before I had a chance to see the king and discuss my mission.

"You see," I explained in the chamber in the Fortress tower where all important business had been conducted that day, "I've finished much of what I was sent to do. But there are two more things I have to settle. One is about the Camden law for succession to the throne, and I think I've worked out what the problem is. The other is a few oversights in the Old Laws. Once I get those squared away, I think I'll be done."

"What flaw is this that you speak of in the succession?" he asked, taking a sip from his goblet. I had gathered so far that wine was the medieval version of coffee.

"Oh, the fact that it stipulates that the ruler can only be the firstborn son of the house of Camden. The crown cannot be passed to a daughter, or to a cousin, or to a second-born son. It can only be the firstborn son. That in itself is bad enough, but it gets better. I made it be so that the heir had to be descended from the firstborn son of the Ancient King." I propped my elbows on the table and rested my cheek against my hands. "I mean, what would happen, for example, if you died childless? Or with only a daughter? No one outside the family could inherit the crown, but no one in the family could either. Then where are you?"

"That has been a near thing in the past. I have wondered what possessed anyone to make the law so specific."

"I was young," I said, grinning and shaking my head. "I didn't realize then how precarious it would be. It seemed simple enough at the time. But that was part of the problem here. It made it too easy for Jodeh to take control, once you were missing."

Right then, before my own eyes, we got out the old records, brought in a few witnesses, and revised the law which thankfully was not set in stone and irreversible. The king drew up a document stating that as long as the heir claimed provable kinship to the royal house of Camden, the crown would pass to the firstborn in line, and made arrangements for if the heir should die without leaving a successor to whom the crown should pass. Then I said we should put in something in case *no* heir could be found, since we didn't want the last several years to repeat themselves. So the king added a clause stating that should no heir be found to rule, the people could select a king from among the nobles by course of election and the crown would follow his family. Satisfied, it was signed by the king and the witnesses and sealed.

"Check," I declared with a feeling of great relief. "Only one more thing left."

"I sent a message to the leader of the Remnant," the king told me. "A delegation of theirs is on their way and should be here by morning. You can arrange with them then about their Old Laws and set everything straight."

"Sure," I said, stifling a yawn. "If I can stay awake. Goodnight." I left, not realizing it would be the last time I saw him. When I got up the next day, he had ridden off on business.

Despite how late I'd been up the night before, I was unable to sleep long the next morning, especially since Dixie wasn't short on sleep and was practically bouncing off the walls, eager to get going. *You should rest yourself,* I told her as I splashed my face with water. *You were in a pretty bad way after the battle, and you'll need everything you've got. I mean, I sure hope I'm wrong about the next world, but if it is Harlan... These last two worlds will look like a joke.*

"*Whoa, take it easy, kid. It can't be as bad as you make out. You were pretty doleful about this world and Bliss, but neither of those were more than we could cope with after all. Just try to be optimistic for once.*"

You don't know Harlan, I thought darkly.

My meeting with the wizard delegation was short but complicated. I found myself with the old woman I had met at the Tryst and was introduced to her husband along with four other wizards from the Remnant. Together we went through the Old Laws with a fine tooth comb, making minor adjustments here and there. We organized a training method for new wizards, instituted a hierarchy system of leadership, and added a little local gathering for every moon, dividing up the island into regions to meet together between Trysts to help keep each other in line with the rules. "*Rules and accountability birth justice and right. Begin the change,*" the diamond had said, and I had done it.

"I'm not asking you to forego your reclusive ways," I said. "It is part of your tradition and there is nothing wrong with it. It does pose risk, however, for if anyone in future were tempted to meddle in the Dark Arts again, living cut off from other people aside from a yearly Tryst would make it fairly easy to get away with, at least for a time. This way that risk is reduced, and if a time ever comes when wizards take to paying each other occasional visits, that risk will be reduced even further."

"It is to be hoped that Xerxes' and Artemis' movements and sorcerous habits have died with them, but one cannot be sure," the leader of the Remnant said. "I think we have taken every precaution possible to prevent anything of this kind happening again."

When at last we were all satisfied and I had done all I thought was necessary, I went to find Dixie, who had been saying goodbye to the last of the wolves as they set off for their home in the Jungle. I found her a little way from the Fortress walls, frisking about as the first snowflakes of the year drifted down to the ground, enveloping the world in a clean fresh softness of icy down. To my surprise, Lynx was crouched nearby, studying the large flakes unlike any on earth.

"So you show up after all the work is done?" I asked dryly, dropping down onto the ground beside him.

"Oh yes." Lynx straightened and leaned back against the tree. "I did my part already. Technically I should probably move on… But first maybe you can explain to me about what happened in the

Inner Sanctum."

"Oh." I blushed and looked away, watching Dixie. "You caught me with the diamond." I took it out again and let its light flash, dazzling between us.

"*What are you doing?*" Dixie whipped around and bounded over. "*How are you going to explain that? Why?*"

Whatever I tell him is better than how things stand at present. He saw me with it. I have a lot of explaining to do. Besides, I trust him.

"It's magical. It shows me my missions that I need to do in each world. I was given it by the Phoenix." I wasn't sure the last part would mean anything to him, but if it didn't, he could ask.

"I see. What do you mean by 'each world'?"

"Oh, well, I was supposed to go help three worlds that tottered on the brink of darkness and stuff like that. Now I'm pretty sure that it's *my* three worlds I have to take care of, since I did Bliss already, which was my first world, and now I've done my second world, Secret. Which only leaves one..."

"Really? Which one?"

I hesitated. I was reluctant to admit ownership of the last one. "Harlan."

Lynx shook his head. "You'll never leave Harlan alive."

"I know. I mean, it seems like since I made the world, I should be fine if I'm careful enough, but..."

"Yeah, try telling that to the Goths. That world is beyond saving, though. I don't see what you could do." He was right. What chance did I have? And what could I possibly hope to do to save that world? "So you created that world?"

"I – well, yes. I did." My cheeks burned as I realized that Lynx had already encountered the incarnate version of my darkest self. Goodbye to this friendship.

To my surprise, he gave me a long, thoughtful look and said, "I think I know that story." I was instantly transported back to the moment I had said those same words, when as we fled from the Tryst he had told me of his worlds, of his own "willful darkness". Relief and gratitude filled my heart.

I hugged my knees to my chest, hating to think about Harlan. I wished I could go back to that feeling of peace and forgiveness I'd had in my dream. *I'm changing*, I promised myself. *I'll make sure I don't make that mistake again.* I cleared my throat. "Um, so Lynx? You come from

Earth, right?"

He quirked a smile. "What gave it away, the alarm clock or the dentist appointment?"

"All of the above plus your shazam when I first met you. But anyway, my home, Timberwood Ranch, is not far out of Austin, Texas. My parents' names are Sean and Sarah Bell. When you go back, if you could find a way to get a message to them or something and tell them —" I broke off and added in a whisper, "Tell them goodbye from me…"

"Sure. But don't go holding your own funeral yet. It might work out all right."

"I doubt it." I couldn't meet his eyes, instead twirling a twig through the snow. "I'm fading to a ghost already, and as you said, I'll never leave Harlan alive."

"Fading to a ghost?" He was still trying his understand-by-repetition method.

I held out a hand in front of me, but it looked as solid as he did, though not much more tangible. "I'm wondering how long it will be until I can pass through walls like you can. I'm dying, and I know it, and I can't stop it. I'm not sure how long I have left."

He opened his mouth to say something, hesitated, and shook his head. "Fight," he said at last. "Fight for solidity. It works sometimes for me, and it might help you. I spend most of my time intangible, but if I really need to for some reason, I can focus and if I work really hard, I can maintain a physical presence for a time. It might be the same for you. That's all I can say."

"Thanks," I said, not sure exactly how one fought for solidity, but the conversation had spent long enough in depressing waters already. I decided to change the subject. "You know I finished everything here. The kingdom's squared away, the steward's dead, his nobles locked up, and the rightful king on the throne. The assassins are out for good, the wizards and their laws are set straight, and of course, we gave Jeduthiam's blade to the king. I'm done now."

Lynx nodded. "Good luck in Harlan then. Or wherever you're off to."

"Thanks," I said, and meant it for more than just the good wishes. I was never good at expressing myself, and this was the second goodbye I was fuddling.

"*You are a little weird,*" Dixie remarked. "*Just say what you think, and then you'll make the other person feel special."*

Except that I can never find the words, Dixie girl. You can.

Lynx held out his hand. I stared at it, not wanting to ask what I was thinking: *Dude, you're as solid as mist. How can I shake your hand?* He smiled encouragingly at me. "Consider it a demo."

Uncertainly, I reached out for his hand, half expecting to pass right through him with that eerie chill. Instead, it was just like any regular handshake, solid, warm, and reassuring. I relaxed a little, smiling back.

"You can do it, Alex. I know you can." And then he was gone. I was alone under the cold gray sky of winter Secret. Blinking away tears, I reached for the diamond.

As the world swirled and my stomach lurched, it occurred to me that for the first time, Lynx had used my real nickname. Then everything went blank.

CHAPTER XXXIV

It was just like when I left Bliss. I floated, caught in a shaft of rainbow light, sucked along into darkness. I was nothing, nothing at all.

I opened my eyes, clutching the diamond. There was no mistaking where I was. The ground was gray, the tree trunks were a lighter gray, the leaves were black, the sky was a dull iron gray, and in fact, though the occasional roguish item of scenery was tinted with a memory of a color, everything that met my eyes was some shade of gray.

I was standing on a small mound in Harlan.

To heighten the eerie effect of this world, I had based it entirely on a grayscale. My skin was white, almost chalk white, my hair was jet black, and I knew that if I had a mirror I would have seen charcoal lips, jet black eyes, cold features. Dixie blended right in, with her black and white fur. This world did not encourage cheery spirits. I was wearing a black tunic, tall black boots, and black gauntlets. Outwardly, I was a pitiless Goth warrior. Inside, I wanted to cry.

"Dixie," I said experimentally, unsure whether any sound would come out.

"Yeah? Is it safe to talk aloud?"

No, probably not. We're not too far from one of the Goth tribes' main camp. Last time I was here I stole their ceremonial amulet, though where it is now, I don't know. I wanted to see if I could speak. Dixie, I can't feel anything. I'm not sure I'm here. Oh Dixie, I'm not dead already, am I?

"You don't look dead." She came over and took a good sniff at me. *"Nope, don't smell dead either. Don't freak out. You'll be fine, I know you will. You just have to hold on long enough to get through this mission, and I know you*

have the grit to do it."

And then what? I lashed out, fear cracking into sudden anger. *Die? Where will I be then?* Dixie didn't answer, probably waiting for me to calm down.

I stalked across to the nearest tree, a ghoulish relic of its namesake. I reached out slowly until my fingers ought to brush wood. Nothing. I jammed them hard against the tree trunk. Still nothing. Not so much as the dim echo of a throb to tell me I was crushing my fingers against wood. I turned to the nearest boulder and repeated the move with no more luck. A thought crossed my mind, and I dropped to my knees in front of it. I put one hand against it – my right hand actually, the one that was broken in Secret but here in Harlan was perfectly fine. Closing my eyes, I tried to focus on the vague feeling of floating (at least that's the best I can do to describe it). It was the complete opposite of touching something and being aware of it and what it was, of standing in a field in bare feet and feeling the dirt squish between your toes and knowing you were on solid ground. This was like being suspended not only from ground, but almost from life. I was almost intangible, and I could feel its ever-present threat creeping up on me. Now I focused on it, and working at the stone with my hand, I opened my eyes at Dixie's shocked exclamation. My hand was gone. My arm was buried in the stone past my wrist. I jerked violently and it came free.

Well, what do you think of that? I asked, turning to Dixie.

"*What are you thinking, Alex?*" Dixie asked. She leapt onto the rock and perched there, glaring down at me. "*You won't help things by trying to be less tangible. You're going to need all of it to do any mission. Your friend told you to fight for your solidity, not unsolidity. You want to get home, right?*"

Of course.

"*And we've got to finish these missions first, right?*"

Probably.

"*How do you think you can accomplish a mission intangibly?*"

I can't! That's the point!

"*So if you try as hard as you can to be intangible, how can you hope to finish this last mission and go home?*" Dixie pointed out triumphantly. Then her tone gentled. "*I know you're simply crazy to be home again, Alex. You're literally going nuts over it. You're losing your senses. You'll have to trust me here. This – what you just did – is not a good idea if it can be helped. Fight, like you just did, but the other way around. Fight to keep your solidity.*"

I sank back, wrapping my arms about my knees, feeling more

hopeless than I ever had in my life. What could I hope to do here? The diamond! I hadn't looked in the diamond to learn my mission yet.

I scanned the area uneasily. Of course, there was nowhere in this world that was safe; it teemed with Goth warriors, all of whom were enemies. But the Black Arrows should be the ones who would most want me dead, since I had just stolen their amulet the last time I was here, and it couldn't have been that long ago. They might still be near and after me, but I saw nothing to indicate it. I was in the Ridges, a region about as relatively safe as you could be in the heart of Goth territory – smack between a bunch of different camps, or tribes, about an equal distance from all the closest ones. I didn't suppose it would get much better. In Harlan, there would be no such thing as a "good time" to be mentally impaired, not even remotely close. And as I knew too well, we didn't have a second to spare.

Dixie, will you keep watch for me? Use your nose, and they might come from anywhere. I slid down the far side of the ridge and sat there, knees drawn up to my chin. I fished out the diamond, wishing desperately I could feel its comforting cold solidness. I watched the colors blur together, saw the image play out, only one scene, but a frightening one. I saw Harlan as if from space, a gray globe spinning slowly, slowly, before my eyes, just like in my dream. A chunk of it, of Harlan itself, broke off and blasted into space as if fired from a gigantic cannon. Water that rapidly froze to ice spurted from the hole; the world was covered with swirling foaming water and ice as it exploded, shooting pieces of itself in all directions. And then it was gone. I heard words too, but the picture was even more clear and potent.

"Darkness rules in Harlan. Nowhere can a child of truth be found. The time of this world has passed; let it be struck from the universe and pass into nothingness. Go to the Deadlands, find the Heart of the evil, and end it once and for all. Face the darkness, and know that it does not own you unless you let it. Destroy Harlan."

It was only too clear. Either the message or the images would be enough – combined, there could be no doubt. My mission was simple, dangerous, and deadly. *Destroy Harlan.* I knew how I had to do it: find my way down into the cold Deadlands where no one ventured intentionally or ever came out from alive, pass through uncounted and horrifying sights and possible dangers down, down, to the very heart of Harlan – literally. Like a living vile creature, Harlan had a grotesque oversized heart in the center of the world that pumped blood to all its far regions. The people drank this blood. It was the source of their dark, corrupted life, and they would do anything for it. It held a certain sway over them, like drugs to an addict, and it was this that was said to be the source of their brutality, and their near indestructability that made them almost impossible to kill. It was liquid evil, the source of Harlan's power, its people's lifeblood, and, like a disease, took control of all who drank it. They became enslaved to it forever. This world was doomed to destruction, and the heart in the Deadlands was literally the heart of Harlan. I would have to destroy that to accomplish my mission.

And then what? I thought bitterly. I'd be brought down with it. I'd never go home. Ever. I was already almost dead, but that would be the nails in the coffin. Except there'd be no one to bury me in one. I blinked away the vision, coming back to myself. Advantages of losing my feeling: my body felt absolutely no pain from looking in the diamond. Even the mind pain was reduced to a dull headache. Disadvantages: well... a lot.

I rose slowly to my knees. I grabbed at everything I had of myself: all the little strength of will, all my courage, all my fire, every drop of determination I had in me. I had been given a job to do, and I was going to be stubborner than an iron mule. I was not going to lie down and quit, I was not going to give up, I was not going to allow myself to give in to the weakness of fear until I was deader than dead. I would drive on to the end with every ounce of tangibility I had until I succeeded or the Goths had trussed me up and chucked me in a blood well and drawn me up again and roasted me. I ground my teeth determinedly. If I was going to die, which was either way, I would die doing something useful. I had messed this world up and now it was my job to fix that and wipe the slate clean of Harlan's existence. I was going to force myself to do it, even if I had to drag myself kicking and screaming through the Deadlands. More than likely. Well, time for me to get busy.

CHAPTER XXXV

I struggled to my feet, and my heart wrenched at the sight of faithful Dixie standing sentinel at the top of the ridge. Poor girl! I would have given a lot to have her safely off in another world. I looked over my shoulder and back, gauging the direction the Ridges ran in. They would act as my initial compass. The Height, as the local Goths referred to the highest ridge, was practically due south in a line from the entrance to the Deadlands and not too far away, as the entrance was in the actual exact center between the camps. I thought I was on the Height, or rather Dixie was, and I was at the bottom, but which was north, the direction I needed to follow it from to get there? Dimly through the clouds I could discern a faint point of light – the sun's attempt to pierce this dark world. It was low on my right, so if it soon became night, I would know I was facing the wrong direction. But if it only got lighter, I would know I was facing the right way. How long could I afford to wait? As much as I hated the idea, I decided I would save myself time in the long run by waiting instead of blundering around. And it would also give me time to fully recover from the diamond's effects.

I slowly climbed the hill to Dixie, relaying the message to her. Idly, I drew my Goth knife, the only weapon I'd ever carried in this world, and scratched an X in the ground while I thought, marking where I stood. Glancing up at the sky, I marked a smaller X on the side where the sun was. I scripted my own name on the ground, then one by one, Dad's, Mom's, and Elliot's.

"*I guess you're right about us probably dying in the ruin of this world,*" Dixie remarked when I'd finished.

I glanced up at her briefly. Dixie seldom agreed with my cynical views. *I don't see how it could really be any other way, unless we go before then.*

"So then, we'd best give it everything we've got, if we won't have anything left afterwards anyway."

I'm surprised at you. Next you'll start a funeral song for us! This isn't like you, Dixie. I scrawled the names of the friends I'd made in the dirt – Kya and Queen Vida, Lynx, King Jed, Queen Mira, Keliel…

"Optimism is only as good as far as it goes. You have to be honest, which I am. I believe that we are in our final act, just like you do. The stage is set, the road leads to the grave, and we can only play our part to the best of our ability and end in glory. In case we get separated and – well, frankly, die, here's goodbye now." She rubbed her furry side against my shoulder and licked my face. I scratched her ears, neither of us having words to say the feelings inside us, not even Dixie, who was never at a loss for words. I rested my head against her and let the tears slip out from under my eyelids, not feeling them course down my cheeks to drop into her black and white fur.

Twilight was setting in, and I realized with a start that I had my direction now. The sun had been in the west, so I'd need to head with that direction on my left to go north, with the little X I'd drawn in the dirt on my left. I sniffed, and peering at the ground, was able to make it out. I stood up, orienting myself in the right direction, and struck off. Dixie didn't follow. She was sniffing the air intently.

The stillness of the evening was shattered by her warning bark. I whirled, and in the darkness I could barely make out her dim shape outlined against the sky. I saw nothing else. Something struck me from the side with a force that drove the breath out of me. I was hurled to the ground, knocking my head hard (which didn't hurt but I figured if I could feel like normal it very much would) and getting my mouth full of dirt. I spat and struggled, trying to draw my knife again, but someone, or possibly multiple someones, was holding my arms firmly. I was screaming without realizing it. I heard Dixie come roaring in like a freight train.

Go, Dixie! Run! You'll do more alone. Get away, and maybe you can finish the mission. I think my time is over. You have to find the Black Heart. Leave me and go! Dixie didn't answer, but her barks died off and the fight ended. I could do nothing myself.

My arms were bound firmly to my sides with an exorbitant amount of rope. Maybe they just didn't want to cut their nice long coil. I wriggled my hands but couldn't reach my knife no matter how hard

I tried, which they hadn't noticed or taken. Judging by the number of hands that hustled at me, there must have been at least a full troop of warriors. I could feel none of them, not so much as a finger, but I was propelled along anyway, like a leaf in a river.

For a moment, the dense clouds overhead shredded fractionally, and I saw something that filled me with utter horror and fear like never before – a moon, golden as honey. It was a Hunter's Moon, and I knew from the lore I'd made up for this world that it only appeared on the night of the Ritual. I tried to hide the shudder that passed through me at that thought. The dreaded Ritual had been the cause of many adventures in this world. Every Goth camp participated once a year in their camp Ritual. It came right at the peak of warring season, which was all but year-round. It involved dancing in the smoke, wailing ceremonial laments, calling up spells for good hunting with their genie-infested amulet, but worst of all, a human sacrifice. The idea was, if you were a good enough camp at fighting, you would be able to capture a high-ranking Goth of another tribe for your sacrifice. If your camp didn't cut it though, lots were drawn among your own people, and one of your own became the victim. *No, please, don't take me to your camp tonight. I can't bear to see...*

But they did. It wasn't more than ten minutes before I saw the rough needled outlines of the pine trees planted in a large circle that formed the barrier for the main dwelling of the Black Arrows' camp. It was for them like a castle wall, and each tribe had their own barrier and their own symbol. If I passed into those trees, I would almost certainly never come out again. It was from the Black Arrows that I had taken the ceremonial genie amulet.

"Hersshiem!" one of the warriors in the troop that had captured me roared in his deep throaty voice. He ducked between the trunks through the lower branches into the circle and the other warriors followed, forcing me along like a wind blowing trash in the road, moving without touching, sweeping me along like a wave of the sea. "Hersshiem!" he called again. I remembered that it was the name of the Black Arrows' chieftain when I was last here. So not too much time had passed, no more than a year, I decided, catching sight of him at last.

"What is it, Hiendrik?" he asked, rising from where he had been sitting cross-legged in the center of the camp, with my archenemy-nemesis-terror of this world, Aeuik the diviner, hovering by his shoulder. "You have been gone barely half an hour. Have you already made your catch?"

"Yes, Chief, and see, she wears the silver." He shoved me forward eagerly, and I obediently stepped out from among them. With a sinking feeling, I realized this man Hiendrik was right. A silver armlet was around my left arm. It had been part of an old disguise in this world, and I had neglected to take it off when I'd finished with it. It marked me as of "noble" blood of a tribe.

"I see," Hersshiem said coldly. "Who are you?" he asked me.

I shook back my hair, standing as tall as I could. I didn't want to die like a coward, even if I looked like a Goth and felt like a mouse. "We've met before, haven't we, Chief Hersshiem? Don't you recognize me already? I mean, you should."

He glared at me, then recognition – and anger – kindled in his face. "Aeuik! The thief is in our hands! The thief who stole the amulet!"

Aeuik moved closer, swaying rhythmically as though in a weird dance. He was stooped, white-gray frizz was all that was left of his hair, but his eyes burnt like black coals and he had some strange power to see through you at times. I was pretty sure he was possessed or something. For all of it, his voice was smooth as oil, sweet as honey, and deadly as poison. "Oh yes, I remember her. Quite the daring prank. You have to admire her nerve, for risking her life sneaking in here and stealing it from my very belt and running off, only to leave it on the Height for us to find." He laughed a cackling laugh, and when he spoke again his voice was ice. "I daresay she'll never play trickster again like that."

"No," Hersshiem agreed in the same icy tone. He gestured to the nearest in the crowd that had gathered around. "Strike her down."

The Goth reached for his blade, but Aeuik intervened. "Hold, my Chief. Allow your servant to speak."

Hersshiem turned a ferocious glare on the diviner, and I hid a small smile. The more they quarreled among themselves, the better my chances would be of escape, and anyway, I didn't care who got mad at Aeuik as long as someone was. He was about as evil as they came.

He was speaking rapidly to the chieftain now. "This is the night of the Ritual, as you know. Your warriors have returned, unable to recapture the rescued Snowdrop princess. We do not have much time left until the hour of the sacrifice. There is no time to capture a new prisoner, and therefore we must offer up one of our own to appease the gods. But now we capture her, and she wears the silver. Isn't she good enough? She will die anyway; why not make her our sacrifice?"

"You are as wise as the stars, Aeuik," Hersshiem said with grudging admiration. "That is why I keep you close." He turned to the Goth warrior, who stood, watching uncertainly. "You there, and a few of you others, chain her to the trees so that she cannot escape and let us prepare for the ceremonies."

CHAPTER XXXVI

Talking rapidly and gargling laughs, a few men rescued their coil of rope from me and hurriedly fastened shackles on my wrists, wrapping the other ends of the chains firmly around different pines in the circle so that I was forced to stand between them, my hands apart and with too little chain to meet. The Ritual was a solemn time for the Goths, but it was also one of drinking and feasting, and they looked forward to it eagerly now that one of their own would not have to be sacrificed.

I stood, watching the herbs burn on the fires, making the acrid smoke for the Smoke Dance. I was numb, completely numb inside and out. I had ceased to feel anymore. I looked at the chains. I could feel their weight, in that it hampered my ability to raise my hand, and if I moved it too far over it would jerk to a stop, but I felt neither the cold of the metal nor the bite of its edge as I pulled against it. Numb, and almost a ghost. I could reach my knife now, but it wouldn't do me any good; I couldn't fight all the Goths at once and its edge would only nick the chain. In a few hours, I would be dead, killed in a pagan sacrifice. *What have I done?* the voice inside me cried.

Perhaps it would be best for me to die now. I couldn't do awful things like this again. But I had a job to do. I had been charged to undo my mistake by destroying this world. I could die then, but not before. I had to live until I'd finished the task given to me, and I hadn't yet. *Dixie, where are you?*

"I can see you, Alex. I don't know what I can do, but I'm ready when you need me."

Will you be able to cause a little diversion when I give the signal?

"*Ready whenever you say! I'm mad enough to eat these guys. Slimly blood-sucking leeches!*"

I didn't stop to ask Dixie why she was here instead of on her way to the Deadlands. It didn't matter right now. She was here, and I needed her, and I hadn't a moment to spare. Closing my eyes, I shut out the wailing voices. I shut out the fluttering of my own nervous heartbeat. I shut out the smell of smoke and the sound of feet drumming in a sinister dance. I focused once again on the feeling of suspension, the floating feeling of nonexistence that I had taken advantage of when I forced my hand into the rock. This, if ever, was the time to use it. The Goths were engrossed in their ceremonies, and if there had been any outward sign of what I was doing, they wouldn't have seen it in the shadow of the trees through the smoke.

I edged backwards, half-step by half-step, as close to the outside of the circle as the chains would let me. They pulled taut. I felt the pressure now against my wrists with a surge of joy. I was not quite gone yet! But I needed to be as wraithlike as possible. I didn't let my eyes open. I concentrated hard on *not* being solid, not being solid at all. I focused it on my wrists, with all the power of my mind and will. I strained, pulling against the chains. My eyes drifted open, and their unfocused gaze took in the sight of my wrists, divided in two by metal shackles that disappeared into the flesh between hand and arm. I pulled harder, straining mind and body against my restraints.

A cry echoed in the camp, out of step, out of harmony with the dark Ritual. "She's escaping! She has witchcraft and she's escaping!"

Now, Dixie! I snapped free of the chains. For a fraction of an instant, all was silent in the camp as the wailing stopped and Dixie hadn't entered. In that moment, the dull clank of the shackles striking the trees filled the air like a bell of freedom.

Everything changed. Dixie blasted in, barking. Warriors caught up weapons and charged. Hersshiem met my eyes as I picked myself up and I heard his voice through the din. "Serve me. Such potent craft should not be wasted!"

I paused only to shout a reply, the words boiling up before I could stop them. "Never! As long as life is in me, I will stand against you! Beware! This night will be your last!" I turned and ran, heedless of direction. Dixie had them fairly muddled by the sounds of it, and she soon joined me. We ran side by side, and before long we were on the Height. I found the mark I'd made, paused to make sure I had my

175

compass right, and took off with all the speed I had due north, Dixie following. We headed straight for the Black Door.

"*Black this, black that. Everything is black. Black Goths, black arts, black doors, black hearts. I am now from binding chains free and will bring this world down with me!*"

I – didn't know – you were – a poet, Dix, I thought. *It's a true one, though. But you say it from my perspective, and didn't mention yourself. How can I bring this world down alone? You should add more lines about my faithful dog.*

"*I'm not the one who can do it, Alex. I know nothing about the Black Heart. You're the one who can destroy it. My job is to get you there, and that's what I'm doing. It's you who's really important.*"

I tried not to think about how I was the one who made it in the first place. I just ran, on and on. My mind thought my body should be too exhausted to keep running, after all I'd done in Secret, but this body was fresh. Also, I couldn't feel any burn of my muscles, no stitches in my sides, no pain or tiring. One problem: oxygen was in short supply, my ragged gasping breaths never seeming to get enough.

The roar of the Black Arrows Goths' war cry pierced the night behind me. I twisted in stride and saw the whole camp of the Black Arrows, men and women alike, in hot pursuit. How much farther did we have to go? I wondered worriedly. I was fast but they were strong. They would overtake me in the long run, literally. Dixie, normally a swift sure runner, was barely keeping pace with me.

Are you all right? I asked her.

"*I'll be fine. You can't be in two fights and not be worn out. How much farther?*"

I think we're close. The only question is if we can get there before they catch up. The ground was flat, hard-packed gray dirt, not bad for running on. My boots were rubbing blisters onto the sides of my feet, but I didn't notice. I pelted harder. Stagger, leap forward, stagger, half-run, leap a few steps more. The Goths were close behind, no more than fifty feet behind me. Dixie was falling back.

Then I saw it. Two heavy black iron doors in the ground, set in a stone doorway. No fancy bells and whistles, no fanfare, just a simple double door. But the sickening overwhelming sense of some lurking evil radiating from the door was fanfare enough. It was the door to the Deadlands, the cold hard icy underworld. I charged, flinging myself at the doors. There was no time to think, no time to process the fear. *Dixie, if you've got anything left, keep them back! It's all you can do. Just buy me time!*

Dixie staggered about and charged wearily at the Goths. What could one dog do against so many? I thought as I scrabbled frantically at the door. There were hundreds of them and only one of Dixie. I hauled the door open an inch. Then a foot. I twisted to look at Dixie. *Quick! Dive!* She had her hands full, darting, feinting, racing in and out, never making herself a target long enough for anyone to strike.

"*Just go, Alex!*" With all my strength I heaved upward on the door. It crashed open, leaving the way for Dixie to follow. I leapt into darkness, evil and cold.

CHAPTER XXXVII

A second later, the feeble moonlight that found its way through the door was blotted out by the stocky bodies of Goth warriors, crowding around the entrance. I lay on cold stone, dragging in painful breaths. I was utterly spent. I could run no farther, not until my wind decided to come back from vacation. If they caught me, they caught me. I was empty of all I had to give just then. I was on the verge of failure, lying there, staring up into hate-filled black eyes.

The Goths hesitated, obviously unwilling to leap in after me. And no wonder. It was as good as a death sentence to go into the Deadlands, where unnamed horrors ruled and roamed. One didn't enter it lightly. Then a voice, cold, crawling evil, smooth as refined oil, slid in between the Goths and me.

"Hold, my Chief, if I may again issue you an order." It was Aeuik.

Hersshiem wheeled on him. "Your insolence is becoming dangerous, Aeuik. Explain yourself and watch your tongue in future."

"She is as good as dead, sir. What need have we to sacrifice her ourselves? The gods speak to me, and they will be satisfied with this. Leave her. Let *IT* deal with her. I assure you, we will never see her again."

Dixie, I slurred the thought. *Slip in before it's too late. Come!* In mounting horror, I saw Hersshiem nod to a group of warriors. They seized the door I'd left open. I tried to move. I tried to get up and stop them, but I was frozen. With a thundering clang, the light was snuffed out, the door shut. Dixie was on one side, and I was on the other. She could not open it from above, and I knew I was too far down to reach it from below. Faithful Dixie, who since I had lost my own world had

178

never left me except once in Secret at my order, was now cut off from me forever. I would never see her again in this world, and after this world, I would be dead. *Oh, Dixie, Dixie, Dixie! Where are you? Are you all right? How can I hope to go on without you?*

"*You have to. I – can't follow you. You have to do this alone, Alex, but you can do it. You showed that when you went into the Cob Grove alone in Bliss and brought down the dragon. You showed it again when you entered the Jungle all by yourself, knowing that no one who went in could hope to get out again, and set changes in motion that rocked that world. You can do this. Don't worry about me. Just destroy Harlan and end this evil. You can do it!*"

Will you be fine? I mean, its teeming with Goths out there.

"*I said don't worry about me. I'll hide from them until you can destroy this world. I don't think I'll care much longer after that.*"

Don't! I almost broke down right then. Darkness was all there was, and its cold embrace was no comfort.

Somehow I did go on, though I'm not sure how. Not only was I leaving Dixie behind, but in this world, the Goths were the least of my worries. My sickest horrors waited for me here, in the otherworldly Deadlands. I clawed blindly to my feet and stumbled forward. I could see nothing, and sight became a meaningless thing. I relied on what I felt and sensed, and that was all that really counted. The gagging sense of heavy oppressive evil, of something powerful, malicious and utterly vile and repulsive, pressed in on me, enfolding me, strangling me. It was a presence; just as the darkness was a void of light, this evil was a presence that filled it. It was darkness with a twisted kind of life, breathing, frightening, deadly, like liquid dark. I was a swimmer, groping my way forward with no hope of light or air again, but struggling against the inexorable flow because a dying man must.

This was the first level. Below this would be the plains of the Sleepless Dead, and below that… the Heart Circle, where I would find the Black Heart and the end of the road. But this level preyed upon your emotions, attacking in an invisible way, harnessing your fear and –

I dropped into a crouch, flinging up my arms to defend myself as a surge of irrational, palpable fear washed over me. I whimpered, waiting for death to take me, my mind a white smudge of terror. Images flung themselves through my mind, everything I loved burning to ash, fading away, destroyed. I watched my family die, one by one. I saw Dixie trapped in a cave, withering away, starving to death, until her breathing stopped.

"No!" I screamed. "No, no, no! Make it stop!" My shoulders shook as tears fountained down my face. Dimly, I remembered that none of this was real. I was going somewhere, somewhere important. Slowly, on my hands and knees, I crawled forward, as the horrible images and overwhelming fear poured on.

People screamed my name. Blood and horror ran a river through my mind. My arms and legs trembled as I struggled to keep going as the fear threatened to drown me completely.

Will you serve fear, or let it serve you? The words rang like a long-forgotten bell in the midst of my confusion and terror, momentarily clearing my head. Phrases from the last few days rushed over me. The Phoenix: *Master your fear. Create the change yourself.* Kya: *I'm with you to the end.* Keliel: *Men and means may fail, but the Phoenix never does. If he sent you to do this, then I believe it is possible for you to do it.* Lynx: *Fight. You can do it, Alex. I know you can.*

I let out a laugh, a hysterical sound somewhere between an actual laugh and a sob of fear. "Okay, fear, time to serve me," I said, repeating the phrase I'd used before entering the Jungle. "I'm going to harness you like a bronco. Come on, you want to get away from this horror? So do I! But we're going forward, not back. So what are we waiting for? Let's make a break for it."

I staggered to my feet, waves of fear washing against me. This time, I didn't try to push them back. I let it rip right through me, shredding my breath, firing my steps forward in desperate, uneven strides. Forever. The raw power of fear – harnessed.

The ground sloped down rapidly, so rapidly I took it at a tumble. There were big loose stones all around me, though the ground itself seemed to be all solid stone with no particular landmarks other than the uneven-but-always-moving-downward terrain. When I regained my feet and blundered on, I had completely lost my sense of direction and time. The dark and the overwhelming Presence were getting to me, and my stomach churned and roiled.

With no warning at all, my foot found nothing beneath it, and I was falling into nothingness. I crashed hard on top of something terribly cold. I had known the upper level was chilly if I could have felt it, but this was real cold. Cold as death itself. I had survived the first level, and with it, the irrational fear ebbed.

Ice. I had landed on a pillar of ice. Dim eerie blue light illuminated the area I was in, though where it came from I couldn't tell. I peeled myself up off the top of the pillar and peered down at ground level below me. Only a dozen feet or so. I thought of jumping, but my mind still rebelled against the idea of such a jump being painless. Awkwardly I squeezed my arms around the pillar and slid down like it was a fire pole. I stood on smooth, perfect ice, almost a little blue from the light, the first near-color my eyes had seen in Harlan. I didn't like it despite this.

There were more pillars, hundreds of them, stretching as far as my eyes could see in every direction. They were not decorative pillars. These pillars had a sinister use. In each one was a body, sheathed in ice. Bodies that had once been alive. If my legend served me, these were the bodies of people who had proved troublesome and had been chucked into the blood wells and sucked down here, where the power of the Black Heart had dealt with them. Men, women, even children, caught in strange, contorted poses, their mouths forever silenced now. I choked on a sob of horror, but a voice deep inside me seemed to say, *you did this. This was your creation. How could you deliberately forge such willful darkness and evil? It was your hand that made the Black Heart.*

And my hand will bring it down, I grated back, struggling hard not to cry. I of all people knew that this was not the place to cry, for I must not be found by the

A distant shadow moved, gliding slowly towards me, joined by others. The Sleepless Dead. They were something like phantoms of the ice-caged people, in reality nothing more than channels for the Black Heart to carry out its designs. If I didn't want to be ice-caged myself, I'd have to get moving on a miracle.

I was already running, somewhere, anywhere, as long as it was away from those creatures. I had no idea how to get to the Heart Circle, where the Black Heart was, but the more immediate problem was behind me. I didn't get far.

I could hear the *slap-slap* of the feet of the Sleepless Dead running behind me, getting rapidly closer. I tried to control my panic, to just keep moving forward, but seconds later, icy hands locked around my arms. I struggled in vain, trying to break through, shouting for them to let me go, begging the Phoenix to help me. And that, in the middle of all that confusion and living nightmare, made me remember something: *Will you serve fear, or let it serve you?* In this realm of pure fear, those words again pointed the way. How could I use this fear? My mind must have been truly messed up, because I did the craziest thing in the world.

CHAPTER XXXVIII

I addressed the Sleepless Dead.

"Hey, guys, I guess down here you just have each other for company. Things must get really boring. You want to hear a story?"

Their vacant eyes stared back at me, and I thought: *I'm such an idiot!* Their grips loosened. The shadowy figures bunched close around me, watching my face intently. I drew a long, unsteady breath. Apparently, they wanted a story.

"Okay, so once upon a time, there was a young girl who made some bad decisions. She made a lot of people's lives miserable, though not on purpose exactly, and then one day, she got shown how much sadness she had made and how badly she'd messed up." My voice cracked, but I tried again, continuing. "She was given the job of fixing everything that she had done and starting the change to make it right. She did what she was told and worked hard to make up for messing up in the first place. And then she got to a world that she had created, a world filled with darkness and evil, a world she was supposed to destroy, for everyone there had chosen to serve the darkness and its time of rule was over. So she set out to destroy the Black Heart and so end the horrible evil."

I eyed my audience, trying to see if they were following, and gauge how they would accept the next plot point in my story. They were nothing if not stoic. "But one of the sad things that resulted from her bad decision was a people known as the Sleepless Dead. Their souls were denied rest, and they were cursed to walk forever between life and death. She sought to give their souls their final rest and free them from

182

their bondage, for that was what would happen when she succeeded in her mission. But the Sleepless Dead, as was their custom, waylaid her as she tried to get to the Lost Stair that led to the Heart Circle and her final task…"

I paused. An elderly-looking Sleepless Dead man rolled his hand, gesturing for me to go on. I shrugged. "That part of the story is for you to tell. Did the Sleepless Dead let her go, or show her the way to the Lost Stair, or did they encase her in ice and let her die? You have to tell me that part. I've written my section of the story. Now it's your turn." A shakiness had wormed through all my limbs, and my voice trembled a bit. I waited breathlessly to see what would happen.

The Sleepless Dead took my arms again, a little less firmly. Then, setting a rapid pace, they propelled me through the columns.

I hardly dared hope that I had succeeded, that the Sleepless Dead were actually helping me. But I was forced to accept it when they released me in front of an ice wall, and the elderly man pointed at it, miming punching it and it shattering. The secret wall that hid the Lost Stair. So I was here. I turned to them, fear and gratitude making a strange combination in my stomach. I'd never imagined myself thanking zombies, but here I was.

"Thank you," I said. "I'll do my best to free you. I'll destroy the Black Heart and end what should never have started. And I'm sorry."

The lead Sleepless Dead put a fist to his chest and then raised it over his head, and all the others followed suit. I blinked away the tears that were trying to form in my eyes and turned to face my greatest evil.

Turning my shoulder, I threw myself against the wall, and it splintered like a glass curtain, falling in tinkling shards around me. I was falling myself, but only a few feet. I crumpled onto stairs – a spiral staircase leading downward. I didn't stop to think, didn't allow myself the luxury of dread or wonder. I had no time to lose. I plunged, half running down the stair, half rolling down in a ball, the eerie blue light soon lost to sight in the darkness.

It was then, stumbling, almost sobbing with the strain of mind and nerves, surrounded by the thick blackness, that an odd thought struck me. As I became less tangible, the darkness became more tangible. It was taking on more of a body, a form like a living being, and an evil one. It wrapped itself around me, pulling me down, trying to stop me. Sight meant nothing again, and this Presence and I were engaged in our own combat that it had no part in. I was cut off from everything, utterly alone to fight this thing. My mind reached out for Dixie, but my thoughts were caught in the net of the black fog and couldn't pierce it.

I groped down the stairs as time became nothing. The deeper into the fog of evil I stumbled, the less in touch with reality I seemed to be becoming.

On Earth, my world had consisted of blacks and whites – life and death, tangible and intangible. In my worlds I had created, I was meeting a new level of gray area. Things neither alive nor dead exactly; things, including myself, neither strictly tangible nor intangible. The Presence about me had a body of its own, and on Earth I had never known darkness to take shape, nor evil either, not in the way it was here. I felt it stifling me as I gulped in breaths, clogging my mind, slowing my body. I had lost all sense except that of the nauseating evil. I wanted to throw up, a thing I'd never wanted in the past, hoping it would help me feel better.

When at last my foot struck a landing instead of another stair, I staggered out onto it and collapsed. I wanted to shrivel up and die right there. I was adrift from time, from myself, from everything I had ever vowed or meant to do. All I knew was the pulsing evil drumming all around and through me, and the deeper down I went, the closer to its source I got. I couldn't go on. There was no way I could destroy this world! I was crazy to think I could…

I hadn't. It hadn't been me… It had been the Phoenix. Dixie too had believed in me. She had told me I could do this, just like Lynx had. Poor Dixie! I thought of everything I had ever loved that I was about to lose. My family; playing with Elliot in the yard on spring afternoons in the sun; washing dishes in the sink with Mom and seeing the soap bubbles shimmer and jump; dancing with Dad to "I Wanna Dance with Somebody" and twirling in time like we had since I could stumble a step. Riding Starr across the Texas ground with the deep blue sky as a canopy overhead; laughing and getting soaked by the buckets of drenching rain that fell in the summer heat; listening to the gurgle of a brook and feeling the life of a tree.

All these and a thousand more little joys stood lined up on the line, about to be left behind forever when I took the fatal plunge. But I knew deep inside that they would still go on after I did, and though I would die, they would continue. My family would still be a family, life would still be life, it would still hold joys for those who lived, and though I wouldn't see it, life would go on. But worse was Dixie, standing on the edge of death, waiting, waiting for me to leap, ready to leap with me. She would not go on after I died. She would die too. I would not only bring about the end of the evil I had started and with it my own life, but I would take Dixie down with me too. I couldn't bear that.

My hand groped blindly at the diamond around my neck, and scarcely realizing what I was doing, my thoughts groped out too, but not to Dixie – she was unreachable. *Lord Phoenix, you sent Dixie and me into these worlds. Please, don't let her die with me! I'll go on, I promise, I'll do everything I can to destroy this world, but don't let Dixie be killed with me. Let her go to Earth or something, and I'll fight this evil as long as I have life. But not Dixie. Please, not Dixie!*

I didn't know whether he could hear my thoughts like Dixie could. I could only hope. Dixie was worth doing all I could to save her.

I was no hero – there were no two ways about it. But I hope I can say I was honest. I couldn't be brave for my own sake, but sometimes, when it really mattered, I could be sort of brave for others. It was like that now. I had made a promise – to do everything I could to destroy the Black Heart as long as life was in me. I remembered my determination on the Height when I first brushed with the evil of this world, when I had vowed I would not stop trying no matter what happened as long as I had life in me. I would drive on to the end with every ounce of tangibility I had until I succeeded. If I was going to die it was going to be in wiping the universe clean of Harlan's existence. I remembered my dream in Secret, when I'd seen the light overpower the darkness of Harlan. I'd reach that moment, and everything it stood for.

Lying there on the landing on the Lost Stair, I reached as I had before for all I had left of myself. I reached deeper than I ever had, into reserves I hadn't known existed up until that very moment. I found I was on my feet, fueled by anger at the evil around me, fueled by the love of all I held dear: my family, life on earth – so beautiful for all its sorrows – and everything throughout the universe that was now staked on me and my ability to end this ghastly creation. Anger and love make strange companions, but they were aimed at different things, and the fire in me burned hot, all the hotter for the darkness of the Presence around me.

Swallowing hard, I started descending again, round and round the spiral stair. I wondered momentarily how far down I still had to go. The Presence grew more oppressive around me. I imagined I could feel it wrapping tentacles or arms or something around me, holding me tight, not letting go, trying to quench the fire in me. The throbbing, whether it actually was a sound or just vibrations or something else, grew more and more potent. It seemed to strum me as though I were a string on a guitar. It beat rhythmically, *thump, thump, thump,* right through me, stronger, stronger, beating its own time. I stepped out, into a wide space, not a stair but not floor.

CHAPTER XXXIX

I was suspended, and if one could walk on fog, it might have been that. There seemed to be nothing beneath my feet, or all around. I lost the direction of the stair, and just before I started to panic, a voice throbbed into my mind, beating as if it were with the pulse around me. It was low, barely perceivable as a foreign thought, almost like when Dixie spoke to me, but this was deadly. It was insidious, too sweet, like honeyed poison.

"Welcome."

I was struck by the word. Who spoke it? The voice was horrible and frightening, but the word – oh, how wonderful it was to call me welcome! The word sounded so, so, so welcoming! For an instant, I was aware of my self-possession slipping away, and then I only felt warm inside, warm and *welcome*.

"Who am I?" It almost seemed to chuckle. *"I am your only hope... Alex."*

"How do you know my name?" I shot back, terrified but amazed.

"You told it to me. No, you didn't know, but I read many things in the minds of people that they will not tell me otherwise." The pulsing seemed almost to have music to it, dancing around me, through me. I felt a most wonderful sensation of being happy. I relaxed a little.

"How do you plan to help me?" I asked dreamily.

"I will send you home."

"What! How can you do that?" I took a step forward into the blackness.

"I have magic stronger than worlds. I can cast you back across the gulf into you own world."

"But the Phoenix gave me a job to do," I said, my mind breaking partially free. I couldn't lose sight of why I was here.

"*The Phoenix?*" The voice was half scornful, half patronizingly sympathetic. "*What has the Phoenix ever done for you that you should be his slave, his errand girl? He ripped you from your own world without asking your permission, and has given you nothing but pain and suffering in return. I offer you freedom. You can go home, Alex. Trust me.*"

The words seemed so wise and true, and suddenly everything that had happened sounded unbelievably unjust. I longed to go home so much! "How do I need to trust you?" I asked.

"Relax into the beat, and you will know."

I swallowed, myself again and nervous for a moment. Then I felt as though I was drifting away from the body I had been in and floating in the blackness. The pulsing took me, swirled me into its dance.

"One are all and all are one
We have no need of light or sun
A drop means nothing in the tide
We come alive when we have died

Deep in the dark where none can see
We beat our dance eternally
Individual is an empty word
Unity of mind is far preferred

Your mind shall be my own
Your will shall be my own
Your soul is useless and shall depart
But I myself shall be your Heart

When all are one and one are all
Eternal darkness shall finally fall
Trust the darkness and you will find
Freedom comes when all are one mind."

Grimly, the dark verses beat through me. My heart began to drum in time with the swing of the words. I was not in control of myself anymore. Someone else had taken the helm – the Presence. It was all around me and through me now. I didn't fight it. It was reeling me in like a fish on a line, drawing me into itself. Soon I would be a part of it. Why had I thought it was so horrifying? Here it gave me peace, freedom from decisions, utter surrender of my will to someone else, and they could make all the choices for me.

But what kind of life would that be? I jerked loose a little from the Presence's grasp. Yes, I had made bad decisions in my life – just look at my worlds – but that was part of being human. As the Phoenix had said, *"You've made bad decisions. Such is the nature of fallen man. But you are repenting them, and that is good. It is the only way for healing and change."*

What made humans unique was that we have a soul – we have free will. We're different from all other creatures in that way. If I lost my individuality, if I lost everything that made me "me" and was controlled by another force, what was I but a simple robot, responding to each signal directed by the someone with the controls? I'd no longer be unique. Yes, unique. It was a beautiful word.

Pain blasted into me. I was suddenly aware of my body again, no more floating off from it, but it was not the body that was in pain. It was my mind.

"Wretch!" the voice roared. *"Submit to my kingdom to be. Quiet your awkward soul and bend! You shall be mine. Are you not here? You cannot escape. You can give in now, and it will be easy – you will have peace. Struggle, and only more pain will be your inheritance. Bend! Bend!"*

Somewhere in a void of darkness, I crashed to my knees, writhing in pain. Then it was gone. I sensed the silence, as if the voice was holding its breath, waiting patiently to see what I would do.

I saw now all the falseness, the lies the Presence had been telling me. The diamond had warned me. *Face the darkness, and know that it does not own you unless you let it.* And I knew that I would not let this darkness own me.

"You're wrong!" I shouted, my voice thick with pain. "The Phoenix has done *everything* for me! *I'm* the one who's made mistakes. He's given me forgiveness, a chance to move beyond my past. He's shown me the way to healing and change. He's taught me how to master my fear and use it. He's led me every step of my journey. I might not be able to see him, but I know he's been there, just like he promised. *And* he's given me the hope of a sunrise in myself, too! Beat that!"

I thought my eyes were still closed, but sight was meaningless. I saw the room with other sight. It was huge, circular, and I saw no floor. All I saw was the Black Heart, darker than night, beating out the rhythm that throbbed through me. It was suspended in the air like a moon that devoured light instead of reflecting it, and from it, things like veins ran off and disappeared, carrying the intoxicating liquor of evil to every part of this world. With thundering realization, I knew that it was the voice that had spoken to me, it was the Presence that surrounded me. I had to fight.

Somehow it sensed I knew. A nauseating black wave washed over me, carrying away the sort-of-sight I'd had, but not the truth. That was still in my heart. Then the voice spoke again, but I resisted it, holding the truth of its identity up like a shield against it. *"Listen to reason. I see you intend to destroy me."* Its chuckle shivered through my mind. *"But don't you realize that if you do, you will die?"*

"Yes. I am prepared to die, so there." I braced every spark of strength I had against the Black Heart's overwhelming persuasiveness. "No great thing comes without cost."

"I understand that. But think of your dog." Blast the thing, how did it know about Dixie? *"And think of your family. If you live, you may yet return to them. I have promised to get you back there if you surrender to me. What would they think if you could have lived and gone back, but instead chose to die in some petty fight far from home? I tell you, I can't be important enough of a threat to cost you your family. They would want you to come home, wouldn't they?"*

I struggled for breath like someone choking. The fog of blackness was infiltrating my brain, and I fought to clear it. "No. Not if they understood. I might never be able to explain it to them, but it doesn't matter. I have a job to do, and I'm going to kill you." I grabbed at where my knife ought to have been, unable to find it in the darkness. *Fight for your solidity, Alex.* How much could I fight for at one time? Fighting to keep control of myself was taking nearly all my concentration.

"Then what of your dog?" The Presence challenged. *"If you do this, she will die, and what will you have gained? You will have lost everything for the sake of nothing."*

I didn't answer, focusing on getting my knife. There it was, and with an effort, I found I could draw it and hold it in my hand. The hilt seemed to absorb some of my hand, but I couldn't help that. At least I had it.

"Come, my friend. I know you are a smart girl. Listen to my words, and you will see their wisdom. Think of your dog, if nothing else."

The beating was becoming more persistent and pervasive. My nerves were just about shredded. It jangled against my own heartbeat.

190

It was out of sync, confusing, and muddled my mind. I did think of Dixie, and all she had done for me. All she had ever been to me.

"*Yes, that's right. How can you let her die?*" The voice was getting incredibly annoying.

"You think of nothing but yourself," I told it. "You use hatred and witchcraft and lies to get your way and to protect yourself. But I'm not like you. I am here because of love and truth. You have no power over me."

Then, fumbling through the black fog that stood between me and Dixie, I flung out my last thought to her like a message in a bottle. *Dixie, you are the best dog a girl could ever wish for. You are one in a million, and I'm so grateful that I got to spend the few days with you we had before I died. Since we both have to die, I could ask for no greater honor than to die with you.*

I was ready. I stood slowly. My knife was still in my hand. I closed one hand around the diamond, seeking the reassurance of something solid in this darkness, and with the other I brandished my knife. I directed every ounce of tangibility I had into my hand and the one stroke I would have. As I said, sight meant nothing in the blackness, but I sensed instinctively that I was less than an arm's length away from the source of this world's evil – from its very Heart.

I swung my arm.

"*NO!*"

The single word was like a battle cry, intended to freeze my blood, and it was more terrifying than anything I had yet experienced. But it felt as though it had nothing to do with me. My mind was set and made up, my arm already in motion. Every bit of strength I had, all I had left to give of me, was behind that desperate stroke. The blade fell, the darkness shattered, and the world cracked.

I felt myself hurled back, heard crashes and roars, icy water washed over me, but the voice, the Presence, the overwhelming evil that had threatened to swallow me, was gone. Forever. I felt a feeling of great release, like someone who has carried a heavy burden for a long time suddenly having it lifted. Then there was a moment's struggle against the water, and then it was all blotted out by darkness, and I knew nothing more.

CHAPTER XL

I drifted in space, bodiless, not really sure if I was alive or dead. A spark of light pricked the darkness, swelling, growing, enveloping me. In the spinning fiery gold light, a shape formed, whirling into the Phoenix I had met before all my adventures. He was right: I did know him better now. He was the Phoenix to me still – always would be – but he was also so much more. And I was only beginning to understand.

His golden eyes locked on mine. "My forgiveness was always there. It was your own heart that needed this journey to find it. Well done, child. You have done all that you were asked to do."

Tears pricked my eyes. I wanted to say thank you, but those two words weren't big enough to encompass everything I felt. Just like before, the Phoenix understood me without words. He lifted his head and let out a great cry that pulsed through my heart. "It is done!"

A smile crept onto my lips. I had found peace. My heart was still. I missed my family, but I would see them someday, when their time, too, was over. Until then, I was content. I had truly come home.

"Your life there is not over yet," the Phoenix said gently.

I looked up into his eyes in surprise. "But I died."

"No. I took you from that world before you did."

"I was dying before, too. I was fading to a ghost, while my body was dying in Texas or something probably. How can I not be dead?"

"You were not dying. Indeed, you were waking up. Soon, your mind will return in full. You have finished all that was set before you, even to creating change in yourself. But there is always more to do, more to change, more to heal. And it is time for you to return to your life on Earth, to carry on as you have now begun. You will bear the memory of all that happened with you, and the diamond shall also be a reminder to you, though it shall there have no power."

"So I just go back to what life was like before?" It seemed so tame compared to what had happened, like I wouldn't be doing enough to change things and help others.

"There will always be a way to help and to change, for those who seek it," the Phoenix answered. "But you shall be a Dream Walker, and walk from world to world in your dreamings, much as you did already. You will be a messenger of hope to them."

"Like Lynx was? But how do I do that?" Did I just figure it out instinctively? Was there a special way you did it? I didn't think I'd find a "How to Dream Walk Properly" book at the library.

"Do not fear about that, my child. When you return to your world, I will send someone to teach you. Dixie also awaits you there. It is time for you to go."

"So it's all over?" That thought was hard to wrap my brain around.

"You have created change, in the worlds and in yourself. You have learned much. But there is always more to do. Farewell, child."

The light became impossibly bright around me. That wild wonderful feeling of joyful terror, like being at the beginning of a roller coaster ride, only a million times bigger, stronger, more like the real thing, flooded me. I was swept away by it.

My eyes snapped open to the lights and sounds of a hospital.

* * *

The doctors could never explain why I was out for so long (it had been about ten days since the accident when I woke up). I had no brain damage, no gruesome injuries – it was only a fall off a horse, and that can only be so bad. They said a lot of things to my parents that basically amounted to they didn't know how or why I was unconscious for so long, but I was. If I had any problems in the future, Dad and Mom could pay them lots of money to do a few pointless scans.

It wasn't until I had been released, all the paperwork taken care of, and we were out by the car that we finally got a real chance for a reunion. It was all hugs and tears and stories for a good half hour straight. I couldn't stop pummeling Elliot, so excited to be a sister again and having a shot at being a better one.

"Geez, Alex, what's up with you?" He looked at me like I was crazy.

I laughed hysterically. "Dude, I thought I was dead. You've no idea how good it feels to be back. I'm probably going to be really ticked off with you within the next twenty-four hours, but for now I'm just glad you're my brother."

Elliot was literally speechless when I said that. I wondered why I'd never said it before. But then, I hadn't felt that way before. I did now.

Mom hugged me for the thousandth time. "We were so scared. They didn't know what was wrong. I'm just glad you're back, honey." Dad hugged me again too.

"Um, yeah, about that…" I began, glancing around the parking lot. I didn't want anyone to overhear and wonder if I was crazy. But I was in Texas. Here, you were allowed to be crazy. A slow grin broke over my face. "Just wait till I tell you the true story…"

Back home several hours later, I'd finally finished telling everything that had happened, down to the last detail. We sat in silence for a long time, gathered in the living room, sipping our drinks.

"So… you believe me?" I asked. I didn't see how anyone could accept all that as fact, but they were my family. They deserved the truth.

Dad and Mom exchanged looks. "Yes, Alex," Dad said slowly. "We do. First of all, there's no better explanation for it. And you have the diamond, which you definitely didn't have before. But also…" He trailed off and glanced at Mom again.

She straightened in her chair and set her orange juice down on the coffee table. Pulling her hair off to one side, she cleared her throat. "I was a Mastermind," she admitted. "A long time ago."

I gaped, stunned. "Then are you a Dream Walker?" I asked, remembering how Lynx had told me that a lot of Masterminds ended up as Dream Walkers.

Mom shook her head. "I only ever made one world… and then later had to fix it, a lot like you did. The whole Mastermind thing wasn't really my speed. I did meet some Dream Walkers, but I never had the inclination to become one. But if you ever run across a world called Q'Dai, it's mine."

"Why does Alex always get the cool stuff?" Elliot complained. "I need to get in on this thing too."

"Dream Walking, maybe. Masterminding, probably not," I told

him. "It's way too easy to mess up. Maybe when you're older I can teach you how to Dream Walk or something. But first, *I* have to learn."

I sank back in my chair, taking in the room. My family. Home. Yes, this was where I belonged in this world. Of course, I'd miss things from the other worlds, the people I'd met, especially Kya. And Lynx. But this was where I belonged. *Here.* I was glad I'd gotten to see it again, to be a part of this picture, this family, this moment, again.

* * *

One morning a few days later, I was eating cereal, dressed but still a little bleary with sleep. Mom and Dad were talking, and tuning in, I realized it was about a new ranch hand Dad had hired.

"He's a keeper," Dad was saying. "If he wants to stick around, he gets to. But get this: he told me something weird this morning."

"What?" Mom asked.

"He said he knows Alex."

"Did you know him, Dad?" I asked, interested. I didn't have many friends in Texas yet…

Dad shook his head. "Never seen the guy before, I'm certain of that. He's the sort you remember."

"How would you know him, Alex?" Mom asked.

"I don't know that I know him," I said. "What's his name?"

Dad rubbed his chin. "Uh, don't remember at the moment. Nothing I knew. Wolfe is his last name. Anyway, so I told him we could work something out, offered room and board as part of the package, you know. We need to step up the game around here…"

The conversation moved on to boring topics, and I discreetly left the room. I had to find out just who exactly it was. I descended the porch steps and found no one. It wasn't long before I found him, though. Out behind the barn, I saw a dark-haired young man with the look of someone who knows secrets. He was less mysterious than I remembered him, more like an ordinary person, but his air was unmistakable, and he tossed his hair out of his eyes just the same as always.

He turned with a mischievous grin when he heard me coming. "Ah, so there's the little Mastermind. You look different here. Almost didn't recognize you."

I surprised us both by bounding forward and pulling him into a quick hug. I bounced back, laughing a little nervously, shocked at myself. It was the first time I'd ever caught Lynx so completely off guard, like a cat expecting to land on all four paws who finds himself suddenly on his back. I'll never, ever, forget his face. It was truly priceless.

"You're kidding," I said finally.

Recovering himself, he grinned. "Surprised it's me?"

"No, your name is Lynx Wolfe? Isn't that like being named Cat Dog?"

He shrugged. "Lynx is actually just a nickname. Someone called me that several years ago, and I guess it stuck."

"I can guess why," I said dryly. "You should have introduced yourself to my dad as Lynx. I've told them my story, so he would have recognized your name."

Lynx grinned. "But that would steal the surprise factor. Always the best."

I hoisted myself onto the fence, now towering over him. "You know you can tell them everything, about Dream Walking and all that. My mom's a Mastermind. They'd believe you. I mean, they believed me."

"Yeah, but I didn't know that until just now," he pointed out. He pulled himself up beside me. "Nice to be tangible. It gets annoying in dreams sometimes. But sometimes it's useful, like when I played a ghost at the Haunted Palace, or when I walked through the ropes when we were trussed to that tree." He smiled, looking pleased with himself. "That's also why we're invulnerable to magic; you might not have been technically a Dream Walker, but you were close enough. Dream Walkers are only partially present in the world, so they can't be touched by magic. Sometimes other things too. I'll show you when I give you the grand tour tonight and show you the ropes. I'm supposed to teach you."

"Rough job?" I asked, squinting against the sun to see his face.

He shrugged slightly. "I'll get used to it."

I rolled my eyes. "You know, you really should meet my brother, Elliot. You'd get along famously: two annoying little boys knocking about on a ranch, existing for the sole purpose of getting under my skin…"

Lynx slapped his leg. "I forgot! I really do want to meet your toothbrush-pepperer!" He grinned. "You'll have to introduce us."

I sighed. "Oh, I will."

"Where's your dog, Dixie?" He glanced around. "I don't see her here."

"She hasn't showed up yet," I told him. "But she will. I know that much."

At that moment, I heard barking, and as a thought slipped into my head, I realized the time had come for Lynx to know my last secret.

"*I'm coming, Alex!*" Dixie was home.

"We're starting at Bliss tonight," he was saying. "I'm going there to help a girl named Kya who's having some difficulties. She's been kidnapped and held for ransom or some such, and it's one of your worlds, isn't it?"

"Kya?" I asked. "Of course I'll come. I don't know how, though. But Lynx..." I paused, slipping off the fence and watching a black and white blur draw closer. "There's one more thing I need to tell you."

CITATIONS

(AKA Nods to Famous People)

Elnoth (the Falls of Elnoth) is from an unpublished story of my brother's named *Fight For Athaya*. I thieved the name of a super-cool-secret-volcano-hideout for the name of my falls. You are a great writer and you totally rock! And *no one* could ask for a better brother!

Shelob, as I'm sure you are well aware, is from J. R. R. Tolkien's *The Lord of the Rings* (*The Two Towers*, to be precise), which I am a huge fan of and is a nod of appreciation and acknowledgement to the master of Fantasy, who inspired me so many years ago.

Rhindon is an acknowledgement of another master of the past, C. S. Lewis, and is a sort of inside secret for Narnia fans, who will recognize this as the name of Peter's sword (which is only named once, in *Prince Caspian*). *The Chronicles of Narnia* remain forever some of my favorite books, and I couldn't write this book without giving Lewis a nod of his own, albeit from my young upstart head.

Jadorel (one of Keliel the elf Guardian's ancestors) comes from *Safely Home* by Randy Alcorn. Another awesome book!

Harlan was a catchy name I liked the sound of, from both Harlan Coben and Brad Paisley's song "You'll Never Leave Harlan Alive." I've never read any Harlan Coben novels nor heard that song. But did that stop me from stealing it? Of course not!

And nothing would be complete without a little N. D. Wilson. Dream Walker comes from this great Fantasy Titan, whose books I literally adore! Much thanks, gratitude, admiration, appreciation, and repeated rereading of his books. No more words. Except these two: must read.

ACKNOWLEDGEMENTS

My family, for making this book possible. I love you guys!

Daddy and Mom: You instilled the love of books in me from the time I was a baby, reading them to me and sharing family book reading time every night, even long after I could read for myself. I cherish those memories so much! Resuming a book shall always and forever begin with: "Now, where did we last leave our heroes?" Mom, you still are the only person who can do Gollum's voice right. Daddy, I still remember dancing with you to "Amazing Grace" by Twila Paris. You guys helped sculpt me a life story that I wouldn't exchange. Thank you!

Big brothers: We didn't get along so well when we were little, did we? Now, though, I'm glad I can call you my friends. Our relationship taught me a lot, as much as I might hate to admit it, and I just wish I'd grown up a little faster so I could have enjoyed more time with you guys! You will live forever in my memories and novels, however, so have no fear! (actually, on second thought, you SHOULD be afraid if I'm writing you into a novel. MUAHAHA!)

Big sisters: So I never really thought about you as the typical "big sisters," except for the times I felt like I was living in your shadows. You are two of my best friends, and we're so close now, I'm sorry I missed it before! Thank you for sticking by me through all the hard times, always being there as a listening ear, and patiently allowing me to beat you over the head regaling you with different stories. Thank you for never judging me, and being cool with me being just exactly who I am!

Little brother: Technically I can still call you that, even though you're more than half a foot taller than me. I'll always be older, but probably not wiser, huh? Even though you never peppered my toothbrush (I'm sure you were tempted!), we did have a rocky start. However, now that I have my head screwed on straight, I can see what an epic brother you are, and I'm so glad we can be such good friends! You are an amazing and talented person, and don't let anyone tell you different! Thank you for always being there for me!

I'm proud to call you all my family!

NaNoWriMo: You crazy old put-a-gun-to-my-head-and-see-what-happens month! The only reason I ever completed a novel was because of you. I was a confused fifteen-year-old with no direction, halfhearted dreams, and vague ideas. You slammed me on a track and said, "Here! Take it for a spin!" I achieved the unofficial award of World's Worst Novel Draft Ever that first year. But you changed my life. So thank you. I still do you every November.

Timothy Pike & My Dream Book Team: This program helped me navigate the treacherous waters of self-publishing and saved me when I was on my way to becoming one of the many DIY thrown-on-the-market books. You met me where I was, ignorant, blundering, and without the tools to do this properly, and walked me through the whole process. Honestly, this book (or probably anything of mine, for that matter) would never have seen the light if not for you and My Dream Book Team. Thank you!

All the books in my life: You threw open a wardrobe door to a world of magic and mystery (and Hobbits, too). You led me on crazy adventures through attic cupboard doors, sagas of six worlds tucked away somewhere in our universe, and a magically mist-guarded island. Even though sometimes you disappointed me, from Hogwarts to Redwall, still you always came through, what with Camp Half-Blood and Fablehaven. I owe a lot to you, books. You, in a way, started everything.

And what would a book be without someone to hold it? Thanks to you, reader (didn't catch your name... _____), for reading through this treasure map aka novel. More power to your kind! And know that you can be victorious! You can do it [whatever it is you want to do]. I know you can.